Praise for Michelle Marcos and

GENTLEMEN BEHAVING BADLY

"Marcos gives readers another taste of desire and danger, along with an enticing adventure/mystery in the second Pleasure Emporium novel. Strong and likable characters, as well as a unique setting, should have readers longing for her next book."

—*Romantic Times BOOKreviews* (4 1/2 stars)

"Michelle Marcos infuses plenty of humor and suspense into this historical tale which readers won't want to put down." —*Romance Junkies*

"A talented storyteller, Marcos gives a very human face to all her characters and the moral dilemmas and situations they face. A solid gold read!"

—*Fresh Fiction*

WHEN A LADY MISBEHAVES

"Marcos delivers a refreshing, creative take on the typical Regency, carried by the spirited heroine and buoyed throughout by lively plot twists."

—*Publishers Weekly*

"Her heroine is a spunky delight, and her dark, hostile hero is an ideal foil...Marcos displays talents that are sure to grow with each new title."

—*Romantic Times BOOKreviews*

MORE...

Wickedly
Ever After

Michelle Marcos

St. Martin's Paperbacks

For God

This is a work of fiction. All of the characters, organizations, and events portrayed in this novel are either products of the author's imagination or are used fictitiously.

WICKEDLY EVER AFTER

Copyright © 2009 by Michelle Marcos.

For information address St. Martin's Press, 175 Fifth Avenue, New York, NY 10010.

ISBN: 0-312-94851-4
EAN: 978-0-312-94851-1

Printed in the United States of America

St. Martin's Paperbacks edition / July 2009

St. Martin's Paperbacks are published by St. Martin's Press, 175 Fifth Avenue, New York, NY 10010.

10 9 8 7 6 5 4 3 2 1

PROLOGUE

Not yet twenty years old, and she was dying.

She lay on a street in London, its wet cobblestones perfumed with the ages. Empty and abandoned, the chill night echoed her loneliness.

Not everyone would miss her. Most women wouldn't, especially wives. And some respectable men wouldn't either.

But in her day, she was beloved by men of affluence and influence, men of high birth and low morals. And she loved them back . . . for the right price.

She was a place that had exhaled the air of pleasure. In her salons, the queens of leisure gathered, open to the entertainment of men's fantasies. In her rooms, delights were sought and bestowed. Within her walls, the women ruled the men.

But now her time was at an end. The FOR SALE sign was nailed to her door.

The Pleasure Emporium had enjoyed her last customer.

Like an unmade bed after a night of passion, the bordello now lay desolate and forgotten. Her furnishings were covered in white cloth, her windows were shuttered, and her once open door was tightly shut. Her courtesans were long gone, her clients vanished. All the vivid people with their vivid lives had disappeared.

But she herself refused to go away. Like the wooden sign that swayed back and forth on the rusty nail, there would be a pendulum swing to her life as well. As with all scorned women, the Pleasure Emporium would not keep silent for long.

ONE

Twice upon a time, Athena McAllister thought she had found the man of her dreams.

The first time it happened she was fifteen years old. He was sixteen, blond-haired, and beautiful, the second son of a viscount who was on holiday from boarding school abroad. He spoke to her politely, as a proper young gentleman should, but stared over her ginger-colored head at a lovelier young woman at the ball.

At nineteen she met another man, a viscount in his own right. He was twenty, blond-haired, and beautiful, and he expressed nothing but admiration for her fiery coloring. He spoke of his travels to Italy and America, and when the music started, stepped around her generous form to dance with a lovelier young woman at the ball.

It was, therefore, with some trepidation that she regarded the blond-haired and beautiful Calvin Bretherton, whose manner and clothes bespoke generations of wealth that she now lacked. At twenty-eight, Athena was well past marrying years, and everyone expected her to live out her life in aristocratic penury. But the earl was looking for a wife, and

Athena gave in to that frustrating yet lingering hope that he might be her final chance to marry well—let alone marry at all.

Hester looked over at her friend as she handed her a glass of wine. "You've got the look of a cat that's spotted an unsuspecting bird. Who are you staring at?"

Athena took a sip, and the sweet wine burst flavor into her dry mouth. "No one."

Hester pursed her lips as her eyes scanned the cluster of men across the ballroom. "There's General Thomason, Lord Ryebrook, the bishop . . . can't be the bishop."

Athena smiled and rolled her eyes. "Behind him."

Hester squinted her dark eyes. "Hmm. Lord Stockdale. Very handsome indeed. I know his family well. He gets his looks from his mother, you know."

Athena smirked. "I bet he gets looks from lots of women."

Hester chuckled. "I've always been partial to men with blue eyes. Let's sit down. Perhaps he'll come over and introduce himself."

Athena took her place beside Hester in the knot of chairs near the fireplace—the potpourri corner, she called it—where the dowagers, spinsters, and other dried-out women congregated. She smiled wanly at the conversation between the Baroness Basinghall, a great turtle of a woman, and her unmarried last daughter, an equally grating bore, on which teas are the best cures for headaches and how to make poultices for bunions.

But her own eyes kept drifting to the object of her growing aspiration. Calvin threw his head back and laughed at something the general said. She smiled. His cheeks curled over a row of perfect white teeth, and just for a moment, Athena pictured them smiling at her. The burgundy coat hugged his form, revealing long, muscular arms that would feel heavenly wrapped around her. And those sky-blue eyes, so charismatic and beautiful, gazing at her in smoky desire . . . Athena exhaled, reveling in the imagined pleasure.

Suddenly, Calvin glanced in her direction, and her heart missed a beat. Dream materialized into reality as he broke away from the group of men and walked toward her. Time seemed to slow as she watched him stride over, her pulse racing. Her breath came out in nervous gasps.

His smile widened as he neared, and Athena blinked shyly. He was utterly delicious . . . like a thick slice of marchpane cake. All her confidence dissolved under that assertively handsome gaze. Her customary proud boast that she needed no man, flung to clucking matrons, evaporated in the flame of anticipation as Calvin's perfect body approached her.

And in a blink of her bashful green eyes, Calvin's perfect body passed her completely. He stopped in front of two willowy French ladies on the opposite end of the ballroom and bowed before them.

Athena's heart sank. As an adolescent, being overlooked like that might have punctured her fragile confidence for months. But she was a woman now. Her confidence was no longer rooted in beauty. She was, after all, a well-read and intelligent woman. If Calvin Bretherton would just *speak* to her, maybe she could persuade him that she was worthy of his attention.

"Please excuse me, ladies." Athena set down her glass and stood up.

"Where are you going?" whispered Hester.

"He's not coming over to me, so I shall just have to go over to him."

Hester moved in front of her, blocking her escape. "Are you mad? You can't walk up to a man and introduce yourself! You mustn't be so forward."

"I can't very well hope to snag a husband if I remain shoved up against a wall like an old rag mop."

"Athena, it's been too long since you've been at a ball in London. There are certain rules of conduct you must observe. You must behave with the decorum befitting your years and reduced circumstances."

"You make me sound like an old carthorse. There's life in me yet, Hester."

Hester's delicate black eyebrows drew together as her anxious eyes looked around. "I just ask that you consider what people might say. For someone like you, it's only a whisper from spinster to prostitute."

Athena sighed. Hester was right—reputation was monumentally important. At least as a spinster, she'd still be asked to parties like this one. If she lost her claim to respectability, life would be even lonelier than it was at present. Good manners demanded that she sit quietly in the company of other widowed, single, and unescorted ladies until a gentleman approached her. It so seldom happened, and never by the gentlemen she truly wanted to meet. And that had become her lot in life . . . condemned by propriety to inexperience.

She watched the two brunette sisters, charming Calvin with their singsong zh-zh'd words. As they batted their thick black eyelashes at him and giggled coquettishly behind their mother-of-pearl fans, she sat back down among the black-clad, bunioned gaggle of women.

Prostitute indeed.

If only.

TWO

"You're scowling, Mason."

Her Grace the Duchess of Twillingham perched her cup delicately inside the saucer. Her flinty brown eyes had snapped to Mason Royce, the Baron Penhaligan, and it was enough to make a man of his advanced years feel as uncomfortable as a schoolboy.

"I know my granddaughter, Your Grace." His papery hands flicked open the book and sifted through the pages. "To get her to read this will be like drawing a cat to a barrel of water."

The duchess swung a disapproving glance around the room, her eyes resting on the worn carpet, the unlit fireplace, and a book on the floor that was propping up a crippled sideboard. "She more than anyone I know stands to benefit from its teachings."

Mason sighed into the frayed armchair across from the duchess. "Athena has very strong opinions of her own."

"All the more reason to oblige her to conform. She must achieve a level of sophistication. If you leave her out in the country much longer, it'll be the ruin of her. Heaven knows . . . she'll probably let herself be covered by some farmer or other."

"Athena isn't like that, Maggie."

"Let me have a talk with the girl."

"She doesn't respond to coercion," he warned.

A nest of wrinkles appeared at her mouth. "You always were softhearted, Mason. No wonder that granddaughter of yours is so indomitable. You've done her no favors by being so lenient. Look at her now . . . twenty-eight and perilously unwed. There's only you to blame for that."

"She's not like other girls, Maggie. She's . . . different."

The duchess jerked her head upward, making the curl of feathers in her bonnet wave. "She's no different from any other woman. If she desires to marry into the nobility, she must learn how to behave in polite society. No man will shackle himself to a waspish woman. But if she should desire my sponsorship, she must first gain a measure of modesty, delicacy, and humility. Bring her to me. I know I can get her to see reason."

Mason shook his grizzled head but rang for the servant anyway.

Out in the field, the servant whispered something to Athena. With a brief shake of her head, Athena set down her paintbrush in front of the half-finished canvas and stood up.

Moments later, Athena appeared in the morning room, her artist's pinafore alive with colors.

"You sent for me, Grandfather?"

The old man rose. "Athena. Yes, come inside. May I present Margaret, Duchess of Twillingham. Your Grace, this is my granddaughter, Athena McAllister."

Her Grace was a regal-looking woman, even in her

sixties. Tight curls in streaks of black and gray peeked out from underneath her bonnet. Her eyebrows had almost disappeared, leaving only a wide swath of forehead lined in multiple directions. But when her dark eyes alighted on Athena, the duchess looked at her as if she had suddenly grown a third arm and an extra pair of legs.

"What in heaven has happened to your dress?"

Athena looked down at her smeared frock, smiling sheepishly. "I'm sorry. I was in the field . . . finishing a painting of a dying tree."

"Was it necessary to get into such a state?"

"I'm sorry. I hadn't expected anyone to call today."

The duchess adjusted the ruff of her primrose-colored spencer. "I can see that I have come not a second too soon. You see, Mason, this is exactly the sort of fatal carelessness to which I was referring. Miss McAllister, in polite society, a lady should *always* be prepared to receive visitors between the hours of three o'clock and five. You, on the other hand, look prepared to serve as a pig farmer's hired hand."

Athena recoiled, her full lips thinning. "I have found, Your Grace, that in polite society, people are either charmingly superficial or tediously so. I aspire to be neither."

"I'll thank you to hold a civil tongue, Miss McAllister. A dirty frock does a lady no credit. A woman that does not demonstrate concern for her appearance may as well be dismissed out of hand. As, apparently, you have been."

Mason cleared his throat. "Athena, Her Grace is a very dear friend of mine. We've known each other since we were children. Because of that long friendship, Her Grace has very graciously offered to help make a match for you. She has agreed to sponsor you in Society, and help find a suitable husband for you. Dresses, entertainments, social engagements—she is willing to support you in all facets of this endeavor. And given our limited resources, I'm sure you will be as grateful as I am."

Athena crossed her paint-smeared hands in front of her, suspicious of such unsolicited generosity. "Of course. Thank you for that kindhearted gesture, Your Grace."

Mason collected the book from the tea table and placed it into Athena's rainbowed hands. "And she has already brought you a gift."

Athena looked at the cover and her eyebrows drew together. *"Feminine Excellence, or Every Young Woman's Guide to Ladylike Comportment."*

"If you are to find a husband," said the duchess, "I insist that you read and learn that book."

Athena bristled. "Thank you for the gift, Your Grace, but I think it may be wasted on me. At the risk of sounding immodest, I don't believe I am in need of learning excellence."

The older woman rested both hands on the knob of her cane. "That is more than immodest. That sounds absolutely prideful. Especially when it is apparent how many qualities you have which are in need of refinement. If it will make you feel any better, you are not the only one being given this book. All the unmarried ladies this Season are being required to learn the principles outlined by Countess Cavendish in her book. The Ladies Patronesses of Almack's have given this book their seal of approval. I realize you did not have a proper come-out, and that cannot be helped. But because of the great personal regard I have for your grandfather, and out of consideration for the absence of female guidance in your life, I will personally take it upon myself to introduce you to Society—provided, of course, you do nothing to humiliate me."

It rankled Athena to be thought a charity case. "I'd like to say how grateful I am, Your Grace." But the words were getting stuck in her throat. "I'm just not certain that reading a book like that will make me into the sort of woman I long to be."

The older woman banged her ivory cane on the floor. "The only kind of woman you ought to be is the *married* kind. If dispelling the horrible disgrace of being a spinster isn't enough inducement, then at least think of your grandfather. You're the only daughter of an only daughter. The Penhaligan name will be extinguished when he dies. Do you want his bloodline extinguished, too?"

"Of course not. I shall marry if and when the right man comes along."

The duchess stared at Athena with her cold, dark eyes, increasing Athena's discomfort. "Mason, would you kindly give us a few moments to talk in private?"

"By all means." He rose and walked away from the tense exchange, and closed the parlor door behind him. Athena keenly felt his absence. It was like being left in a room with a growling lion.

"Miss McAllister, let us speak candidly. The prospects you offer as a wife are severely compromised. You're well beyond a desirable age, insubordinate, podgy, and redheaded. You've no title of your own—oh, I know your father was a viscount, but he was a *Scottish* viscount, which in this country is almost a strike against you. Moreover, your grandfather isn't exactly in the best financial circumstances, leaving even a healthy dowry past your ability to produce. Miss McAllister, let us face facts. You have absolutely nothing to offer a prospective husband."

Athena cast her eyes to the floor, her chin jutting in impotent defiance. She knew all these things, and had said these hurtful words to herself many times. But to hear them come out of a stranger's mouth stung far more.

"And to further complicate matters," the duchess continued, "your grandfather has told me that you have cultivated the romantic notion that you would only marry for love. Now, while I do not disparage this concept, like all ideals, it is elusive and unpragmatic."

Athena was about to argue, but the duchess halted her.

"Nevertheless, it has come to my attention that you have developed feelings for a certain man named Calvin Bretherton."

Athena's eyes widened. "How did you—"

The duchess waved her question away. "You will find that there is little that is left undiscovered when one frequents Almack's."

Athena's face colored in humiliation. While true that she had harbored a secret passion for Calvin these many weeks, she suffered to think it was common knowledge. The more she had learned about Calvin, the more she desired him. He was everything she ever wanted in a man—clever, witty, modern in his thinking, and as beautiful a man as she had ever laid eyes on. But the truth was she didn't know how to entice his suit. Her parents died when she was ten, and she had grown up in the company of her grandfather, so the feminine art of seduction was never taught to her. If, indeed, it was something to be learned.

"I know that you have been stunted in your development as a woman," the duchess continued rather astutely, "but this book will show you how to acquire what you lack. I stand in favor of your encouraging Bretherton's advances. But I must warn you that if you wish to endeavor to turn this calf love for Bretherton into a proposal of marriage, you will have some work to do on improving your chances. The competition this Season shall be stiff. I have it on good authority that Bretherton is being targeted by no less than five different ladies of my acquaintance for their daughters." The duchess picked up the book from the table. "Nevertheless, with my personal sponsorship, I think his parents will look favorably upon you, as will he. But only if you can offer him the prospect of a *proper* wife."

Athena took the book from the duchess's silk-gloved hand. Her confidence was in tatters, and this book promised only more frustrated hopes. "If I am up against all these other more qualified women, why would Calvin even consider me?"

"Because unlike them, you will have *me* to champion your cause."

Athena turned the book over in her hand. She knew that men were after more than sparkling, intelligent conversation. She knew she was at fault for doing and thinking things a proper lady mustn't. She knew she was guilty of being herself.

Maybe there was something to be gained after all from Countess Cavendish's instruction. Maybe the reason it all didn't make sense was because she just had never learned the language of artifice and coquetry.

She would give anything to become the wife of Calvin Bretherton. And if all it cost her was the reading of a book, then it was certainly a price she'd be willing to pay.

Page one.

THREE

My dear Lord Stockdale,

Now that you have had the opportunity to meet Athena McAllister on a number of occasions, I trust that you have formed a kind opinion of her. She is a charming companion with many fine qualities to recommend her as your bride. Moreover, you need do nothing more to win her heart—it is already yours.

As for your parents, I have done my part in influencing them. They are prepared to accept your announcement of engagement to Miss McAllister. The path is illuminated for you. It only remains for you to walk down it.

I hope that I have helped to make your obligation easier to bear. But make no mistake . . . Athena McAllister is the one.

Until Vauxhall.

Yours,
Margaret, Duchess of Twillingham

"You remember all you've learned?"

The carriage rolled over a rain-filled hole, jarring Athena inside the carriage. She almost let loose a stream of blue epithets, but remembered why she was there and with whom she was riding. And yes, all she had learned. "I remember, Your Grace."

"That new corset I purchased for you has done wonders for your figure. You look almost normal. I hope you can see how essential it is to suffer for one's beauty."

Athena could scarcely breathe, but it was worth it to be able to fit into the glorious gown that the duchess had ordered for her—a long skirt in turquoise silk, with the scalloped sleeves and neckline festooned with tiny seed pearls. The matching satin slippers also had tiny pearls sewn upon them, echoing the dainty white flowers ornamenting her hair. Pristine white gloves snaked up her arms.

"I suppose there was nothing to be done about that red hair of yours. I told you not to choose such an alarming color for your dress. Yellows and browns would have damped down that ginger coloring. Blues and greens only make it more pronounced."

Athena bit back a rude reply. "Grandfather says that my hair is part of my natural beauty."

The duchess harrumphed. "Natural beauty is what sheep and horses have. We women require more than that." She looked out of the window. "Perhaps there's still time for us to stop off at the milliner's and purchase a turban to match that gown."

Athena resisted the urge to roll her eyes. "No, thank you, Your Grace. I think my hair shall be quite all right for today's outing. Perhaps such an accessory will be unbefitting an evening spent out of doors."

"Hmm," she agreed reluctantly as the coach came to a halt. "I daresay you're right."

If the entrance to the Vauxhall Pleasure Gardens was intended to impress, then it worked its magic on Athena. As she walked through the entranceway, her eyes beheld what she could only describe as heaven on earth. Trees in bloom marched down the wide path like giant sentries. In the sinking daylight, nightingales trilled in the boughs. To Athena's left wound a long, serpentine colonnade, with alcoves fitted into it for people to sit at table and eat. To her right, in the middle of a large courtyard, was an ornately festooned pavilion with a giant gilded cockleshell, under which an orchestra had just begun to play.

She followed closely behind the duchess—*no more than five feet in the wake of an older person,* as Countess Cavendish's book decreed—as the older woman led her to her very own supper box with a magnificent view of the orchestra. Hundreds of people—all persons of quality, from the look of their clothes—strolled about the gardens. Athena was desperate to explore the vast gardens, which she heard had a magnificent cascade, but was obliged to remain with the elder lady, who now took her seat.

A warm breeze ruffled her skirts as she sat next to the duchess, and it waved the fragrance of roses and hyacinths into their alcove. A magnificent painting graced the inside of the supper box, and Athena found every one of her senses overwhelmed with divine delight. Athena hardly had time to check herself before a line of people came up to renew their acquaintance with the duchess. She was surprised by how many people were on nodding terms with her sponsor, and Her Grace was very gracious toward those in her circle. The duchess introduced Athena to each one of those peers and ladies, and Athena could sense her esteem among Society growing exponentially.

But soon Athena grew weary of making polite discourse. As yet another ambitious woman sycophantically petitioned the duchess to implore her cause for a voucher with the Lady Patronesses of Almack's, Athena stifled a yawn. So much of Society was about being admired for who one knows, rather than for what one has done. Athena looked out wistfully across the garden, wishing this part would be over and she could take a stroll among the fragrant roses before night fell altogether.

"Good evening, Your Grace."

Athena took no notice, except for the fact that her sponsor did not return the greeting. Puzzled, Athena turned to look at the woman who had spoken. She was a tall, bony person, with dark hair and modestly elegant clothes. The gown she wore was a strong shade of indigo, but it did not seem out of place on her. She was not an unlovely woman, but far from being handsome. Her sharp nose was very remarkable, and Athena imagined that every joint of her must be just as angular.

The duchess stared beyond her, making no answer.

"You're looking well," the woman continued.

Still no answer. Athena began to grow uncomfortable from the tense exchange. It was rude of the duchess not to speak, but Athena knew that a snub from someone like her was tantamount to a social execution.

"Well, good evening to you, then," the woman said to Athena.

"Good evening," Athena replied.

The woman harrumphed. "At least one of you can

lay claim to some manners." She turned on her heel and walked away.

The duchess's face grew florid with rage. "Of all the impertinence! How dare she come and speak to me!"

Athena's brows drew together in bewilderment. "Who was that?"

The duchess's still-open fan slammed against the table. "That . . . *creature* . . . is a pestilence on this town. If I had known she'd be here, I never would have come!" She whirled on Athena, her eyes wide. "Let me make this perfectly plain to you. You are never to have contact with that woman."

"Of course not."

Her gloved finger stabbed the air in front of Athena's face. "If I ever find out you that have entertained that woman, I shall withdraw my patronage of you immediately."

Whatever offense that woman had given, it was enough to make the otherwise undemonstrative duchess lose her composure. "Yes, I'm quite clear on that point, Your Grace. But don't you think it would be easier to turn her away from my door if I were to know her name?"

The duchess breathed a deep sigh, her face resuming its expression of marble. "*That* is Vera, Lady Ponsonby, though it pains me to use that form of address on her. Don't be fooled . . . she is titled by marriage only. She is actually the daughter of a solicitor. But if you can believe it, it was her mother who was even more disgraceful. When the father passed away, her mother purchased and managed a house of ill repute!"

Athena gasped at the scurrilous bit of gossip. "No!"

"Her mother was a ghastly woman named Fynch

who dedicated her life to manufacturing votaries of pleasure. The whole Fynch family was simply bad seed—I don't know what Ponsonby was thinking when he married into it." The duchess shook her head. "And now *that woman* is the owner of her mother's den of iniquity. For all the good it does her. The building has lain vacant since the awful Fynch woman died, and I hear that they are unable to sell it. I can only express my supreme joy that the dead property is causing a severe drain on Ponsonby's finances."

It surprised Athena that there was so much vitriol in the duchess against the Ponsonby woman, but she suspected there was more to the story than Her Grace was willing to confess. Her husband the duke was known to be a profligate, and Athena wondered if the duchess had lost him behind the doors of Mrs. Fynch's house of prostitution. She looked around to locate the lady that could so disquiet the utterly unflappable duchess. That's when she saw him, standing in a circle of men in the middle of a toast.

Calvin Bretherton, Lord Stockdale.

As handsome a man in person as he was in her memory—and fantasies. Dressed in a tan coat and gold-embroidered waistcoat, he radiated health, wealth, and style. She was unaware how her breathing quickened as she watched him speak animatedly to the group. He looked just as dashing as he had the week before, when the duchess had taken her to dinner at Calvin's family's London town house. The remembered thrill of their long talk hummed in her anew. And now, here he was again, looking every bit as delectable as he had the other night at dinner.

"I can see the course of your thoughts."

By degrees, the duchess's words penetrated her reverie. "Pardon?"

"You heard me. Every lurid notion is printed upon your face. Remember Countess Cavendish's admonitions."

Athena blushed hotly. *A proper lady does not dwell on notions of the flesh. She who aspires to feminine excellence must not let herself be contaminated by corruption, in thought or in deed. Purity of thought is a proper lady's hallmark.*

The duchess gave a curt nod to a well-dressed man. "I have enjoined the Duke of Sedgwick to bring Lord Stockdale to us. Do try to keep your mind from swerving in the direction of Lady Ponsonby's domain."

Athena felt her face redden even more. She hated to blush, because it made her auburn hair appear that much redder. She fanned herself to cool the heat in her face. She took a deep breath, and prepared herself to receive him. Her gown was lovely, her hair was immaculate, and she was wearing the manners of a proper lady. She was no longer the unpolished hoyden that she was a month ago, before Countess Cavendish's book elevated her to the realms of proper social conduct. Tonight she was a lady . . . and Calvin would take notice.

Calvin came over, a brilliant smile spreading across his face. "Your Grace," he said, tipping his hat. "How very nice to see you again. I hope you are well."

"Quite well, thank you, Lord Stockdale. You remember Miss McAllister."

"Of course," he said, bestowing that charming smile upon Athena. "Miss McAllister, it is a joy to see you again. How ravishing you look."

There went her face again. Her only consolation was that at least when she blushed, her freckles disappeared. "Thank you, Lord Stockdale. Will you join us?"

"Delighted." He came round and took a seat on the duchess's left.

They chatted amiably about the beauty of the gardens and the persons that they had met. Each time they spoke, Athena came to know another exquisite level of happiness. Calvin's charm drove all thought out of her head, and she found herself smiling more and talking less. Just as well, she thought—as Countess Cavendish pointed out, *no man wants a parrot for a wife. A lady who speaks overmuch, or at least more than a man, shows a deficiency of character that points to a future as a shrew.*

Calvin glanced in her direction as the duchess spoke, and when those blue eyes met Athena's, she couldn't help but smile.

"I must say I'm beguiled by Miss McAllister's accent, slight though it is. Miss McAllister, how long have you been away from Scotland?"

"Too long a time. I left Scotland when I was ten." Athena stuttered when she realized she had inadvertently pointed to her advanced age. "My parents died then, and I came to live with my grandfather in England."

"I've never been to Scotland. I should like to see it."

"Oh, you would have loved Tigh na Coille. It means 'House of the Woods.' Oh, it was a bonnie house, with fields as far as the eye could see. A river coursed through the forest, and on Sundays we would go—" She was about to say "go fishing," but the constraints of

Countess Cavendish's book schooled her. *A proper lady does not participate in the leisurely pursuits of the male. Hunting, fishing, archery, horseracing, boxing matches, etc., should remain the exclusive purview of the man. It is considered most unbecoming behavior for a lady to join men in even conversations about these activities, let alone participate in them herself.* "Go walking and look for songbirds."

"Sounds an enchanting place. We should take a drive up soon. Provided, of course, Her Grace is free to join us."

"Well, we no longer own it, I'm afraid. My father lost the property before he died."

"Oh, I *am* sorry. Have you nothing to call home in Scotland?"

She jerked her head. "My father acquired a parcel of land for my dowry. I'd like to be able to brag about it, but it really isn't much. Thirty acres of rough hills in the Highlands not far from the sea."

A dimple appeared in his cheek. "I should still like to see it. Perhaps one day you'll take me there?"

She shrugged shyly. "If you wish it."

"Perhaps we'll picnic there . . . after we're engaged."

Athena's eyes grew wide as saucers. "Did you say 'engaged'?"

His eyes blinked dreamily. "I shall speak to your grandfather to get his permission, of course, if you've no objection to becoming my wife."

The duchess turned to her, a triumphant look upon her face.

Athena could hardly believe her ears. Married to Calvin Bretherton, the most handsome, charming, wealthy, noble, and desirable man in all England. If she wasn't cinched in so tightly, her heart might have burst with happiness.

"Why, no, Lord Stockdale. I have no objection whatsoever."

He mirrored her smile. "Then you've made me the happiest of men."

"Lord Stockdale," remarked the duchess, distracting him from Athena's furious blush, "will you be staying in London long?"

"For a fortnight more, I think. I promised some friends in Cornwall I'd pay them a visit."

"Perhaps you'd be good enough to visit us at Almack's next Wednesday. A ball has been organized in my honor. It shall be my last engagement in London, as upon Saturday, I shall be going abroad for the rest of the Season. You're most welcome to join us for the party."

His warm blue eyes floated to Athena. "I'm afraid I must decline . . . unless Miss McAllister will pledge one of her dances to me."

Athena could hardly contain her joy. Marriage to Calvin was a dream come true. And more than that, she had ceased to be an object of ridicule, a spinster left upon a shelf . . . now she was desirable enough to become a countess. Countess Cavendish was right. *When a lady behaves properly, all men take notice.* "If a dance with one such as myself will persuade Lord Stockdale to grace us with his presence at the ball, then I am honored to agree to the proposition."

"Then we are all agreed," she said. "Lord Stockdale, we shall look forward to seeing you at the ball."

Calvin held out his hand to Athena, and she placed

hers in his. "I shall dance with no one but you." Athena watched as his head descended over her hand, and she felt the warm press of his kiss on her gloved hand. She held her breath as his lips lingered on that spot, and she memorized the pleasurable sensation.

His eyes lifted to hers, and she exhaled. His gaze held her captive, and his soft smile promised heavenly delights upon Wednesday. Too soon, he returned his attention to the duchess, and he placed a perfunctory kiss on her hand as well. "Ladies, *adieu*." She watched him as he dissolved in the sea of people in the orchestra courtyard.

"You were very gracious," said the duchess. "I must say your comportment exceeded my expectations."

Nothing could erase the smile from her face. "Finally," she breathed. "I'm becoming betrothed."

"Gold is made more valuable by its refining. And so it is with a woman. A sophisticate like Bretherton desires only the best in life . . . the best carriages, the stateliest homes, the loftiest friends . . . and the finest quality of female. The greater a prospect you present to the world, the more of a magnet you become to men like Bretherton."

Athena nodded slowly, absorbing the duchess's words. Clearly, Athena had been far too ignorant to know what a man truly wanted. It was a strange game, this courtship ritual. If she hadn't been so thrilled by the victory of snagging Calvin, she would have condemned all the pretense of it.

Dinner was served, a cold repast of flavorless chicken, thinly sliced ham, and boiled potatoes. Though utterly insipid, the disappointing meal did nothing to tarnish her gilded happiness. She looked up from her plate, and spotted a face in the crowd she recognized.

"Hester!" Athena called out from the box, waving a hand wildly.

"Sit down!" admonished the duchess. "You're making a spectacle of yourself!"

"I'm sorry," she replied, but was gleeful that Hester was approaching the box.

Although Athena was drawn to Hester's regal shyness and serene wisdom, she envied her everything else. Hester had a dark, ethereal beauty and a tall, slender figure, whereas Athena—did not. She was demure and polished, the consummate lady. Even if Hester's family hadn't been steeped in wealth, every landed nobleman and peer would still have offered for her. But Hester had fallen for a gentleman scholar and investor named Thomas Willett three years before and had become his wife.

Hester's mother, Mrs. Bermondsey, greeted the duchess. "Your Grace, may I present my daughter, the Baroness Willett?"

The duchess held out her gloved hand. "How do you do, Lady Willett? Is your husband not with you?"

Hester lowered her eyelids. "No, Your Grace. Regrettably, estate matters keep him from accompanying me tonight."

"I have not seen him at Almack's for some time. How does he?"

"He is in good health, Your Grace. His duties consume much of his time. I shall tell him you remembered him."

"Thank you. Tell me, Mrs. Bermondsey, how did you find Greece?"

As the older ladies struck up a conversation, Athena leaned over and whispered to Hester. "I have delicious news to tell you!"

"What is it?" she asked, her large doe eyes imbued with excitement.

"Not here," Athena said, craning her head behind her conspiratorially. She waited for a lull in the older ladies' conversation. "Your Grace, would it meet with your approval if Hester and I were to take a turn about the gardens now?"

The duchess straightened. "If Mrs. Bermondsey poses no objection, then neither do I."

The shadows deepened along the elegant planes of Mrs. Bermondsey's face. "As long as you're back for the lighting of the candles. And Hester, steer clear of the dark walks."

Hester nodded obediently as arm in arm, she and Athena disappeared into the flowered groves.

"My goodness, Athena," cried Hester. "Have you lost weight?"

"No," she replied, her hand resting on her midriff. "It's this bloody armor I've got on. But I've never been happier to wear such a torturous article. You'll never believe what happened tonight!" Excitedly, Athena recounted all that had happened earlier with Calvin Bretherton, weaving each succulent sensation into the telling.

"Oh, Athena. How absolutely wonderful! I'm so jealous of you I could scream."

"Don't be silly. You're already married! It is I who am jealous of you!"

Hester shrugged apologetically. "I'm just happy that it's finally happening to you. Gosh, whoever thought you'd become a countess? What a picture you two would make!"

Athena smiled, and imagined herself with Calvin in a wedding portrait. She saw herself seated in a chair in a garden, much like this one, with him standing behind her, his head held high. It would be a self-portrait, she decided, because she wanted to paint him herself. He would emerge from her canvas perfectly handsome, while she—well, she'd paint herself a few pounds lighter. The colors would be vivid and spectacular, and the faces would be softened to enhance the romantic effect. Tomorrow she'd practice. It was no problem trying to paint Calvin from memory. She was certain she'd be able to capture that peculiar turn of his mouth, the slant of his jaw, the fall of his hair. The only thing that might give her trouble would be his eyes . . .

They walked until the orchestral music grew faint. Dusk had fallen, and the path grew dim.

"It's getting dark," Hester noted. "Shouldn't they be lighting the lamps soon?"

It was a spectacle that Athena had looked forward to seeing. Thousands of lights throughout the garden were somehow connected by common fuses, and just before nightfall, servants would stand at strategic points in the garden and simultaneously light all the torches, as if by magic bringing the entire place to light with just a single spark. It was a fantastic display that by all accounts seemed to beggar description, so Athena was keen to see it for herself. "It shouldn't be long now. Come along, I want to see more of the gardens before I have to return to the confinement of the supper box."

They meandered along the garden paths, but Hester stopped dead when they reached a garden arch. "We can't go in there."

Athena turned to face her. "Why not?"

"Because that's the entrance to Lover's Walk."

The bower where paramours went to make secret love. A gleeful smile spread across Athena's face. "I've heard about this place. Let's go inside."

"No! Mother said I wasn't to go in there."

"Don't be such a wet goose. We'll only take a quick peek round."

"Someone will see us. I don't want my husband to learn I've been in there."

"I can hardly see my hand in front of my face. Who will recognize us? Come along, I know you want to see what's happening inside." A gentle tug was all it took, and Athena and Hester were swallowed into the overgrown copse.

If it was dim outside, it was positively dark inside. They tiptoed through the neglected trees, and pushed away the long clinging branches of some sort of bush. The air was thick and close, and the canopy of leaves muted all sounds. Except one.

"What's that?" whispered Hester, panic rising in her voice.

Athena paused as she listened to it. "It sounds like an animal in pain." Curiosity prodded her forward.

Hester didn't move. "Animal? What sort of animal?"

Ignoring her, Athena advanced slowly, her footsteps dampened by the brown and yellow leaves littering the path. The sound became clearer the closer she got. It was no animal making that sound. It was a woman.

The path opened up onto a small clearing, but Athena remained behind one of the bushes. From this point, Athena could make out some movement in the clearing. Through the darkness, Athena saw the wide figure of a man, made more evident by the lightness of his cravat. Beneath him came the soft moaning sound, a whimper of pain-pleasure that riveted Athena's attention. Once her eyes formed the figures, it became clear that she was observing a woman bent over a garden bench, while a man knelt behind her. Back and forth his hips drove, the woman's gasps and moans hanging in the muted enclosure.

Blood suffused Athena's face. It was utterly wicked to be witnessing such a thing, but she was unable to turn away. Though the figures were shadowy, Athena's own imagination supplied what she couldn't see. She envisioned the bodies colliding with one another, the heat from the one's intense pleasure infusing the other. The muffled sounds they made painted their own picture of what she was watching. Her own body grew warm from the thrill of being part of this stolen moment.

The man hissed something at the woman, but Athena could not make it out. His grunting grew louder and his rocking more exaggerated, and the woman's moans became gasps. Wide-eyed and breathless, Athena watched as their passion mounted.

A sound from outside the bower penetrated the silence inside. It sounded like champagne corks popping one right after another. Athena thought it was the beginning of the fireworks display, but the sound was rapidly coming closer. She turned around, and from behind the leaves, she could see the interconnected torches flaming to light through the garden like a snake of fire. The snake ignited behind her, and for the first time, the two lovers were cast into light.

The woman, surprised by the light, looked up from the bench.

Athena gasped. Lady Ponsonby!

Her ignominious position was made more shocking by the folds of her indigo skirt draped over her waist. Behind her, buried to the hilt inside her, was a man in a tan coat.

"Stop!" cried Lady Ponsonby, looking at the bush where Athena was hiding. "There's someone there!"

The man lifted his gaze in Athena's direction. And Athena blanched.

His features were contorted into a mask of lust. It was not an expression she recognized. But, oh, it was a face she knew well. Those were the eyes she had so lovingly gazed into, the hair she had longed to touch, the mouth she had craved for her own.

Calvin.

The monument to happiness she had built in her mind began to fracture and collapse. As she looked into that face, the face of the man who had pledged his troth to her barely an hour ago, huge pieces of debris began to rain down upon her. Only one thought filled her head.

Run.

Her knees buckled, and she scrambled to right herself. Light from the torches illuminated the serpentine path, but it blurred as tears pooled in her eyes. By the time she had made it out to the open air, she was sobbing.

Hester gasped as Athena fell into her arms. "What's the matter? Athena, what did you see?"

The image was scorched into her mind. She could describe it in a thousand nauseating details. But she didn't want to. She wanted to bury it forever.

"Get me away from here," she breathed. "Please."

She let Hester guide her down a new path. The over-tight corset made Athena gasp for air, and she stumbled toward a garden bench facing a fountain. Athena collapsed in Hester's arms, uncontrolled sobs racking her body.

Everything in her was screaming for help. It seemed an eternity before Athena could breathe deeply enough to form a sentence. She wiped her moist, puffy face on her wet gloves and haltingly described what she had seen.

"Oh, Athena," Hester said, rubbing her friend's back. "I don't know what to say."

Athena shook her head. "I thought he loved me. I thought he loved *me*. I feel such a fool." In the trees, a choir of nightingales warbled, but to Athena they sounded like sirens calling men to their doom. "Why did he go off with that . . . that . . . horrible woman? Why did he desert me for her?"

Athena was drowning in a sea of betrayal. She felt an utter fool for thinking she was worth matrimony. She had no wealth, no title, no prospects, and the blush of youth was gone—and no corset was going to change any of those realities. What pride to think she could capture the heart and admiration of a man like Calvin. She wanted to hate him, but instead she hated herself.

"Athena, what happened hasn't changed his proposal of marriage. He'll still marry you."

"I don't want to marry him!" she exclaimed, too loud for discretion. "He's just proven the measure of his love for me. Do you honestly expect me to shackle myself to a man who's going to leap from my bed into that of another? To sit at home waiting for him to return to me still reeking from the likes of that Ponsonby woman?"

Hester's gentle hand stroked Athena's shoulder. "I know you're upset, but think about what you're saying. Calvin Bretherton is an earl, and he's a very good catch for any woman. Your comfort and that of your grandfather would be established for life. You mustn't pass that up."

"Hester, you sound just like the Duchess of Twillingham. What about marrying for love? What about living in mutual adoration? What about marrying a man who intends to honor you with his body and sacrifice for your happiness? Isn't that more important?"

Hester shrugged uncertainly. "Mother says that the greatest joys a lady can hope for are to be married and to become a mother. As long as a man treats us with all the respect due those stations in life, he has fulfilled his duty. You can't expect men to be chaste to only one woman. They aren't made that way. That's why they have mistresses."

Athena was too worldly not to recognize the truth of those words. But now that they applied to her, she refused to accept them. "Why must I content myself with only half of a man's ardor?"

"I don't know. Some women—the lucky ones—get

to be wives. The rest must content themselves with being whores. It is the way of things."

Athena looked out at the gardens. The lights had made every tree, path, and structure glitter as if they were made of stars. It was spectacular, it was exquisite . . . but it was not real. The true beauty of the gardens was masked by a brilliant if deceptive conceit.

Compromise. She tasted the word as if it were a slice of a strange fruit on her tongue. Can it be true that half a marriage was better than none? Didn't most women make concessions to matrimony out of a need for protection and provision? Didn't even queens marry not out of love but out of duty, to men they barely knew because it enlarged their dominions? Did she really think she was better than they?

Athena bolted out of the garden seat, swiped her last tear from her face, and stormed back in the direction of the courtyard. "It shan't be *my* way. I'm through playing the lady. If the prize for all this playacting is nothing more than a beautiful wedding followed by a cold marriage bed, then I don't want any part in it. To think I changed myself all over for that, that . . . pile of pig vomit. As if *all* a man wants is someone prim and proper. That's the biggest load of cow pats I've ever been told. Just ask Lady Ponsonby."

"Where are you going?" Hester called after her, racing to keep up.

"Home. To make myself a cozy fire courtesy of Countess Cavendish's *Feminine Excellence, or Every Young Woman's Guide to Ladylike Comportment*."

FOUR

"So the little French boy runs home shouting, 'Mama, Mama, Papa's on the roof and he's threatening to jump!' And she says, 'Tell your father I put horns on him, not wings.' "

The admiral laughed heartily at his own joke. Marshall Hawkesworth chuckled, too, making the gold epaulettes on his shoulders ripple.

As smoke from the admiral's cigar swirled between them, Marshall was flooded with memories of the England he had left behind before he shipped out to sea. Roasted duck, good port, cigars—these were all remembered flavors of home. Some things had changed—the face in the shaving mirror was weathered from his many months at sea, his blond hair had grown lighter from exposure to the sun, and he was all hard lines from the many battles he'd fought. Other things were the same—namely, that joke.

The admiral wiped his laughter-moistened eyes. "How's the port, my boy?"

Marshall set his empty glass on the table. "First-rate. It's a damn sight better than the swill we drink on board. That stuff is tastier than hemlock, but with much the same effect."

"Then have some more," he said, filling Marshall's glass with the ruby-colored liquid. "Wait, wait," the admiral said as his large frame sank back into the chair. "Here's another one. A little French boy comes home from school and tells his mother he has been given a part in the school play. 'Wonderful,' says the mother. 'What part is it?' The boy says, 'I get to play the part of the French war hero!' The mother frowns and says, 'Go back and tell your professor you want to play a real part, not a fictional character.' " The admiral's jowls shook with merriment. "The Gaul of some people, eh?"

Marshall cracked another smile.

The admiral stopped laughing. "Sorry, old chap, I was just trying to cheer you up."

"With all due respect, sir, I don't need cheering up. I need answers. Why have you ordered my ship back to port? We were on our way to rendezvous with the *St. George* when I got your orders to return to England. Quite frankly, I'm concerned for the safety of our sister ship and all her hands."

"They're quite well, my boy. I sent the *Triumph* in your stead. I've already had reports that they captured two French vessels carrying ammunition and supplies and sank a third."

"But why pull me away from the operation?" Marshall followed the admiral's gaze to the black armband halfway up Marshall's sleeve. "It's not because of my father, is it, sir?"

The admiral's voice became somber. "He was a good man and a dear friend. And I want you to have time to grieve his passing."

"I loved my father, sir. And I will mourn him. But not now. I have my duty."

"Your ship has been on active duty for fifteen months straight. Your men need rest."

"They're hale and hearty," Marshall said defensively.

"They're human beings who need to tend to their bodies and souls. They must have leave to refresh their morale. As you haven't requested a furlough on their behalf, I decided to give you one."

"But Napoleon is being driven back. We've already severed his supply routes. We were keen to push on, sir."

The admiral's eyes narrowed on Marshall. "Are you sure you're not trying to numb yourself to the loss of your father by driving yourself harder?"

"No, sir. I am trying to honor his memory by winning the war."

The admiral's mouth thinned. "*That* is the very thing I was afraid of. I don't need a captain out there who's trying to make his dead father proud. I need a leader who is able to retain objectivity and clearness of thought in the midst of battle." The admiral's tone softened. "Marshall . . . you've won many battles for the Crown. You're a first-rate officer, the finest captain His Majesty commands. You've already honored your father's memory. But have you stopped to consider that it is your family that needs you most now, and you can best pay tribute to your father by taking charge of his affairs?"

Marshall ground his teeth. Admiral Rowland was a man Marshall had always admired, in many ways more of a father to him than his real father had been. And because the admiral had never had children, Marshall was like the son who understood him and followed in his footsteps. "I'm needed out there, sir."

"Your mother and sister need you too." The admiral held up his hands. "I'm not asking you to give up your naval career. I'm just offering you a chance to detach yourself for a short time, so you can put your father's affairs in order. And I must say that a little gratitude from you would not be amiss. I wouldn't be making such an allowance for just anyone. But you are unlike most of my officers. Most of them are second or third sons, not heirs to the estate. And none of them have just become a marquess and peer of the realm . . . my lord."

Marshall shook his head. He doubted he'd ever get used to being addressed as Marquess of Warridge. He was never fond of titles of nobility. To him, they always implied undeserved honors. He had known too many nobles that led dissolute, dishonorable lives, and yet expected to be treated as though their titles somehow entailed worthy accomplishments. "Captain" carried much greater weight with him than "Marquess."

"How's your mother bearing up under the strain?"

"Very well, sir," Marshall replied, regretting the honesty of those words. He suspected his mother was only too happy to be finally liberated from the other half of her unhappy marriage. "I'll convey your kind thoughts to her."

"And your sister?"

He shook his head. "Justine was very attached to Father. It was she who took to nursing him during his long illness."

"Poor girl. She passed up many offers of marriage, did she not?"

"In a manner of speaking. Truth be told, she rather didn't try very hard to encourage them."

"I see. Well, as your father was unable to concern himself with finding her a suitable husband, that duty must now fall to you. Maybe while you're at it, you might even pick up a wife for yourself before you ship out again."

Marshall doubted that *he'd* try very hard. His men often joked he was married to his ship, and there was much truth in that. Women of his station in life were all so colorless and unexciting. One was much the same as any other, all of them a blur of coy smiles, feigned sensibilities, and uninteresting small talk. They dressed alike, they talked alike, they even acted alike. It seemed that they were all contestants in some unspoken challenge, a race to see who would become the Epitome of the Lady. It was not a prize he desired.

He found far greater interest in the low-class women who worked at inns and mercantiles along the wharfs. They did not shed their personalities in trying to fit the mold of a lady. Their concerns were centered on keeping food on the family table, not on what shade of jonquil was considered unfashionable that season. He was drawn more to she who was a real *woman* than she who was a real *lady*.

The admiral extinguished his cigar and stood. "I have nothing but the highest regard for you, my boy. That's why I'm ordering you to live your life. Mourn your father. Comfort your mother. Get your sister married. Take a wife. In a few months' time, return to me for reassignment."

Marshall came to his feet. "And my ship, sir?"

"I'm putting the *Reprisal* under Captain Hedway until you get back. He'll take care of her for you."

Marshall hung his head. He now felt as though there were two deaths in the family.

The admiral seemed to perceive his sense of loss. "Come now, man. You don't expect me to leave one of our ships of the line in dry dock, do you?"

"No, sir," he muttered. "Thank you for dinner, and for your company, sir. And for this leave of absence. I am beholden to you for your consideration of my family tragedy. Good night."

Marshall executed a formal salute, and turned toward the door.

"Hawkesworth?" called the admiral.

"Yes, sir?"

"Don't be too long. We can't let little French boys play real heroes in school plays."

Just like Admiral Rowland to say precisely what Marshall needed to hear.

It was a gorgeous day at the height of spring, one of those peculiarly perfect days without a single cloud in the sky.

Hester exchanged a few pleasantries with Mason Royce before walking uncertainly up the stairs to Athena's bedroom.

Softly, she knocked on the door. "Athena?"

Hester poked her head into Athena's darkened bedroom. Though it was after eleven o'clock in the morning, the curtains were still drawn. The air in the room was stale. Athena was lying on her bed, staring into the dying fire.

"How are you feeling?"

Athena glanced at Hester, but didn't acknowledge her.

"I called for you yesterday, and you wouldn't even come down to see me."

"Go away, Hester. I'm not in the mood for you today either."

"No. I'm not about to let you wallow in your gloom for one moment longer." She drew back the curtains, and pushed open the window. "Come on. Get up."

Athena cringed, shielding her eyes. "If you don't leave right now, I'll tell Grandfather."

"Who do you think sent me up here? Come on. Time to start the day."

Athena sat up, and looked at Hester in irritation. Her friend was looking clean and perfectly arranged in her pink dress and white shawl and slippers. The ribbons in her hair were white and pink. Even the rosy cheeks in her fair skin matched her ensemble.

"I'd like to see how cheerful you are with my chamber pot on your head."

"It might improve the smell around here. How long has it been since you've bathed?"

"I don't know," she said sarcastically. "What day is it?"

Hester pursed her lips. "I'll tell you what day it is. It's the day you and I go for a ride in Hyde Park."

"You go to Hyde Park. I'll just hide."

"No," Hester said firmly. "It's time we leave what happened at Vauxhall behind."

Athena swung a warning glance at her friend. "Hester Willett, if you so much as mention the name of you-know-who, I shall shove my parasol up your bottom."

"Agreed. Now go have your bath. I'll lay out something sensational for you to wear. I'm taking you hunting for fresh game."

As Hester's landaulet rambled toward London, Athena breathed in the cool spring air. The sun felt warm on her face, and she inclined her head to receive its rays. She felt like a wilted flower that was slowly coming to life once more.

By the time they reached Hyde Park, she was feeling quite herself again. Hester stopped the carriage to greet everyone, and Athena was drawn into polite conversations that, though superficial and frivolous, were just the sort of triviality she had needed. There was something to be said for the ladylike pursuit of inconsequential discourse; at least it kept one from pondering the blacker concerns of life.

The afternoon had grown sunny, and they took to walking alongside the lake. Couples walked arm in arm, and small groups meandered by twos down the paths. As Hester walked beside her, prattling idly about this party or that dress, the fragmented pieces of her life started to find their rightful place.

As her eyes casually scanned the gentle rise of hills dotted with clusters of picnickers, something snagged her downy mood. It was a fleeting thing—an ephemeral thought, perhaps—but it dampened her airy humor as surely as a dip in the frigid Thames. She looked again, wondering what it was that could have so disturbed her. Nothing. She shook her head at her own silliness.

And then she saw it. Indigo. It was a color that for Athena seemed to have set off bright sparks of irritation. In the far distance, on a path beyond the trees, a woman in an indigo dress was stepping onto a carriage.

Athena's eyes narrowed. She recognized the dress . . . and the woman in it.

A tide of rage roiled within her. She had some choice words for Lady Ponsonby, and by God, she would have her say.

"Hester, wait for me here. I'll bring the carriage back round for you."

Hester's baffled questions were left unanswered as Athena raced toward the landaulet at the Stanhope Gate. The driver had slumped to one side, fast asleep. Athena charged into the conveyance, startling the old man.

"See that carriage over there? Go where it goes. There's a sovereign in it for you if you remain on its tail."

"Yes, miss," he said, scrambling to put his hat back on his head as he urged the horse forward.

Blood raced through her veins as she struggled to find just the right words for Lady Ponsonby. She wanted to spit and kick, but she knew that it would not do the damage she wanted. She wanted to hurt this woman far deeper than just to mar her appearance. She wanted to inflict her with the same poison of pain she herself had suffered with for the past week.

Athena tossed aside the remembered promise to the Duchess of Twillingham to stay clear of Lady Ponsonby. She pursued the woman relentlessly as her carriage wended through the London traffic. Finally, after what seemed about five miles, Lady Ponsonby's carriage came to a halt in the middle of a Whitechapel street.

Lady Ponsonby alighted from the carriage and paid the driver. She walked up the front steps, opened the red door, and disappeared into the redbrick building.

Athena jumped out of the carriage, bounded up the stairs, and paused at the door. A wooden sign hung on the door from a nail. It read FOR SALE. Beside the door, on the brick wall, was a tarnished bronze plaque that read THE PLEASURE EMPORIUM, EST. 1795. She felt a moment's hesitation. It was a monumental thing she was about to do, and she was certain it would change the course of her life. But Athena had rarely regretted the things she did—only the things she hadn't done. With the same aplomb, Athena threw open wide the door and stepped through.

Instantly, she was enveloped by darkness. Her eyes widened instinctively as they gradually adjusted to the dimness inside. Through the foyer there was a parlor with windows facing the street. A needle of light from the shuttered windows pierced the darkness of the salon, and Athena could see inside.

Though white sheets were draped over the clusters of chairs, and the air was thick and musty, the house did not seem to have been boarded up for very long. There was a peculiar scent to the place, a strange mélange of cigars, liquor, and jasmine perfume. The walls were stripped of paintings and sconces, but the cornflower-blue paint was undiminished by time. At the far end of the room, a door opened.

Athena folded her arms in front of her. "Well, if it isn't Lady Pounce-on-me."

Lady Ponsonby's angular face registered surprise. "Who the devil are you?"

The question made Athena's blood boil. "Who am I? I am the woman whose future happiness you stole."

Her eyes narrowed on Athena. "I *do* know you. You're the protégée of that haughty cow, the Duchess of Twillingham. I spoke with you at Vauxhall last week."

"That's not the only thing you did at Vauxhall last week. I saw you in Lover's Walk with Calvin."

Her chin lifted defiantly. "That was *you* behind the bushes. Didn't your benefactress teach you that spying on people is considered rude?"

"That's rich, coming from you. How would Society look upon someone who had intercourse on the ground like a rutting sow?"

Lady Ponsonby advanced upon Athena slowly. Her dark eyes had depth and shallowness all at once, as if they hid some secret . . . and it was not a happy one. "In the first place, my little Scottish miss, I care bugger-all what Society thinks of me. And in the second place, what's my private life got to do with you?"

Though Lady Ponsonby was a good deal taller, Athena stood her ground. "Because that man in your 'private life' wasn't yours. He was mine."

The fierce look in the older woman's eyes softened in colorless humor. "Oh, so that's what this is about. You're jealous of me for that milksop. Well, I didn't break him. You can have him now." She turned to walk back through the door.

Athena seethed at her cavalier manner. She grabbed the first thing she could find, an unlit candelabra, and threw it against the empty fireplace. The heavy silver branches clanged against the bricks, making a fearsome racket as the candelabra bounced to the hearth.

"He was to be my fiancé! And you took him from

me!" Angry tears threatened to leak from her eyes, so she cast her face away.

Lady Ponsonby didn't speak for several moments. Her face never lost its composure. "If it's any consolation to you, he doesn't love me. We don't mean anything to one another." She chuckled hollowly. "I can't even remember his last name."

That only twisted the dagger in Athena's heart.

Lady Ponsonby bent over to pick up the now deformed candelabra. "He is still yours."

"I don't want him anymore."

"Why? Because he wanted to make love to another woman?"

"Exactly."

The bony shoulders shrugged. "Well, then, be happy I spared you from discovering the truth about his infidelity after you bound yourself to him for life."

There was some truth to that. But the colors on the palette of Athena's life had already been muddied beyond recognition.

"I just don't understand why on earth—"

"He would seek the bed of another? Wake up, my pet. Men have only two states of being—dead and unfaithful."

"But what on earth did he see in—" Athena didn't need to finish the sentence. Illumination dawned on Lady Ponsonby's face.

"Oh, now I understand. It's not that he betrayed you for another woman. It's that he chose me." A cold smugness rose on Lady Ponsonby's face, and despite it all, Athena felt small. "And here you are wondering how your dashing prince could choose the withered old crone over the fair princess." Sarcasm dripped from her thin lips. "Well, that, my pet, is because of what I have to offer him that you simply can't."

It was a question that cost her every last shred of pride, but she had to know. "What?"

Lady Ponsonby grinned jadedly. "Well, you're not going to find it in the pages of that ridiculous instruction manual all you debutantes are reading."

Athena's breath caught in guilty surprise. She raised her head defensively. "I am not a debutante."

"No, you're not. And therein lies the problem."

"What do you mean?"

"How old are you?"

She wasn't about to admit her advanced years to Lady Ponsonby. "That is none of your concern."

"Very well, don't tell me. But I think it a rational assumption to say that you have collected a fair bit of dust sitting on the shelf as long as you have."

Athena's face colored in spite of her defiant attitude. "Am I right in thinking there is a point to all of this?"

"My point is that here you are, ripe for the plucking, and yet you choose to remain on the vine for want of a skilled gardener."

"And what is the alternative? To fall into the hands of any passing field hand? I am not one of your mother's harlots."

Lady Ponsonby chuckled hollowly. "Oh, but you are, you just can't see it. You and every other Society rosebud have been raised with the express purpose of being hawked to the first moneyed gentleman that shows an interest in you, whether you like him or not. There is no difference between the likes of you and the likes of me. Except that I get to enjoy the fruits of my labor, whereas you . . . you get Society's permission to condemn me for it."

Athena couldn't deny the truth of her words. To take an opinion one way or another would make her either an ignorant or a hypocrite.

"But by all means," continued Lady Ponsonby, "go back to your morning room gossip over the embroidery hoops. Go back to the Countess Cavendish's most excellent tutorial on getting and keeping a husband. Keep your head buried in the sand as to what men are truly looking for in a wife. All of London will join you in celebrating the fantasy. But don't be surprised if women like me find their way into your lace-covered lives."

Her words burned within Athena. Whatever it was that Calvin had found lacking in her, she certainly didn't know what it was. And she wanted to. Quite desperately.

"Very well, then. Educate me. What is it that a man truly wants in a wife?"

The woman threw her head back and laughed. "Ask them . . . if you dare. I can promise you that they'll be delighted to show you. Just know this: you can't lay hold of a man without ever touching him. If all you do is play hard to get, other women will play with what gets hard." With an indigo flourish, Lady Ponsonby's skirt twirled as she returned to her parlor.

Dejectedly, Athena sank into a sheet-covered chair. She was no closer to learning why she could not win the heart of Calvin. Whatever it was, she would not find what she needed to know in Countess Cavendish's book. Despite her abrasiveness, Lady Ponsonby was right. Those pages were a waste of pulp.

She looked around at the empty room, full of the ghosts of pleasure-seekers and pleasure-givers. Athena would wager that those courtesans knew what men wanted in a wife, and they were entirely prepared to give it to them . . . for a short time and for the right price. If only she had been here when the bordello was in full bloom. Within these four walls was a veritable academy of knowledge as to how to nurture a husband—regardless of whose he was. Athena was no debutante—she was a dilettante, a mere amateur in the pursuit of a man's devotion. Had she been a courtesan, she would have long since learned the secret to snagging a man's heart.

She sighed. But men don't marry courtesans, do they? They marry ladies of quality. She shook her head. That's all wives were fit for, it seemed: breeding. Men sought wives only to bear children; they gave their affection to ladies of the night. Was it possible to have both? Was it possible to be the one he loved and the one he made love to? Was it possible for a woman to become both wife *and* mistress to a man? Was it possible for Athena to learn to be exactly what a man like Calvin desired, and still remain above reproach?

Suddenly, an idea occurred to her, one that she almost didn't want to claim. But it seeded in her despairing brain and began to grow before she had a chance to uproot it. There *was* a way to learn to become a lady-courtesan. But it would require capital. And cleverness. And, above all, daring.

Athena walked out the front door, and lifted the FOR SALE sign off the hook. She came back inside, walked to Lady Ponsonby's parlor, and flung open the door.

"Teach me."

FIVE

"A school for spinsters?"

Mason Royce lowered his newspaper and peered at Athena. She sat down on the upholstered chair opposite him.

"A *finishing* school, Grandfather. An academy for marriageable ladies of a certain age, wherein the gentle art of the acquisition and nurturing of a husband is taught. All using Countess Cavendish's methods." But there was a hidden curriculum, one that she had absolutely no intention of telling him.

His grizzled eyebrows drew together. "But I thought you said that the book was a monumental insult to literature."

"No." She thought quickly. "I said it was a monument to the institution of literature."

He removed his round spectacles. "But you don't know anything about running a school."

"Well, I didn't know how to paint until I tried it. I'm only thinking of the great need there is for this sort of learning. There are many ladies in Society who are believed to be past marrying age, and I want to offer them another chance at refining those advantages they possess and improving the ones they lack. Take, for instance, Joy Isley—she can play the piano and sing, but would be totally inept at managing a gentleman's household. Or Violet Teasdale, that Baron Whatsit's oldest daughter. She's a complete bluestocking on all things Egyptian but a grating bore at the dinner table. Countess Cavendish's book will work wonders on them."

"What about Calvin Bretherton? Aren't you going to marry him?"

Athena stiffened. "Calvin will have to wait. This is more important. If Countess Cavendish's book can improve me so much that I can get a handsome earl's proposal, I owe it to women like me who have lost all hope." She put on her most earnest face, the one she used when her lies were greatest. "I've already written to Countess Cavendish to get her blessing, and she is most excited about the prospect. She even said that once we get the school up and running, she might be able to lecture there from time to time."

Her grandfather ran his hand through his sparse hair. "What sort of things will be taught?"

"Only the most ladylike pursuits. Art, literature, and keeping gentlemen entertained at the dinner table." But Athena had other things planned. The lectures would also focus on the art of seduction, the literature of Eros, and keeping gentlemen entertained *under* the dinner table.

"It's a noble endeavor, to be sure," he said with a sigh. "But we don't have any money. How much is this going to cost?"

Athena smiled inwardly. "Nothing at all from us. Hester has the wherewithal, and has already agreed to invest in the school. I already have the location picked out. It's in the heart of London, not far from the City. The building is for sale, and from the look of it, no renovation will be necessary. And the owner is anxious to sell. If all goes well, as I predict it will, I may be able to start classes in a couple of weeks."

"Very well." He disappeared once more behind his newspaper.

Athena stood up and gave him a kiss on the cheek, then walked off, afloat in victory.

"What does Her Grace say?"

Defeat replaced triumph. "I . . . wasn't aware she had to be consulted."

"Well, she's your sponsor now. She's done us the favor of helping you get affianced. Until you're married, you must make certain that any enterprise you undertake carries her blessing."

Athena didn't even have to ask. She knew the duchess would not approve, especially if Lady Ponsonby was anywhere in the vicinity of this idea. It was time for another little white lie. "I had mentioned the idea to her at one point before she left on her voyage to Italy, and she sort of crinkled her nose at it. You know how these Society matrons are. They frown upon a lady being anywhere but a parlor room. But the more I explained the benevolence of teaching other women what she had taught me, the more she grew to like the idea. I'd say she was even quite flattered by it."

"I wish you'd just marry Bretherton and forget these notions."

Athena walked over and perched herself on the arm of his chair. "Do you remember the stories you told me when I was little? About Cinderella and the prince?"

Mason leaned back, awash in pleasant memories. "Of course I do."

"You used to tell me how poor Cinderella never got noticed, living as she did in her rags. But when she put on that exquisite dress and slippers, the king's son couldn't help but fall in love with her on the spot." Athena put her arm around her grandfather. "There are princes aplenty for women such as these Cinderellas. They just need a godmother to show them what to wear to the ball. Do you see, Grandfather?"

He sighed audibly, patting the arm that embraced him. "I suppose I'm just a stupid old man who loves you very much. You have my blessing."

My dear Lord Stockdale,

I have just learned the reason Miss McAllister has not been receiving you. Apparently, she chanced upon you in flagrante delicto *with a woman at Vauxhall.*

Whilst I am in no position to pass judgment on the morality of your actions, I do take exception at your carelessness. To undertake such a tryst in public with our protégée in the vicinity was a foolish mistake. You must understand the sensitivities of a woman such as Miss McAllister. Although her reduced circumstances may have tainted her appeal to a man of means, her spinsterhood is not a result of them. In fact, even if she were to be endowed with wealth, position, and beauty, making her the most attractive prospect in Society, she would still not marry for any reason but love.

She already has calf eyes for you, so you must nurture this. Express your own devotion to her, or

*she will seek her love elsewhere. You must not let that
happen.*

Please apprise me of your progress.

Yours,
Margaret, Duchess of Twillingham

Within a month's time, Athena and Hester had opened
the doors on Countess Cavendish's School for the
Womanly Arts. And had made a grand success of it.

Athena had conscripted a series of brilliant lecturers to speak on a number of relevant subjects: an estate
manager to discuss the intricacies of household and
servant management; a deposed French countess to
talk about deportment and high fashion; a well-known
American author and bon vivant to illustrate the flair
of discourse; a curator from the British Museum to
teach the substantive aspects of art appreciation; and
several others. This collection of lectures comprised
fully one half of her tutelage for shaping a woman into
a charming and sophisticated companion and marriage
prospect.

But the other half of the curriculum was much more
clandestine, and those lectures took place after the sun
set on the former bordello. Athena had sent discreet
missives to Mr. Gallintry and Lord Rutherford, gentlemen of a certain notoriety who were renowned for
their powers of seduction. They were men whom no
self-respecting lady ever entertained alone but whom
no self-respecting hostess ever left out of her party.
Athena engaged these rogues of the realm to teach her
students the right way to seduce a man: what words to

use to inflame a man's desire, how to kiss a man like bad girls do, how to touch a man without going too far.

Her inaugural month-long course had drawn a small number of interested applicants, half of whom were older governesses, and the other half, ladies of Athena and Hester's acquaintance. Within a few weeks of the end of that course, six of the seven spinsters were either engaged to be married or had strong prospects. Word had spread; at the beginning of the second course, Athena and Hester had three times as many applicants as before.

Miss Athena McAllister had become headmistress of a school that taught good manners—and wicked conduct.

And things were about to get a little more wicked. She put quill to paper, and penned an advertisement for the *Times*.

Marshall Hawkesworth crumpled the letter in his large fist and stormed out of his study.

"Justine!" he shouted up the grand staircase, pacing the marble floor like a caged lion. "Justine!"

A maid had emerged from the dining room, but wisely turned back until her master had done away with whatever had displeased him.

"Justine, get down here this instant!"

A woman with sandy brown hair and caramel-colored eyes leaned over the banister. "Yes, Marshall?"

"I want a word with you, please. In my study."

Justine tightened the shawl around her shoulders as she gingerly stepped down the staircase. "What is it?"

He placed the rumpled piece of paper into her

hands. "Read this. It seems your fiancé has called off the wedding."

She glanced at the disfigured paper. "Herbert? But why?"

He crossed his arms in front of his chest. "That's what I would like for you to tell me."

She preceded him into his study, a room of dark wood and polished brass. She perched herself on a leather chair. "I don't understand any of this. Why would he cancel our betrothal?"

"The letter puts it plainly. He questions your morality and your character."

"My morality?"

"That is a gentleman's code word for saying that he thinks you a loose woman."

"But that's preposterous. I'm not a loose woman."

"I am aware of that. What did you do that would have given him cause to believe that you are?"

Justine was silent a long time. "I was . . . demonstrative."

His brows drew together. "Demonstrative? How?"

Justine's face sank. "I don't want to talk about it."

"You bloody well will talk about it."

"Marshall, you're my brother, not my father. I don't owe you any explanations."

He leaned forward over his desk. "Now you listen to me. When Father died, I detached myself from the Royal Navy—in the middle of a war, mind you—just to look after you and the estate. My one remaining duty, before I can return to my ship, is to see you married off advantageously. And now that I've convinced Herbert Stanton, a man who owns half of Buckinghamshire, to ask for your hand in marriage, you turn him away with your 'demonstration.' Do you now think you don't owe me an explanation? I suggest you reconsider."

Justine's chin trembled. "I am not some task for you to tick off your list, Marshall. Go to your precious ship. Just leave me be."

"You know perfectly well I can't go back to sea until you are under a husband's protection."

"I don't need a husband. Miss McAllister has no husband, and she is perfectly respectable just as she is."

"Who's Miss McAllister?

"She's the headmistress of the academy that Mother sent me to, Countess Cavendish's School for the Womanly Arts. I completed her course last month."

Illumination dawned on Marshall's features. That was the trouble with educating females. Some dry old spinster pretends to be better off for never marrying, and all the impressionable girls decide they too don't need to be wed. "What else did this 'Miss McAllister' tell you?"

"She taught us that there is much more to being a lady than just what can be done in the parlor room. A lady is someone who plays by her own rules."

"Is that what you were doing with Herbert Stanton? Playing by your own rules?"

"As a matter of fact, it was. Herbert always thought of me as some sort of living doll . . . just some ornament to festoon his drawing room. I wanted to show him that I was a living, breathing woman with needs and desires . . . someone who could be a partner and companion to him, an equal in thought and reason."

Marshall shook his head. "Herbert Stanton is one

of the most conservative traditionalists in all of England. He doesn't want an equal . . . he wants an obedient wife to sire his children."

She banged the arm of the chair. "Well, in that case, I'm not sorry he called off the wedding. I don't like him, Marshall. I never have. I want a man who will love me and who will let me love him."

"Justine," he said, his teeth grinding, "you don't have the luxury of waiting for an advantageous marriage that happens to inspire love in both of you. You have an obligation to marry when we find you the perfect man."

"And Herbert is the perfect man? A man who wants his wife to be no more than a glorified servant or some brood mare to sire his purebred foals?"

"He's your only choice, Justine." His voice softened. "Your only chance."

Tears pooled in her eyes. "Well, if he's my only *chance,* then I won't be married to any man." She balled up Herbert Stanton's letter and dropped it in the wastepaper basket before she slammed the door behind her.

He was not accustomed to such insolent behavior, even from his own sister. Discipline and respect— those were his hallmarks, as well his men knew. He would have gone after Justine to make her take her leave in a more civilized way, but the poor girl had left in tears. And he didn't know how to handle women with leaky faces.

Marshall threw himself in the chair behind his gleaming mahogany desk. He stared across the expanse of desk at the ship in a bottle he had fashioned, an exact miniature replica of the *Reprisal.* As smelly and uncomfortable as life aboard a ship was, he missed it dreadfully. He found the parlor rooms of England far more tedious than muster at sea, and the rebelliousness of his sister infinitely more tiresome than an insubordinate sailor's. With Justine's engagement, he was mere weeks from getting back aboard his ship and being called Captain Hawkesworth again. He held up the glass bottle and peered inside. Now, his greatest desire seemed to be floating farther away.

It was all the fault of that academy for girls. A finishing school indeed! It certainly finished *his* plans. Imagine telling a woman that it was acceptable for her not to marry! It was outrageous. A perversion of society. A flagrant and intentional upset of the established order. Well, he wasn't going to allow this to go on. That headmistress had a lot to answer for. And if she failed to satisfy him, well . . . his ship would not be the only Reprisal.

SIX

Marshall Hawkesworth jerked on the reins, forcing his horse to an awkward stop. He curled his gloved hand around the pommel and flung himself off the stallion.

His scowl blackened as he looked up at the redbrick structure. The door was painted a cheery blue, and geraniums lined the windows beneath lace curtains. But he had just been made aware of the house's sordid past, and irritation threatened to choke him all over again. This was no place for his sister to be *seen* in, let alone *taught* in.

He took the stairs two at a time, and rapped on the door with his riding crop. A diminutive maid opened the door and curtsied. "May I help you, sir?"

"I'm here to see the headmistress." He gave her his crop, hat, and gloves.

"This way, sir," she said.

Marshall reluctantly followed behind the maid, who had the stature of an overgrown pixie, though he was more inclined to jump over the girl's head and charge ahead of her. But as he didn't know where the headmistress was, he thought it best to school his temper. Until, of course, he met the woman responsible for giving his sister a scandalous education that had rendered her unmarriageable to a most advantageous prospect.

They came to a door at the far end of a grand salon, and the maid knocked on it. "One moment, sir. I'll announce you."

"There'll be no need," he said, and opened the door himself.

Sunlight streamed in through the windows at the far end of the sitting room, casting squares of light onto the green carpet. The walls were papered in a light green silk frothing with tiny pink and blue blooms. A cherrywood table sat in the middle of the room, its legs curving down to the floor. Sitting behind the desk was a redheaded young woman who looked up from her ledgers to frown at him.

"You're late," she said, placing her quill into its stand. "I was expecting applicants at noon."

He shook his head dismissively. "I'm here to see the headmistress."

"Then it is a happy coincidence that you've found her. I am Miss McAllister."

Marshall blinked in a shudder of surprise. "You? You're in charge of this school?" He expected a bookish lady, wizened in face and feature, her curves disfigured by the ravages of time. Not someone like—

"Yes, I am. Now kindly close your mouth and take a seat."

He flinched at her impudence. "Young woman, I am here on a matter of great importance, with nothing less at stake than family honor."

Her posture stiffened. "In the first place, you may call me 'Miss McAllister.' I'll thank you to remember to whom you are speaking. And in the second place, I know precisely why you are here."

An angry retort died on his lips. "You do?" he said slowly, wondering how she could possibly ascertain his intentions.

"Of course," she replied, rising from her chair. The fabric of her blue dress cascaded to the floor. "You are not the first man to step over our threshold who has found himself experiencing some degree of financial embarrassment. You might even say that gentlemen who have fallen on hard times provide our stock-in-trade."

His eyes narrowed suspiciously. "Do they?"

"There's no shame in earning an honest wage. A good hard day's work would do many gentlemen a world of good. Including you, I daresay."

The affront was almost more than he could stand. It was bad enough that the saucy woman had mistaken him for someone else. But to upbraid his character without the benefit of even a formal introduction was beyond tolerable.

"Nevertheless," she continued, crossing her arms at her chest, "we more than anyone appreciate the importance of tact. After all, modeling has been a much maligned profession."

He almost laughed. Tact was something this girl knew nothing of. As he debated how best to put her in her place, something she said buzzed in his head like an angry hornet. *Modeling?*

"You will find that at this school, educational candor is valued above all else. These young ladies are taught a broad range of subjects, without capitulating to what is deemed acceptable for members of our sex. To the outside world, however, our curriculum may raise a few eyebrows. Your involvement in the program will be treated with discretion for as long as we have yours."

Marshall had not ascended to the rank of captain in the Royal Navy without learning how to deal with an adversary. And something told him that it would be far more effectual to get the information he sought by concealing his intent rather than disclosing it.

"Indeed. That had been a concern of mine."

"What is your name?"

"Marshall."

The woman returned to the desk and pulled out a fresh piece of paper from a box of stationery. She laid it upon a graph she had been working on when he had arrived. "Well, Mr. Marshall, have you ever done any modeling before?"

"I can't say that I have, no. But I have been told that I'm not too hard on the eyes."

"Hmm," floated back her pert response. "I suppose if the room were dark enough."

Marshall shifted in his seat uncomfortably.

She scribbled something down. "Your hair is flaxen, your eyes are blue . . . how tall are you?"

"Six feet, three inches."

"A large fellow."

"I come from good Oxfordshire stock."

She glanced up from the sheet. "I've no wish to discuss your relatives. No matter what manner of farmyard species they came from."

He chuckled in spite of himself. This girl was a complete surprise to him. Proper ladies of his acquaintance rarely disagreed with him, let alone offended him. She had a nerve—no, the bloody cheek—to treat him this way. He looked around the room. There were paintings hanging on the walls, each one made intriguing by a mysterious image—an idyllic countryside with a darkened wood to one side, a woman cradling a locked box, two people at a ball wearing masks. All of them seemed to be painted by the same hand.

"Will you be the one I shall be posing for?"

"Not exclusively. I lead a class on art, and I will need a model for our next lesson. Seeing as you're the only applicant who has presented himself, I expect you may have to do."

He pursed his lips. "Please don't flatter me. It goes to my head."

She smirked, and it lent her face a wicked charm. Her skin was lovely . . . fair and luminous, offset by her striking red hair. Her eyes were like cut emeralds, sparkling with a lively intelligence. Her mouth was like a rosebud, pink and kissable, and he experienced a rogue desire to make that mouth moan instead of smirk. This meeting had completely veered off his intended course, but he was intrigued by the prospect of the fresh adventure. This woman warranted exploration.

"The job pays a guinea an hour. If I engage you, I'll want you to pose for no more than two hours at a time."

It was a generous wage. Clearly, this woman had no idea that anyone off the street would pose for a twentieth that price.

"When shall I start?"

She stiffened. "I said *if* I engage you. You haven't been given the position yet."

He couldn't help but smile. He was beginning to understand how her mind worked. There was another volley of mortar fire coming, and he had to let her launch her attack. She wasn't about to give an inch without first taking a foot.

He clasped his hands. "What must I do to be hired?"

"I'll need a proper look at you. Stand up."

He ground his teeth at her commanding manner.

"Over there, in the light." She strolled up to him and took a closer look. She walked around him, examining him from all angles. The top of her chignon came to just below his shoulder.

"Well, Admiral?" he quipped. "Do I pass muster?"

"I haven't even begun my inspection yet. Take off your clothes."

The sardonic grin was torn from his face. "I beg your pardon?"

She looked him squarely in the face. "Take off your clothes so that I can get a better look at you. You can't expect me to hire you on the basis of a smile."

"You want me to pose *nude*?"

"Why should you appear so surprised? My advertisement called for a male model to pose *à la française*. Did you think that meant I would serve you up with croutons?"

Marshall shook his head in amazement. "Miss McAllister, aren't you afraid of what this compromising situation will do to your reputation? Or to that of the school?"

She walked over to the window and untethered the drapes. The fabric swished over the window, muting the light in the room. "There is no one else watching."

His rational judgment began to dissolve in the

rising tide of his fascination. What an audacious woman this was. And yet, as he began to tug at the knot of his cravat, her eyes drifted to the floor.

He studied her intently as he pulled off his coat. A muscle in her throat tensed, and color suffused her face.

He pulled the linen shirt over his head and dropped it on the chair with the rest of his clothes. Naked to the waist, he waited for her to look up at him, but her gaze was riveted to the floor. His hands went to unbutton his trousers when a soft voice stopped him.

"That'll do for now," she said. Finally, she looked up at him.

Marshall watched as her eyes traveled nervously across his broad chest. She was too uneasy to assess him properly, and he wondered briefly if this exercise was just a childish display of power. But she was visibly shaken by what she saw, and despite her bravado, he wondered if she had ever before beheld a man in a state of undress.

He watched in growing amusement as she timidly inspected him from different angles. Her rushed, unsteady breathing betrayed her nervousness. Though her crossed arms attempted to communicate a distant reserve, her whole body was as tight as a manrope knot. It was as clear as daylight. She was *attracted* to him.

"You may have the job," she said finally from behind him.

"Thank you."

"On one condition."

He turned around to face her. "Yes?"

"You must tell me how you acquired those scars."

"Perhaps."

She blinked up at him.

"If you ask me nicely."

The haughty expression returned, and her full lips thinned. "You may get dressed now. I shall open the drapes."

As she walked past him, he reached out and grabbed her forearm. Her body jerked back and collided with his. "Just a moment," he said, snaking his arm around her waist. She looked up at him in equal parts panic and fascination. She tried to push herself away, but everywhere her hands touched his bare flesh. In the hollow of her throat, her heartbeat fluttered like a trapped bird.

He lowered his head to within inches of hers. "I have a condition or two of my own."

"I beg your—"

"First, I will want to know more about this institution of yours. I have a keen interest in the sort of education you offer, especially when I am asked to be a part of it."

She tried to pull herself free, but his arm was as immovable as a branch of oak. "And second?"

"The second I shall reserve for a later time. I wouldn't want you to think me too presumptuous." He softened his arm, and she slithered away. For the first time, her sharp tongue was silent.

The girl retreated behind the desk, presumably to gather her wits. He grabbed his shirt and slipped it over his head, the voluminous fabric falling below his hips.

"Shall I begin Monday?"

She nodded.

"Ten in the morning?"

"No." Her voice cracked and she cleared her throat. "Eight in the evening. You must use the servant's entrance through the back. Is that understood?"

"Of course. We must observe the strictures of propriety."

"Precisely."

"Speaking of propriety . . . would you mind terribly?"

"Would I mind terribly what?"

One corner of his mouth lifted. "Turning around. I must unbutton my trousers in order to tuck in my shirt."

Wide-eyed, she glanced between his legs before spinning toward the wall.

Once she was facing the opposite direction, Marshall leaned over her desk and stole a peek at the chart she had been working on. He caught one phrase— "Erotic Literature"—and knew he had to take it. Gingerly, he pulled the sheet out and flattened it against his abdomen before tucking his shirt into his trousers.

"Miss McAllister," he began as he buttoned his waistcoat down the front, "I do hope that I will prove satisfactory in my commission. The last thing I wish to do is disappoint your students—or you for that matter. You will of course let me know how to best please you."

She turned around to face him, and he saw that it had happened again, that telltale blush that darkened her cheek. It was like reading her thoughts—and lascivious ones they were.

"Perhaps there is one thing you can do to accommodate me, Mr. Marshall."

He jerked on his coat. "Anything."

"Do try to leave your colossal arrogance at home. Copernicus has already decreed that you are not the center of the universe."

He smiled in spite of the cut, and bowed curtly. "If I were, I would no doubt be incinerated by the warmth from your sunny disposition."

Marshall tethered his horse outside the Hart & Hound. Although his father had been a longstanding member of White's Club, Marshall himself preferred the more pedestrian drinking establishments. There was nothing like the smell of sawdust and roasting ham while one downed a swift half.

A trip to the water closet let him remove the pilfered cache from inside his shirt. He sat down at a table, ordered his ale, and began to read.

His blue eyes danced over the schedule, which outlined all the lectures for the week. There were classes scheduled during the day, which centered on history, music, and myriad other mundane subjects.

But his mouth fell open when he read what was being organized for the evenings. Monday's class was *Painting the Nude Male Form.* Tuesday's was *Bringing Erotic Literature to Life,* followed by Wednesday's *Sensual Kissing,* and Thursday's *Using Your Hands to Bring Pleasure to His Body and Yours.* His mind turned to his sister. Now he knew why his sister was accused of being "demonstrative." Miss McAllister was teaching her pupils to become seductresses!

His drink arrived and he took a large swallow. School for the Womanly Arts indeed! The education

that Justine received had cost her her fiancé and him
his freedom from the tedium of the London Season.
No doubt to his sister these lectures were an awakening of sorts, opening her mind to the seamier side of
social interaction. But even at her age, she was better
off remaining an innocent. It was difficult enough to
find her a potential husband at twenty-nine, but it
would be impossible if she started to let attraction determine her choice of prospective husbands.

Attractive. Marshall took a slow sip of his ale as he
reread the names of the evening lectures. That sassy
Miss McAllister had awakened every nerve that had
lain dormant since he left his ship. She was a tangle of
contradictions. Strait-laced and haughty, but far from
being a lady. Fiery red hair that accounted for her
incredible daring, but cheeks that blushed with the
awareness of being discovered. A buxom figure that
would fill a man's hands, but he doubted she'd allowed
any man access to it. The face of a good girl, but the
mouth of a bad one. He chuckled. That mouth, at once
impertinent and alluring—the thought of it ignited a
slow burn in his trousers. The corners of his lips lifted
at the thought of the exciting venture she presented.

He sighed, folding the sheet of paper and slipping
it into his coat pocket. If word of this school ever
got out, Miss McAllister would not be the only one
to suffer. Every student who'd ever matriculated would
be tainted, his own sister included. They would be
shunned by Society, ostracized by any decent family. Despite her dowry, no upstanding gentleman
would ever marry Justine. But any bounder and cad
would. He would never allow that to happen.

The school ought to be closed down, quietly and without incident. But how on earth was he going to get the indomitable Miss McAllister to see reason? He had to find a way to force her to close, short of burning the place down.

SEVEN

All day Monday, Athena kept glancing at the clock on the mantel. At first, she could not wait for evening to come around. Mr. Tremayne, the lecturer on the subject of servant management, whom she had scheduled to speak for two hours that morning, droned on for more than five. All twelve of her students were valiantly fighting drowsiness. Only the promised art class with a live male model kept them alert.

But after the apothecary had left, Athena began to dread the appointed hour with Mr. Marshall. It was bad enough that she had dropped her chilly reserve of authority with him; worse still was the way she lost her composure altogether. Instead of a mature woman of years in a position of authority, she dissolved into a weak, virginal *female*. His embrace had completely robbed her of any aloofness. How formal could she remain in the arms of a partially naked man? But the real humiliation was in his ability to read her discomfiture. Even now, when she thought of it, she groaned inwardly.

The ladies had practically raced through supper to be ready in time for Mr. Marshall's arrival. The most eager was Miss Drummond, a woman of over thirty who lived as a virtual recluse in her brother's household. Her eyes lit up behind her round spectacles as she repeatedly asked Athena, "Is he really going to be naked?" with the same bubbly enthusiasm as a child waiting for a sweet.

At the stroke of eight, Athena heard a knock on the back door. She tensed, unaware she was holding her breath. She asked Gert to answer the door.

A few seconds later, Gert opened the door to the parlor and announced him.

Mr. Marshall strode in, wearing a quiet intensity and a crooked smile. He was dressed in a dark green jacket and a skintight cream-colored waistcoat. He looked significantly larger than the last time she saw him, but she suspected that had something to do with the way his body filled the doorframe.

Their eyes met, and he smiled. He effected a curt bow.

"Miss McAllister, I bid you good evening."

She steeled her haughty reserve. "Mr. Marshall, you're looking well."

"Thank you. May I sit down?"

"No."

His blue eyes darted to hers in curious surprise.

She stood up. "This is not a social call, Mr. Marshall. There are a dozen art students upstairs. I've no wish to keep them waiting. Through that door is a hallway, and the next door down leads to a water closet. Please use that room to disrobe. There's a towel inside which you can use to protect your modesty as we go upstairs."

"I was hoping to be introduced to your students first. Fully clothed, preferably."

She folded her hands in front of her. "I'm sorry to disappoint you, Mr. Marshall, but perhaps I failed to make you understand your position. What you do outside these walls is of no concern to us. It matters not whether you are a Member of Parliament or a chimney sweep. Within these walls, you are a servant for hire, pure and simple. So there is no need for introductions. You have no name once you go upstairs."

A muscle tensed in the hollow of his jaw. "You have an annoying habit of putting people in their place."

"And you have an annoying habit of forgetting yours. To the washroom, if you please."

He made no move. His eyes stormed over as he stared down at her, as though he were warring with the urge to defy her. Without a word, he strode off in the direction of the door.

His absence from the room filled her with relief. He was clearly not a man accustomed to taking orders, less so from a woman. Hard luck, she reasoned—he was going to have to get used to it. She was proud of the way she stood up to him, her frosty equanimity fully intact. It was the best way to deal with presuming subordinates.

A short while later, the door to the salon opened. In the doorway stood Marshall. He was unclothed from head to foot, with only a narrow towel wrapped around his narrow hips. His wide shoulders practically spanned the doorway, and she realized he looked no less substantial without his clothes. A hood of sinew cloaked his neck, ending at the cannonballs of muscle that formed his shoulders. His chest was smooth and sculpted, like the statues of Greek soldiers in the British Museum, but there ended the comparison, for there was strength and life beneath the sun-kissed skin. A trail of golden hair led down his ridged abdomen, disappearing behind the white towel.

She tried to walk past him through the door, but he did not budge. She came to an abrupt halt just under his downturned face.

"Move," she commanded.

His expression hardened. "Servant or no, I believe the polite thing to say is 'excuse me.'"

Any hint of mischief or teasing on his part would have earned him a severe tongue-lashing. But his expression was serious.

"I beg your pardon?"

"Both an MP and a chimney sweep deserve your polite civility. And so do I."

Her nostrils flared. Even her grandfather never upbraided her in such a manner. "Stand aside, Mr. Marshall."

"Stand aside, *please*."

She had half a mind to ram her way through the wall of muscle in the doorway. But she knew that if she touched him anywhere on his naked flesh, she would crumble all over again.

"I'm not in a playful mood."

"Nor am I. Address me with common courtesy, and I shall treat you with the same."

She stared up into his face, her face heating with contained anger. "Very well," she said through clenched teeth. "Stand aside, please."

A civil smile graced his face. He moved away from the doorway and let her pass.

She turned to face him and sank into a deep curtsy. "Now if my master would graciously condescend to following one such as I, I will gladly show him to the art room."

He leaned his back against the doorjamb and crossed his arms. "Sarcasm is just as rude as brusqueness. But I shall give you the benefit of taking your words at face value."

Athena straightened. It was like being with a schoolmaster. She hitched up her skirt and led him upstairs to the lecture room.

From behind the door, she could hear the ladies chattering. She knocked twice and breezed in.

The room had been arranged according to her specifications. A semicircle of easels had been positioned in front of a platform, upon which a single ottoman stood. The room was alive with the familiar, sharp smell of charcoal, and Athena felt once again in control.

"Ladies, class is about to begin. Please take your seats behind your easels. All smocks on? Good. Now, remember what I've told you. Mr. Marshall, you may come in."

Marshall took a step into the room, and twelve women gasped. Wide-eyed and slack-jawed, they took in a quick look before retreating behind their sketchpads to giggle nervously with one another.

"Ladies, please control yourselves. Show some decorum. Mr. Marshall, please have a seat on the ottoman."

In front of the platform were two pedestal candelabra casting light upon the cushioned seat. Uncomfortably, Marshall padded along the carpeted floor, and stepped up onto the platform. He puzzled over how to sit down on the low upholstered bench without revealing what was underneath his towel. Only one thing was to be done. He unhooked the towel and held it to his groin as he crouched onto the seat.

The sight of his naked hips made a woman gasp audibly. Athena walked along the semicircle of easels until she found the guilty party.

"Lady Katherine! Control yourself. This is a man, not a circus freak." But the heavy lady could not overcome her shock. "Oh, for heaven's sake! Mr. Marshall, would you mind closing your eyes?"

He frowned at her. "Close my eyes?"

"Just for a moment. Please," she added meaningfully.

He sighed, and shut his eyes.

"Now, ladies—Alice, stop snickering—take a good, long look at your model. He can't see you, so don't be bashful. This is what a man looks like with no clothes on. Although men vary greatly in size and build, and your model here is physically among the finer specimens of males, all men are equipped alike. The reason I hired a model for you is twofold. Artistically, we are going to perfect our techniques of shading contours and conveying textures, and a human body has many curves and textures that we can practice with. But I also wanted you to see what a man's body is like. Your parents and protectors would have you go to your wedding night in complete ignorance of what to expect your husband's body to look like. This puts you at a disadvantage, since his more worldly education has already taught him what a woman's body feels like, let alone looks like. Consequently, many young brides are so astonished by the overwhelming experience of seeing a man nude for the first time that they seldom enjoy the act of intimacy. This shall be your primer. See what you can expect in your marriage bed. Permit your visual senses to feel the hard curve of his muscled shoulders and the wooliness of his body hair. Learn the ridges of the grooves and sinews, and the sharper angularity of a man's form. Let your eyes drink their fill of this man's body, and then translate that image to the paper."

Athena looked around at the ladies' faces. The giddiness had vanished. Now they were able to look at the body with a more analytical and probing eye. She smiled inwardly. This exercise had let the girls take a great leap forward in becoming confident and self-assured women.

"There isn't enough time to draw the whole of your model, so tonight, you will focus on one feature of his body and sketch it. You may begin now."

Athena walked up to him. "Mr. Marshall?"

He opened his eyes and looked up at Athena. "That was a very moving speech. This class of yours is certainly very interesting."

"It's about to become more interesting. Please remove the towel."

EIGHT

Marshall's eyes darted around the room nervously. "In front of all these women?"

Athena found she enjoyed seeing him squirm. "That cocksure attitude of yours melted awfully quickly."

His eyes sparked blue fire. "Miss McAllister, are you sure this is wise? These ladies are innocents."

"They are all elder of twenty-five. Old enough to be married, and therefore old enough for this."

"Inexperienced, then."

"Not after tonight."

He shifted uncomfortably in his seat. "I don't wish to be responsible for corrupting these ladies."

"It is an attitude that does you credit, but you're not corrupting anyone. That is the point of this exercise. Ignorance of a thing increases the fear of it. When these ladies finally do see a fully naked man—on their wedding night, presumably—they will be in the midst of a situation over which they will have little control. This is an environment in which they can feel safe. Safe to look, free to enjoy, without the threat of any impending violation."

His sandy brown eyebrows drew together. "Violation? Is that what you think of lovemaking?"

Athena shrugged. "It is a fact. For some of these girls, whose marriages will be arranged to a complete stranger, it is the way they will feel about their marriage bed."

A guilty expression came over his face as his thoughts turned to Justine. He cast a concerned glance across the ladies' expectant faces. "I hadn't . . . quite considered it . . . from that point of view."

"Perhaps you should. Ask them yourself." Athena turned around. "Lady Penelope, you once described to me the man that your father intended for you to wed."

Lady Penelope, a woman of tepid beauty but possessed of a lovely figure, shuddered. "Lord Chesley. Oh, he was awful. He was old and gouty, and he spat when he talked. I couldn't stand to be in the same room with him. One time, I saw him flog his horse just because she went lame. The poor beast bled torrents, and even I couldn't stop him from hitting her. One night at a ball, he began to kiss me. I tried to be accommodating, really I did. But no matter how many nice things he whispered in my ear, all I heard was the sound of his horse screaming."

Athena returned her attention to Marshall. "When she refused to accept the gentleman's offer of marriage, her father expelled her from the house without a penny to her name. Now she lives on her uncle's modest estate in Dorset, forced into spinsterhood by her father until she relents and marries Lord Chesley. It's the height of injustice that a woman as bright and caring as Lady Penelope is given in marriage to one such as he. That's why her uncle asked her to come here . . . to break down her resistance and get her to accept the betrothal. And each of these ladies has her own story to tell. Quite frankly, I don't know if I can rescue them from a loveless marriage. But the least I can do is ease their way through a ghastly nuptial experience."

Marshall hung his head to think how Justine must have felt when faced with a marriage prospect of *his* choosing. He knew she didn't like Herbert Stanton, but he had forced her hand anyway. How poor Justine must have tried to make the most of a bad situation by learning how to *endure* marriage to Stanton rather than *enjoy* it.

Marshall sighed deeply. He didn't know if it was guilt or compassion that spurred him to it, but he lifted the towel and let it drop to the floor.

His nakedness was a blur as Athena spun around and stepped off the platform. Despite her admonishments to her students, Athena could not help feeling a bit flustered herself. "Ladies, if you would, avail yourself of the sight of this obliging model. We will discuss the topics of sensuality and lovemaking in depth next week. For now, feel free to appreciate a man's form in its natural state."

A couple of the women giggled furtively, their smiling mouths hidden behind their nervous hands. Athena walked around the room, watching the faces of her students quickly transform from a look of bashful tension to timorous curiosity. They began to gaze unabashedly, their heads tilted to one side in thoughtful study. Within moments, all were sketching furiously.

Athena was also eager to gaze upon him. But each time she glanced up at his platform, she found him looking straight at her. Any hint of embarrassment at his own nudity had been replaced by a challenge that seemed spoken only to her. His eyes followed her everywhere, as if she were the most important thing in the room. Consequently, she felt far too self-conscious to look at his body for any length of time. His confident, teasing smile seemed to hide some secret knowledge, and it made her feel as if she were the one with no clothes on.

Athena walked behind the semicircle of easels, offering guidance and correcting her students' techniques. Under the guise of the art teacher, Athena found she could study his nudity without her face coloring. After bending over Miss Drummond's moving pencil, Athena finally satisfied her curiosity. She stole a long look at the place between Mr. Marshall's legs.

This part of him was wholly unlike the Greek statues she was familiar with. Those were smooth and polished, and showed miniaturized, aesthetic representations of the male sex. But the man on the platform had a nest of light brown hair between his legs and a thick tube of muscle that grew from it. The size of the sex was particularly surprising, and she marveled at the fact that such a substantial organ could be accommodated by a woman's small opening. For the thousandth time, she wondered what such a thing would feel like inside of her. Soon she became conscious of a hushed erotic whisper inside, inaudible to anyone but her. Later, perhaps, she would give it full voice. But for now, she cradled the sensation, and secreted it away like a stolen sweet.

He was a beautiful man, no doubt about that. Handsome in face and form, a perfect artist's model. There were points of interest all over his body. Curve upon curve of muscle flowed down his arms. His golden-brown skin seemed to absorb the candlelight rather than reflect it, but a dusting of blond hair gave his shins and forearms a soft shimmer. The ridges of muscle on his abdomen folded at his narrow waist. One long thigh was partially obscured as he leaned over it, his elbow resting on his left knee. But the other showed clearly just how long his lap was.

Her hands itched to sketch him. She went to a side table and began to sharpen a pencil with a blade.

"I'm beginning to feel a slight draft," he said.

She glanced up at him. "No doubt it has something to do with the fact that you have no clothes on."

He rolled his eyes. "Isn't there a fireplace behind me? A fire might make me more comfortable."

"Question asked, question answered." Athena picked up her sketchbook and her pencil and retreated to the rear of the room. Here, behind the platform, she could see Marshall from the back, but he could not see her.

"That's quite all right, Miss McAllister. Your tenderness alone warms me."

"Well, I mean really. Why a man would complain about being naked in a room full of women absolutely defeats me."

"You'd sing a different tune if you had to change places with me."

"Now there's a silly idea. A naked artist painting a clothed model."

He snickered. "Perish the thought. The whole fabric of society would become unstitched."

Athena smiled surreptitiously at his joke as she leaned against a table. There was great freedom from her vantage point; here, she could scrutinize him without feeling the weight of his perspicacious stare. She cocked her head to one side, tracing the contours of his back with her gaze, and let the pencil fly over the blank paper.

In no time, the white paper showed an outline of his masculine body. She began to sketch the details of his form: the waves of his blond hair, the expanse of his wide shoulders, the tapering of his narrow waist, the spread of his heavily muscled legs. There was a texture to his skin, not smooth like silk, but rough like sketch paper. And then there were those scars on his back . . . long, jagged lines that marred the beauty of his body.

"How did you get those scars?"

He chuckled. "Such fatal curiosity."

"Oh, very well, then. Don't tell me." She meant to come off as flippant, but instead sounded petulant.

"It's almost a joy keeping a secret from you."

She pursed her lips as she darkened the contours of his back. "I can only presume you were stabbed in the back by women you kept secrets from."

He turned around and looked at her, the muted light giving his features a lethal edge. "Weren't you taught that it's unseemly to comment on a person's deformities?"

She felt her face go all red again, but put forth an air of displeasure. "Mr. Marshall, please retain your pose. If you remain still and don't move, perhaps our relationship will be less painful than I find it at present."

"As you wish," he said, resuming his pose, a wicked grin spread across his face. "May I have leave to speak just once more?"

She sighed heavily. "I shudder to grant it without a due sense of alarm."

"I'll tell you about the scars if you tell me what meaning is behind the sinister elements in your paintings in the sitting room below."

Her mind turned to those paintings. The locked treasure chest, the masks, the dark woods. Those symbols were emblematic of her own secret pain—the inaccessibility of love, the inscrutability of men, her own loneliness. She could never confess those intimate details with someone like him. "Then I suppose we shall never discover each other's secrets."

"Pity. I should have liked to become more intimately acquainted with you."

It was impossible to ignore the double entendre, and it made her feel a bit giddy.

His left shoulder was next, and her pencil delineated the hard lines. She appreciated the way the light disappeared under the curve of muscle and used her fourth finger to blend the graphite into a soft shadow.

Gradually, her mind began to drift. As her fingertips smoothed over the contour of the muscles on his shoulder and back, she began to imagine the feel of his skin against her hands. Softly, her fingers brushed the long line down his spine, wondering what it would look like in movement over her own body. She traced a line across his back to his right shoulder, imagining it braced beside her head as he positioned himself over her. Her darkened fingertips smudged the shadow down his right thigh, absently wondering what such a thing would feel like against the soft inside of her own thighs. Pensively, her fingers warmed the hard planes of his buttocks. They were firm and square, calling forth images of it rising and thrusting into her own wetness, again and again and again . . .

"I said, 'Excuse me.' "

The interrupted pleasure was almost painful as the heated vision vanished into cold reality. She looked up at the source of the voice. Marshall had turned in his seat to peer straight at her. "It's ten o'clock. Time's up."

It took her several moments to reconnect with her surroundings. "Oh." She set the sketchbook facedown on the table. "Of course." She stood up on unsteady legs. "Ladies, have you all finished?"

"Yes, Miss McAllister," they answered in unison.

"Very well, then. You may leave the smocks here on the table and retire for the night. Alice, please ask Gert to bring up Mr. Marshall's clothes."

Marshall stood up and stretched. Athena watched in fascination as his magnificent naked body extended to its full length.

"That was rather more grueling than I expected," he said, fastening the towel around his hips.

She busied herself collecting and folding smocks. "Yes," she droned. "Sitting idly must be absolutely exhausting work for you."

He shook his head. "I wish your mouth would sit idly." His feet pounded on the wooden floorboards as he stepped off the platform. He padded around her to get a look at the sketchpads.

Marshall moved slowly from one canvas to the next, regarding each one thoughtfully. With his arms crossed in front of him and a contemplative look on his face, he looked as if he were walking along the Prints and Drawings Room at the British Museum instead of a ladies' academy lecture hall covered in nothing but a towel. "This is very interesting."

"What is?"

"The artists' choices of subject."

"What do you mean?" She looked at each drawing, stopping where he did. "There's nothing untoward in these sketches."

"That's what I mean. Look here," he said, moving back along the semicircle of easels. "This one drew my hand, and she did a damn fine job of it. This one drew my foot . . . even though it looks more like a sea lion's flipper than a human foot. This one did my head. That one did my chest. Sitting up there naked as a jaybird, I was sure I'd find twelve interpretations of the sight of my *arbor vitae*."

Athena snorted. "It's quite in character for you to think that the naughty parts of your anatomy are uppermost in a woman's mind. Perhaps the women that you are accustomed to dealing with would think so. But these ladies are more serious about their art than your body, as you can see from what they have honed in on."

He cocked an eyebrow. "Really? Well, let's see what *you* have honed in on." He strode over to the table where she had left her sketchbook and picked it up.

Athena followed him, and tried in vain to snatch the book from his hands. "Mr. Marshall, give me back my book!" She jumped up to grab the book from his outstretched hand, but missed. "Mr. Marshall, I'm warning you—"

"Hmm," he said, studying the sketch while holding her at bay. "You seem to have portrayed my bottom quite accurately. I suppose that puts you in with the legions of women you claim I deal with."

"Certainly not," she said, seizing the sketchbook and walking to the table, her pride sorely bruised. "I was merely perfecting my craft."

"Is that what you call it? Looks more like you were preserving the image of me for you to enjoy alone later."

That made her face go red, but she spun around to stare him down. "Oh, you really are a conceited oaf. Just so you can remove that smug look from your face, I'll have you know that this was an artistic study of contrasts. I was trying to capture the look of a solid object on top of a delicate one."

He took a step toward her, wedging her against the table. "Perhaps I can offer a more tangible example."

Her pride rebelled at his arrogance. How dare he accost her in such an ungentlemanly manner! But his nearness rekindled the flame that had ignited when she was caressing his image. Now, with his body towering above her and his legs lodged between hers, she was living the very fantasy she had enjoyed just moments before.

The amusement vanished from his face. Thick eyebrows hooded his eyes as they gazed intently into her face. His hand came up and caressed the nape of her neck. Athena held her breath as his thumb traced a line across her slack jaw. His fingers came round and brushed her open mouth.

The tender touch on such a sensitive place heated her body all over. Like the lights at Vauxhall Gardens, a series of sparks ignited each part of her body in turn, until she was aglow in pleasure. His hot breath on her face quickened as his fingers trailed down her neck slowly, provoking vivid new sensations. His touch was both soft and hot, soothing and enraging, and it made her mad with longing. Her mind skipped across the daydream she had enjoyed. As fantasy and reality collided, she lost all presence of mind. She wanted him to kiss her, to put an end to her sensual curiosity. But when one fingertip crossed the sensitive hollow of one shoulder and wandered to the other one, her patience was at an end.

"What are you doing?" she breathed, her words claiming innocence but her expression begging for more.

"Perfecting my craft," he said, the backs of his fingers caressing the slope of her breasts above the neckline of her dress.

She looked down at his wayward hand, wondering if it would ever make it down to the nipples that were now rising in expectation. Her heart beat so strongly she could almost hear it. But another sound echoed in her ears . . . someone was knocking on the door.

She pushed him away and flew to the opposite end of the room. "Come in."

The maid opened the door bearing Marshall's clothes folded in a neat pile on her arm. "The gentleman's clothes, miss."

"Thank you, Gert. Mr. Marshall can dress himself here in the room. Tell him to meet me in my sitting room when he's done." Without another glance, she rushed out the door and into the safety of solitude.

NINE

Marshall chuckled softly at Athena's swift retreat. There was no question which of them emerged the winner from that particular skirmish, and he was going to savor every moment of his victory.

He shook his head as he thrust his legs into his breeches and buttoned them up the front. It had been all he could do to keep his towel from tenting upward as he touched her. She was absolutely maddening, in every sense of the word. If she wasn't cutting into him with her razor-sharp tongue, she was inflaming his desire with her innocent allure.

He drew on his stockings. She was full of claws and teeth, that one, and woe betide any man who was foolish enough to corner her on wit alone. But he had found a way to keep her from unsheathing her weapons, and learning her vulnerability finally made her seem like a real woman.

He threw the white shirt over his torso, reveling in the familiar warmth. It was puzzling that such a self-assured woman could so completely founder when it came to matters between a man and a woman. It was hard to imagine a woman as old as she was completely naïve about the touch of a man. But when she was in his arms, he could *feel* her inexperience . . . and he knew she had drifted into unfamiliar waters. As he wound his cravat around his neck, he realized that there was more to her school than he'd first surmised. Athena McAllister was not just trying to expose her students to relations between the sexes. It was she herself who was in search of understanding.

He shrugged into his waistcoat. Justine had been tutored by one just as innocent as she. Nevertheless, Athena McAllister had opened his eyes to something he'd never considered. He had been with women who had been with men before him. They had enjoyed the act of lovemaking just as much as he'd had. But for a sensitive woman like his sister, a heated embrace with a man she wasn't attracted to must seem like a revolting and offensive thing. And Athena had taught him the depth of his sister's suffering.

He slipped on his shoes and coat, and wove a loose knot in his cravat as he went downstairs. He found the sitting room door, and swiping his hand against his hair, knocked.

"Come in."

He smiled inwardly at the frigid command. She was back in familiar waters, her distant reserve back in place. He opened the door, and stepped in.

At night, her cheery sitting room, with its light, airy colors, looked more somber. There were darkened corners to it now, and her intriguing paintings were cast in shadow. Nevertheless, the images were engraved on his memory, and the room still gave him a secret thrill. It was here that he had learned how his touch was able to take out Miss Athena McAllister's rudder and make her run aground.

But no one sat at her writing desk. His eyes scanned the room, and he found not one but two women sitting on the settee near the hearth. Beside Athena sat a very attractive woman who was older by about five years, with dark hair and dark eyes.

"Good evening. I hope I'm not interrupting, but Miss McAllister asked me in to . . . conclude matters."

Athena's neck stiffened. "You mean 'settle accounts.' There's no need to be enigmatic, Mr. Marshall. Hester knows you're an *employé*."

"Athena, don't be so rude. Mr. Marshall, I am Hester, Lady Willett."

Marshall bowed over her outstretched hand. "Delighted to make your acquaintance, my lady. I'm glad to see that manners are not completely absent from this institution." He ignored Athena's expression of pique.

Hester smiled graciously at him. "Thank you for sitting for our students this evening. I've just come from seeing to them upstairs, and I must confess that you are quite the sole and exclusive subject of conversation."

"I hope I did not shock them."

"Not at all. I believe one of the more frequently used descriptives was 'handsome.' "

"Then I'm flattered. Thank you for saying so."

"Would you care for a glass of wine?"

Athena stood up. "No, Hester. I wouldn't want to keep Mr. Marshall from his other appointments." She held out a small pouch. "Here's your pay, Mr. Marshall. Don't let us detain you."

"Not at all, Miss McAllister. I'm quite enjoying my conversation. With some of you, anyway."

Athena pursed her lips and sank slowly back into her chair.

Hester handed Marshall a glass. "May I ask what brought you to us? Apart from Athena's advertisement?"

"You mean, why was a gentleman such as myself reduced to taking on employment?"

Hester shrugged. "In so many words, yes."

Marshall's eyebrows drew together. It was contrary to his nature to be deliberately deceptive, especially to one as pleasant as Hester. "My father died recently, and I've been required by duty to take on the running of the household. Naturally, one does what one has to."

"Of course," she said, her face wreathed in sympathy. "It seems that is something the two of you have in common."

"Oh?" he said, turning to Athena.

Athena shook her head. "Hester, I'm sure Mr. Marshall would prefer to retain some measure of secrecy about his private life."

"To the contrary, Miss McAllister," he said, settling himself more comfortably in the chair. "I could go on and on about my life and adventures."

Her words barely made it out between her clenched teeth. "Not with this pouch stuffed into your mouth, you couldn't."

He laughed, a robust sound that filled the room. "Temper, temper. Whatever would your students say?"

The corners of Hester's eyes crinkled. "You know, Athena, I wonder if Mr. Marshall would care to return to the school as a replacement for Lord Rutherford."

She gasped. "Absolutely not. As I said to you before, Hester, we'll postpone that lecture until he's fully recovered."

"But why?" she asked. "Mr. Marshall is perfectly charming. And the ladies have already taken an immense liking to him."

Athena shook her head meaningfully. Hester nodded, mirroring Athena's intensity.

Marshall set his glass down. "Er, have I missed something?"

Hester returned her attention to him. "Do forgive us—it's terribly rude to speak of you as though you were not here. You see, Lord Rutherford is one of our lecturers. He conducts sessions on the art of kissing—a practicum, if you will. There's not much to it, really. The main purpose of the first session is just to help the ladies overcome their initial shyness. Lord Rutherford has been taken ill these last two weeks—a violent bout of influenza, I'm sorry to say—and we'd just been discussing what to do for his replacement. I thought that if you would be so disposed, perhaps you could lead that lecture yourself."

Marshall knew this Lord Rutherford. He was an overindulged, narcissistic dandy, and a profligate to boot. He grew furious to think that this man had been hired to teach his sister how to kiss. If Athena had also been tutored by that fop, it was no wonder she was so inhospitable to men.

"I'd be honored," he said, secretly wishing Rutherford were right in front of him so he could punch him squarely in the mouth.

"Mr. Marshall," objected Athena, "I'm not convinced of your qualifications on that point. Lord Rutherford is rather renowned for his ability to romance a woman."

A smirk dimpled his cheek. "Oh, I don't know. I've

no wish to boast, but I've been known to turn a few heads in my day."

"And a few stomachs, no doubt. Lord Rutherford is a master at his craft."

The amusement melted from his face. "Miss McAllister, Lord Rutherford's 'craft' is at being crafty. His fame—or infamy, I should say—is wholly deserved, but not for the reason you think. It isn't his ability to seduce women, but his ability to beguile them—generally out of more than just a claim to chastity. He is an opportunist and a scoundrel, and more than one lady has found herself in the unenviable position of being forced to purchase his silence after a madcap indiscretion, leaving her both financially and morally bankrupt. Whether or not you engage me as his replacement, my advice to you is to scrape him off while you have the chance, before anyone at this school falls victim to his nefarious schemes."

Hester's eyes grew round as saucers. "Athena?"

Athena pursed her lips. "I'm sure that's not the case, Hester. I have never heard such pernicious slander in the whole of my life."

Marshall leveled his gaze at her. "You would have, had you spent more time among the discerning circles of English Society and less, as your accent suggests, in the remote backwoods of Scotland."

Athena's mouth fell open. "How dare you belittle me! Had *you* spent more time in Scotland, you would have learned that a remark like that would earn you a sound pulping from a civilized Scottish gentleman."

"After dealing with you, Miss McAllister, I've learned that the word 'civilized' and 'Scottish' should never be used in the same sentence, let alone the same breath."

"Oh!"

Marshall stood and scooped up the pouch containing his coins. "Ladies," he said, bowing, "I shall importune you no further. Thank you for a delightful evening. I'm pleased that I proved satisfactory. Good night."

Hester bolted out of her chair. "Mr. Marshall, wait. In light of what you've told us about Lord Rutherford, we cannot in good conscience let him remain in our employ. Please reconsider accepting the position. We would be eternally grateful."

"We?" he repeated, staring fixedly at Athena, challenge glinting in his eyes. "Your headmistress has already voiced her objections. I sincerely doubt your invitation is echoed by her."

"Athena," urged Hester. "Ask him!"

She turned her nose in the air. "I suppose, once again, being the only candidate, you will have to do."

For a man accustomed to hearing "no, sir" and "aye, sir" nearly all of his life, he was not about to subject himself to any more of her rudeness. "Oh, no, Miss McAllister. When dealing with me, you will have to cultivate a more civilized tone to your demeanor. You will have to ask me politely."

"Who do you think you are?"

He wanted to tell her exactly who he was, but his identity did not matter in the present confrontation. "I am a man entitled to your respect."

Hester glowered at her. "Athena—"

Athena growled, biting out each word. "Will you fill our vacant position, *please*?"

He crossed his arms in front of him. "Yes, I think I shall. For ten pounds."

Athena gasped. "Ten pounds! Rutherford did it for five!"

Hester jumped in. "We'll pay it. Thank you. Until Wednesday then?"

He bent over her proffered hand. "I look forward to it." He swept his hat onto his head as he turned his attention to Athena. "I shall content myself, Miss McAllister, that you've learned the proper uses of 'please' and 'excuse me.' I would ask you to exercise the words 'thank you,' but I fear that you would probably perish from showing so much courtesy. And I would hate to be the one responsible for your untimely demise."

He left her retort in her mouth as he walked out the door.

TEN

My dear Lord Stockdale,

   I can scarcely describe my frustration at learning that there has still not been any progress on your betrothal to Miss McAllister. I need hardly impress upon you the gravity of this situation. You and I made an agreement, and I expect you to fulfill your obligation. Miss McAllister must at all costs be married to you and no other.

   I shall return to England very soon and I expect to read the banns of your upcoming nuptials upon my arrival. Enough time has passed for her to have forgiven you for your indiscretion. It is time to woo her once more. Promise her whatever she desires, but see to it that she gives you her hand.

   Do not fail me in this regard, for you will find me a formidable adversary when I am disappointed.

   Yours,
   Margaret, Duchess of Twillingham

Justine Hawkesworth dashed out of the house. Suffocated by her mother's disappointment, she sought the sanctuary of the rear garden to clear her head.

She had felt so far from home since her father died. Outside, the air was cool and clean, and smelled of damp grass. Though taking a walk through the gardens used to make her feel liberated, her troubles seemed to remain upon her now, like a heavy cloak that she couldn't take off.

It was a profound humiliation to be rejected by Herbert Stanton. Although she'd met him only three times before, he seemed a fine enough gentleman. A bit staid, perhaps, and too rigid in his manner, but attractive nonetheless. She didn't object when Marshall told her of his intentions. Even though she'd always imagined that she'd marry a man with whom she'd fallen in love, she expected she would most likely marry a man she hardly knew. The difference was that she had been *willing* to love Herbert Stanton. And his rejection hurt not only her feelings, but her reputation—and her relationship with her family.

The garden path behind the house wound past the kitchens, and the smell of baking bread drew her attention to the doorway. Two young kitchen maids were bringing baskets filled with apples toward the kitchen. Justine sat on a bench near the lavender beds to stare at them. What a simple life girls of that station led. In the grand scheme of things, whom they chose to marry didn't matter in the slightest. Reputations weren't ruined and families weren't rent because of their choice of husband. Duty, honor, and wealth played no part in their betrothals. Perhaps their toil earned them the right to marry freely. Justine felt keenly a stab of envy.

A young groom ran past them and snatched two apples from one of the maid's baskets. She admonished him in mock displeasure, broadcasting her mixed sentiments with a fist pressed against a swaying hip. Walking backward, he touched a hand to his cap in gratitude, and then sprinted toward the kitchen garden.

Justine watched him as he walked through the carefully tended rows of carrot and potato plants. He was new to the staff—a hard worker, from the stable master's account to Marshall. He was a handsome man, with the smooth skin and thick hair of all men of twenty-four. Though he was only about five years younger than she, he seemed of another generation altogether. He had a ruddy complexion, made even darker by a day's growth of beard, and his unshaven cheek barely concealed a mole above his square jaw.

He went up to a raspberry bush and pried away a branch of it. Just then, he caught sight of Justine, watching him from the flower garden, and stopped. He tipped his cap in deference, nearly dropping the apples he still held in that hand.

"Mornin', miss," he said, his voice sounding as rich and jaunty as his manner.

"Good morning," she responded, for the moment mesmerized by the thick, long lashes that outlined his hazel eyes.

He glanced guiltily at the stolen items in his hands. "These are for Captain Hawkesworth's horse. We exercised him a long while this morning. I wanted to give him a special reward . . . apples and raspberry leaves are a fair treat."

"That's very kind of you," she found herself saying.

He grinned, and a long dimple creased his cheek. "Can I be of help to you, miss?"

Yes, she wanted to say, but there was so much that followed that word. And he was unable to help her

anyway, so it was pointless to speak it. "No, thank
you," she responded with a forced smile. "I wouldn't
want to delay Lancelot his treats."

"I see," he said, though she knew he didn't. "Well,
I'll be off then. Good morning to you."

She stared at him as he sauntered toward the stables.
Young men such as he possessed their own innate
eroticism. The strong back, the confident walk, the
firm buttocks . . . there was no time quite like the dawn
of manliness. How she would have liked to practice on
him some of the things she learned at the School for
the Womanly Arts. Lord Rutherford had taught her one
technique in particular that would no doubt enrage the
passions of that young man . . .

But as she wondered how salty his skin would taste,
she heard two voices in her head. The first belonged to
her mother, and it sternly reminded her that a man of
his caste was far beneath her station in life, and that
she was not even to look at such men, let alone talk to
them. The second voice was more intimate and infinitely more hurtful. *You are old enough to be that
man's aunt*, it said—*his maiden aunt. Even if it were
not prohibited, he would not be interested in the likes
of you. He's young and handsome and vibrant, and
you're—*

She didn't let herself finish that sentence. A spike
of self-reproach stabbed at her, and tears threatened to
come. They were words she'd said to herself many
times in the past. She'd inherited none of her mother's
beauty or her father's confidence—Marshall alone
had been blessed with those qualities. All she had was
the desire to be desirable.

She started toward the rose garden, but was halted

by a glimpse of the young maid coming out of the kitchen door with something wrapped in a tea towel. She bounced over to the stable, and strode up to the handsome groom. A gentle breeze waved through her pinafore as he unwrapped the steaming bread. She said something to him, her body swiveling in exuberance. He flashed a smile at her, those lovely dark-rimmed eyes crinkling in appreciation.

Justine lowered her face. This is how it is meant to be. Fresh young maids take up with fresh young grooms. Her chance to attract a dashing young man like him had passed long ago, frittered away by self-consciousness disguised as concern for her father. Now it was too late. She had to accept whomever Marshall put in her bed, whether she liked him or not.

Her pride in tatters, she trudged back to the house . . . completely unmindful that she was being watched by a pair of concerned hazel eyes.

Athena lay slumped against the arm of the divan, munching on marchpane cakes as she read to Hester a wedding invitation from one of their former students.

"You know, Hester," she said, sucking the icing from her fingers, "there's a Roman bath in the cellar of this building. The courtesans used to bathe men in there for a steep fee. What do you think of doing a class there next term?"

"Teaching what?"

Athena plucked another piece of cake, and shoved it into her mouth, smiling wickedly. "How to bathe the beast."

A sharp rap at the back door startled her, making her choke.

"That will be Mr. Marshall," Hester said, straightening in her chair. "Gert," she said to the maid, "go and answer the door. And bring a fresh pot of tea."

A coughing fit strangled Athena's voice as her eyes watered. "Oh, no. Speak of the beast, and the beast appears. I don't think I can bear another evening under the same roof with that man."

Hester pinched her cheeks. "What on earth is the matter with you? You act as if he were the very devil. He's extremely handsome."

Athena wiped her moist eyes as the last spasm subsided. "Handsome, yes. It's the horns and the pointed tail I mind."

Hester began to collect the correspondence, bills, and schedules that lay scattered about the room like forgotten confetti. "Don't be ridiculous. He's only a man."

"That's like saying a tiger's only a very large kitten."

Hester smirked. "Nonsense. He's well mannered and charming. Not to mention considerate and noble to have gotten us out of a potentially disastrous situation with Lord Rutherford."

Athena straightened in her chair and smoothed out her skirt. "Inconceivable such a mythical creature could exist. Did you forget that he also managed to get himself another post with us at double the going wage?"

Hester shoved the papers into Athena's writing desk. "Don't be so cynical. That was not his intention and you know it."

"I wonder. The man is completely overbearing. To have our students exposed to another evening of Mr. 'Look-What-a-Perfect-Body-I've-Got' Marshall may skew their expectations of what gentlemanly comportment is supposed to be."

"If I didn't know you better, I'd think you were trying very hard to resist an attraction to the man."

Gert opened the door. "Mr. Marshall here to see you, ma'am."

"Thank you, Gert. Show him in," responded Hester as Athena cut her a nasty look. "And ask the ladies to assemble in the main parlor for tonight's lecture."

They heard him approach before they saw him. His boots pounded his full weight onto carpeted floor, and Athena sensed her own anticipation at seeing him.

Marshall strode in, his carriage characteristically purposeful, as if he were leaning into the wind. He wore a navy blue coat, silver-threaded waistcoat, and a snowy white cravat. Athena took one look at him and her face flushed. He looked even more fascinating with clothes on than with them off.

"Good evening, Lady Willett," he said cheerfully. His voice then took on a subtle edge. "Miss McAllister."

"Good evening, Mr. Marshall," said Hester, her pinched cheeks blossoming in a smile. "Do sit down."

"Thank you."

Athena couldn't help but notice how many colors made up his hair. Tangled in the wheat-colored locks were streaks of lemon and gold, with just a hint of silver at the temples. The colors in his hair danced and shimmied, like sunlight on the surface of a lake. And his eyes were absolutely riveting. Their color was harder to identify. They were of a crystalline blue, rather like a Scottish sky on a clear summer day. The blue circles were surrounded by cobalt rings, the color of the depths of a Highland loch. Brown eyelashes radiated from the gently smiling eyes. His complexion was most puzzling, considering its tawny, nearly swarthy tones. What call does a gentleman have to have been exposed to so much sun? Maybe the hard times he had fallen on had forced him to take on outdoor labor.

"We were just remarking how very kind it was of you to fill this post on such short notice? Weren't we, Athena?"

Athena cleared her throat. "I seem to remember another motive, one that had something to do with ten pounds."

"Athena, really!"

Gently, he shook his head as his intense blue eyes smiled into Athena's. "A man is motivated by a good many things, Miss McAllister. Fame, money, accomplishments . . . but seldom does a man come by an inducement as pleasurable as revisiting two very beautiful women."

Athena blinked in surprise. She hadn't expected him to be so gracious. But when the tea arrived, he and Hester skipped down a melodic conversation of small talk, and their rhythmic chitchat evoked a feeling in her she couldn't name. It was as if they had their own language, and Athena felt like a foreigner amid compatriots. He never spoke so comfortably with Athena. Their words were exchanged with épées and gunfire. Suddenly, she knew what that feeling was. Envy.

Maybe if she let down her guard a little, and allowed him over the drawbridge keeping her isolated from men . . . Although he was handsome like Calvin, and charming like Calvin, he wasn't Calvin. Though the memory of Calvin's betrayal was still present, the man chatting amiably with Hester was not at fault for it.

"You seem a bit distracted, Miss McAllister."

She grew flustered. "Distracted? No, I was merely noticing that . . . you're looking well."

"And you're looking well *at me*. Does my appearance offend?"

"Not at all. I . . . your presence called to mind a man I know."

"Oh? How do I compare?"

"I don't believe that's any of your concern."

"Ah. A lover."

"Certainly not," she said, her back straightening. "Quite the contrary, in fact."

"A spurned love."

She turned her head, and yanked the drawbridge back up. She wasn't prepared to debate the issue of Calvin with this particular man. "If you must know, I have spurned all men. Quite frankly, I don't believe anyone of your sex is worth the trouble."

"I see. This man must have really hurt you to have soured you on us all."

Her heart twisted inside her. "This may sound shocking to you, Mr. Marshall, but I prefer to live life on my own."

"That's not what you teach your students."

"Not every woman is strong enough to make the decision I have made."

"To embrace spinsterhood?"

"*Singlehood,* Mr. Marshall. I choose freedom."

"I should deem it unfair of you to curse all men as

scoundrels on the basis of one alone. Perhaps you ought to give the rest of us a chance."

"Starting with you, presumably."

"Well, you might allow me the chance to redeem the rest of my sex."

"Honestly, Mr. Marshall, your ego is about as large as an elephant and just as difficult to tame. What makes you think I have any but the most professional interest in you? In fact, I question the wisdom of hiring a teacher of your untried expertise."

"And did Lord Rutherford offer you a firsthand demonstration?"

"Certainly not. His reputation preceded him."

"Reputation wields a powerful force. Both to exalt and to crush."

Athena rose imperiously. "Well, see to it that your performance tonight exalts. We expect you to earn every penny of your exorbitant wages tonight."

Slowly, he came to his feet. "I shall endeavor to please."

The ladies had all assembled in the salon, chattering like small birds. Marshall opened the door, allowing Athena and Hester through. Suddenly, the chatter silenced to a hush.

"Good evening, Mr. Marshall," said Miss Drummond, her bespectacled face widening in a smile. The rest of the women echoed the greeting, each wishing they had been the first to say it.

"Good evening, ladies," he replied. "How becoming all of you look tonight."

Athena watched the women giggle like girls fresh out of the schoolroom. Their eyes were drawn to him, as if his face and body exerted some magnetic force over them. Even when Hester stood in the middle of the room to address them, their gaze was riveted on him.

"Tonight, ladies, we begin the first of three lectures on the sensual art of kissing. Mr. Marshall, with whom you are all acquainted, has agreed to demonstrate the nuances of erotic kissing. This is your opportunity to improve your skills in pleasing a man—all without fear of reprisals or repercussions. Remember that this is your academy of learning. No one outside these walls will ever learn about what has gone on here tonight, so feel at ease to make mistakes, ask questions, voice your concerns, and to understand the world as it is and not how it is presented to you. So without further delay, Mr. Marshall, the floor is yours."

"Thank you. Ladies, I feel privileged to be your instructor tonight, so it is with much remorse that I must begin my discourse by disagreeing wholeheartedly with Lady Willett. She has implied that it falls upon your shoulders to develop your skills in kissing, as if there should be some technique that you must acquire to please a man. Speaking as a man, I hope I put your anxious minds at ease by explaining that your pleasure pleases us more than any skill you could possibly master."

The ladies looked at one another, smiling. Athena sat down in the back of the room, silently fascinated by his opening remarks.

"Kissing is a display of affection. How much you care for the gentleman will become evident in the intensity of your kiss. Having said that, I advise you to not be concerned if your first kisses are awkward.

Kissing is a dance—a movement in concert between two people. Not a country dance with regimented steps, but a flowing, unfettered interchange, like a waltz."

Lady Katherine cleared her throat. "But we are strictly prohibited from dancing a waltz in public."

Marshall grinned and crossed his arms in front of his chest. "You're prohibited from kissing before marriage too, but that's not going to stop any of you tonight."

The women glanced at one another in guilty titillation.

Marshall continued. "A man's kiss is his signature. By the emotion of it, you can tell what he is feeling for you. When you are untried, as I expect you may be, it is easy to mistake passion for love. When a man is aroused, the intensity of his words, his embrace, his kisses, could easily confuse you into believing he cares for you. Do not make that mistake. A man—especially a young man—may confound the ardent response of his body with a cry of the heart.

"But do not exempt yourselves from that failing. Women are guilty of that too. Let us put you up as an example, Lady Penelope. How many times have you been to a ball and spotted a handsome man on the dance floor? Have you not looked him up and down, admiring his form and the fit of his clothes, and wondered what it would be like to hang in his embrace as he kissed you passionately?"

Lady Katherine jabbed at Lady Penelope mockingly while the other girls laughed. Penelope blushed to red. "Mr. Marshall, please!"

"Don't let Lady Katherine embarrass you, Lady Penelope. She is just as guilty of it as you are."

The laughter rose in the room as both women hid their burning cheeks behind their hands.

"The point is, ladies, that you did not feel love for these men you admired. Desire, yes, but not love. Love begets desire, but desire does not always beget love. Therefore, as the worldly women you are becoming, you must learn the difference between infatuation and love. When a man truly loves you, you will know it not from his kiss, but from his actions."

Athena was mesmerized. Lord Rutherford never said anything like that. Neither, for that matter, did Calvin.

"So then. Let us suppose that I am your suitor. I have been courting you for weeks, and now you are ready to let me physically express my feelings for you. Who shall be my first volunteer?"

Six hands shot into the air. Miss Drummond's hand went higher as Marshall's eyes scanned the room.

His eyes fell on a spot in a darkened corner of the room. "Miss McAllister."

Her eyes widened. "Yes?"

"Thank you for volunteering."

"I did not—"

"Wish to be presumptuous? How considerate."

She was not about to be manipulated. "No, thank you. Choose another for your demonstration."

Marshall lowered his head like a bull about to charge. "Come, come, Miss McAllister. A teacher leads by example."

Alarm rattled her insides. "I said no."

Amid the girlish cheers, Marshall strode straight toward her. He reached down and encircled her wrist in his large hand. She tried to pull away as he dragged her to the center of the room, but his strength was far greater than hers.

Lady Penelope applauded. "Miss McAllister, now you can show us how *you* would kiss a man."

"I'd rather punch that mouth than kiss it."

Candlelight danced in his darkened eyes as he regarded her. "Coward."

She straightened. "Never accuse a Scotswoman of being a coward."

"Then come and kiss like a Scotswoman would." He stood in front of her, a mischievous smile lifting one cheek.

Dread elevated to panic. Never had she felt less a headmistress and more like one of her students. A woman of her advanced years should know better, but all her practical experience had resulted in monumental failure. She had no wish to be exposed to teasing by the beautiful man looking down at her.

"I don't know how . . . that is, perhaps you should explain to the students how to go about initiating a kiss."

"Very well. First, your suitor will take your hand, like this." Marshall took her hand in his, her fingers curling into his large palm. It was warm and dry and firm.

"Next, he will probably tell you what he thinks of you. Miss McAllister," he began, and his pause increased her anticipation of what he was about to say. "I'll be damned if you're not the prickliest woman I've ever met. You personify the 'mean' in 'demeanor.' " Athena rolled her eyes and started back toward her seat, but he held her fast. "But you're also the most beautiful and most fascinating woman I've ever met, and I think about you constantly, even when we're apart. I don't know how a woman like you escaped a man's attention, but I bless my good fortune that you are still free to claim my admiration. Merely being with you gives me far greater pleasure than anything else I know. When I'm with you, I laugh—mostly at myself—and you seem to teach me things about myself I never knew or had forgotten. The days without you are sharp, and the nights are like daggers. Let me know by your kiss that you feel some small measure of affection for me."

His words were softspoken and tender. Athena studied him for even a hint of mockery, but in his eyes there was only earnestness, as if he were suspended between hope and fear. An intense current passed between them, and the world outside their circle melted into the soft candlelight. He took a step toward her, obliterating any distance between them. She looked up into his face, unsure of what to do. He just stood there, his eyes drinking their fill of her expression. His lips were tantalizingly close, just a hairsbreadth from hers. She was almost on tiptoe, almost close enough to touch him. Just a little bit more . . .

His head descended, and their lips touched.

A soft press, that's all it was. Innocent, tender, affectionate. But his mouth lingered upon hers, increasing exponentially the emotion behind the kiss. She felt something unleash inside him, and his hands traveled up her arms. He took possession of her arms, and pulled her whole body toward him. The kiss deepened, his lips capturing hers one by one.

She was sure she was supposed to do something. It was a dance, he had said, and she was supposed to perform her steps. But she was so enjoying the sensation, the pure pleasure of his touch, that she didn't want to ruin it with a hamhanded maneuver.

His mouth opened over hers, then smoothed closed. Again and again his mouth caressed hers in the same rhythm, as if trying to communicate something to her. Her mind could not read him, but her body understood what he'd been trying to say. *Taste me.*

Gradually, her jaw dropped, her lips softened, and her lips mirrored his motions. He tasted like tea, the same tea she had shared with him moments before, except on his lips it was sweetened by the taste of him. *Delicious.*

His arms came around her and she was engulfed in his embrace. He was like a soft, warm blanket, and his great, heavy arms made her feel totally protected.

Something went into her mouth, startling her. She knew people kissed with tongues, but she had been unprepared for the sensation. His pointy tongue peeked between her lips, and the searing heat of it surprised her. He burned his way into her mouth, tasting her from within. His tongue stroked hers, and she retreated shyly. But the pleasure and adventure he offered was too enticing, and she began to stroke back. She didn't know when it had happened, but the drawbridge of her heart was smashed to ruins. Only it wasn't he who'd torn it down . . . it was she.

His tongue lit a fuse that sparked all the way down her body and ignited a flame of pleasure between her legs. Her hands went up to push him away, but they lost their purpose when they stopped to absorb the feel of hard muscle at his sides. She knew what he looked like naked, and she had wanted to touch his body since the moment her eyes had taken their fill of him. Now he was inside her and she wanted more. She wanted all of him.

He must have sensed the same thing, because she felt the beginning signs of his sexual arousal against her tummy. Suddenly, she became conscious of a delicious sense of victory. His arousal made her feel attractive, seductive, desirable . . . *wanted*. All the things she had desired to feel from Calvin.

Before she could dance down that train of thought, Marshall pulled free. He held her still, his eyes still closed shut. He had a concentrated look, and Athena could see that he was forcing himself to dispel the pleasure. For some reason, as Athena stood panting, she relished seeing that look on his face. It was a sign of her power over him. Although he always seemed to be in control of himself and her reaction, she too could claim some dominion over him. But when he opened his eyes and looked at her—and *smiled*—it was she who surrendered.

"Miss McAllister," said Miss Drummond tremulously, "are we expected to do all that?"

"We're not being graded on this, are we?" asked Alice.

Athena blinked away her dulled senses, her surroundings materializing once more. "Um, the purpose is for each of you to be exposed to . . . er . . . to take a hard look at . . . that is . . . I want you to get a firm grasp—"

Marshall chuckled at her bruised composure.

She gave him a withering look, and stomped off to resume her seat beside Hester. "You may continue your lesson, Mr. Marshall."

"Notwithstanding what's on your headmistress's mind, let's bring our attention back to the lesson at hand. No, you will not be graded on this, and no, this exercise is not compulsory. The point is, ladies, that no technique, no attempt at pretense, can ever be more pleasing than a natural, candid response to my advances. Just like Miss McAllister's."

Athena felt her cheeks burn. She turned to Hester and was surprised to find her hunched forward, tears streaming down the clenched fist she held at her mouth.

"Hester? What's wrong?"

Hester snuffled and darted out of the salon.

Athena called after her. Unable to leave the girls unchaperoned, she could not follow her out of the room. "Hester!" Though she shouted under her breath to avoid undue attention from the girls, she need not have bothered. Their full attention was focused on Marshall as they stood around him, each taking her turn as Marshall kissed her chastely on the lips.

Worry crumpled her forehead. What had upset Hester? She leaned against the doorjamb, wondering what to do about Hester. Then she glanced up at Marshall, remembering the way her heart came alive in his embrace.

And wondered the very same thing about him.

ELEVEN

The blue sky had angered to black, and in an instant, the heavens poured forth a deluge.

Justine had been out riding in the meadow. When the weather turned, she urged her bay colt into a gallop, but the rains overtook her.

She was walking alongside the horse by the time they reached the stables. A figure ran out to meet her, his shoulders darkening as the rain soaked through his brown jacket. It was the handsome young groom she'd spoken to the other day.

"I'm so sorry," she said as he steadied the animal, "but I fear he may have gone lame. Something happened to his right foreleg out in the meadow."

The groom took the reins from her. "I'll handle the colt, miss. You should go into the house and out of the rain."

She ignored him. "Is he going to be all right?"

The groom crouched low and examined the leg. "Looks like a shoe's come loose. Not to worry. I'll take care of it in the stable."

"It hasn't split his hoof, has it?" she asked, worry etched onto her wet forehead.

"Let's have a look inside."

Rain pounded on the stable roof, creating a deafening noise. The young man led the hobbling horse into the stable, and cross-tied him so he wouldn't fidget. He lit a lantern and placed it on a small stool beside the horse. He lifted the horse's hoof, wedging it between his knees, and gave it a thorough examination before setting it down gently.

"The nails on one side have come loose, miss. But there's no damage to the hoof. Once I pull out the shoe, he'll be . . . well, right as rain," he quipped, wiping his dripping face with a wet sleeve.

"That's a relief. Thank you, Mr. . . ."

He touched a hand to his sodden cap. "Keane, miss. Elliott Keane."

"Thank you, Mr. Keane."

His smile dissolved. "Pardon me for sayin' so, miss, but have you been crying?"

Justine blinked in disbelief. Every inch of her head and body was dripping with rainwater. How on earth could he observe that she had been weeping?

She could dissemble. Or she could upbraid him for his impertinence. But concern was written all over his face. "It is nothing to be concerned about, Mr. Keane."

"It's not about the shoe, is it, miss? Because I promise he'll be ready to ride in no time."

She pasted on a smile. "No. I was just a little melancholy this morning, and I shared my feelings with Thunder here."

"Horses make good companions, but awful quiet ones. It sounds as if you could do with a friend right now, miss."

"Perhaps you're right. My dearest friend lives in Canterbury. I could arrange a visit."

"My mum used to tell me that in times of trouble, better a neighbor nearby than a brother far away."

"What are you saying, Mr. Keane?"

He shrugged, but measured his words carefully. "I know it's not my place, miss. And if I'm being too familiar then you just have to say so. But I don't believe a lady ought to be sad. Every tear a woman sheds is a shame on all men everywhere."

His hazel eyes stared at her from beneath thick eyebrows that expressed a worry for her that was greater than fear of losing his job. The eyelashes, wet with rain, together with his clean-shaven cheek today, took even more years off his young face. She could easily see how the maids would be taken with him.

"You're very kind, Mr. Keane," she said, pasting the smile back on her face. "But there's nothing you can do to help."

He nodded quietly. "Very well, miss. You don't have to say. I'll just ask Thunder here what's troubling you. He's not as tight-lipped as you are."

She laughed. It was the first genuine laugh she'd had in a long time.

"But if you ever feel like you need a friend, miss, one that isn't so far away, you only have to send for me."

Justine extended her gloved hand. "Thank you, Mr. Keane, for looking after Thunder—after both of us, actually."

But when he reached out and took her hand, an insidious and desperate idea germinated in her head. She knew this would be the only moment they would ever touch, and she silently cursed the glove which stood between her skin and his. There was only one other way she could steal a caress before this moment passed forever.

Forbidden, her mind kept telling her, but that made her want it all the more. Among the stifling trappings of a lady in which Justine lived, she could barely breathe. But with her dress plastered against her body and her hair matted on her face, she had never felt *less* a lady. Here in the stable, with no one around, and the heavy rain outside forming a curtain of privacy, there was an opportunity to take a step toward the wicked. Here, she became a thing of instinct and feeling, like the horses that watched from the stalls.

Just one kiss, her body begged. Highborn men expected too much, but lowborn men asked for nothing. The practice sessions on erotic kissing with Lord Rutherford traipsed through her memory, but they seemed ill-fitting now, as if her experience with that man had all been a sham.

Tremulously, she closed the distance between them, and with a hesitant rise of her face, placed a soft kiss on his lips.

Immediately she cast down her eyes. She felt foolish—worse, depraved. He was a servant. She had taken advantage of her superior position. He'd be fearful of losing his post now. To make matters worse, she was about to turn thirty, and he was at least five years her junior. It was inappropriate, scandalous— *forbidden.*

She waited for him to hem and hedge, and back away with some muttered excuse about mucking out the stable. But he didn't budge. She glanced up at his face, and gasped at his expression.

It was a look of such intensity that it stole her breath

away. He was not judging, but *understanding*; not fearing, but *feeling*. A gentle tug on her hand pulled her closer until she was underneath his gaze. His eyes swept over her face, just inches under his. He brought his lips down upon hers. And gave her a *real* kiss.

His full, warm lips caressed hers in a way that made her feel wanted, desirable. Never had she experienced such a heavenly sensation, as if she were drenched in warm honey. For all Lord Rutherford's expertise in awakening erotic sensations, nothing he had taught her had made her feel like this. It was as though Elliott Keane were making love to her from the inside out.

She wanted a moment, and he had given it to her in full. It was the eternity after this moment that she was now afraid of.

TWELVE

Marshall's boot landed in a puddle as he jumped from the hansom cab and ran up the stairs to the front door. The rain sliced sideways, needling his face.

Gert opened the door and let him pass. The maid took his drenched cloak and hat and led him to the study. Within a few moments, Hester came in.

"Thank you so much for coming to see me, Mr. Marshall. I hadn't expected you, considering the inclement weather."

"The letter you slipped into my wage parcel last night sounded important. I did not dare miss the appointment."

"You are soaked to the skin. Please sit here by the fire." Hester wrung her hands. "I shouldn't have summoned you. Especially in so furtive a manner. Do forgive me. I was impetuous and stupid."

"Lady Willett, you strike me as neither impetuous nor stupid. But I did detect an elevated sense of urgency in your note . . . and of unhappiness."

"Yes. Yes, there was that." Hester perched herself on the edge of the opposite chair. "I had thought to speak to you—in private—when Athena took the students to the museum today. But I've since reconsidered. I really shouldn't burden you with my troubles."

He leaned forward. "Tell me what has happened to cause you such dismay."

Hester chewed her lip. "It was something you said during the lesson last night which gave me pause. You said that when a man truly loves us, we shall know it by his actions. Do you really believe that?"

Surprise registered on his face. "Well, yes, I do. I have always found that the character of a man is spoken by his deeds, seldom by his words. Men may proclaim their wisdom or goodness, but the true test of it is in the fruit of their life."

"And what if a man's actions don't speak of love, but of indifference?"

Marshall sighed. "Lady Willett, it is difficult to discuss these matters in the abstract. Is there something specific that is troubling you?"

Hester's eyebrows tented. "It is a delicate matter . . . concerning my husband. I love him very much, and I believe he loves me. But I do not know if he loves me in the same way that I love him." She glanced uneasily at him, and shook her head. "I'm so sorry. I must be embarrassing you. It's just that . . . last night you stood in front of us all stating with such authority that inspiring love wasn't a technique to be learned, and yet . . . I do not know how to win my husband's affection."

"If I can be of help, I am at your disposal."

"Your counsel is all I seek." She worried her lip some more. "My husband is . . . inscrutable to me. He is a responsible man who provides for my needs in every way. But I fear that he doesn't care for me . . . outside of the bedchamber, that is."

"I see."

"When we're alone together at night, he is all attention. But in the light of day, he changes. I don't seem to matter to him anymore. I seem to vanish, as if I were of no more significance than the furniture. He rarely goes out with me, and he hardly shows an interest in anything I do. I thought perhaps that I wasn't being alluring or distracting enough. That's why this academy became so important to me, why I invested so heavily in it. I wanted to learn from our gentleman teachers how to overcome my inadequacies and become the woman my husband desires. Certain lovemaking techniques were explained to me . . . things I was told would please Thomas. The kiss of flesh," she admitted with a timid shrug. "He enjoyed it very much, but the very next day, all was as before. I had become invisible once more." A look of consternation clouded her delicate features. "I feel as if I'm living between parentheses. I don't know what to do. So I ask you, Mr. Marshall. Is there something else I must do for him, something that will inspire him to love me better?"

Marshall clenched his teeth. It was lamentable that a woman as beautiful and tender as Lady Willett could wind up with a cold and distant man like her husband. And yet Marshall was too honest to ignore the commonalities he shared with the baron. Did he too not consider marriage to be a vapid and inconvenient obligation? Did he too not regard wives as little more than fixtures in a home? Had he not arranged his sister's marriage to a man who presented a socially advantageous match, rather than a caring and attentive matrimonial prospect? Personified in this brokenhearted woman was the product of his own careless attitude.

He regarded her thoughtfully, her brown eyes brimming with unshed tears. She expected him to tell her some secret or heretofore undisclosed lovemaking technique. How like Athena's way of thinking it was. It was foolish to believe that by learning how to please a man in bed that a woman was going to make him fall madly in love with her. There was more to it than that. Much, much more.

But in Lady Willett's case, something had to be ruled out first.

"Forgive my indiscretion, Lady Willett, but is there a chance that your husband might have become unfaithful to you?"

She sighed. "I do not think so. He has not shown any outward sign or inclination, nor has he left the house for any stretch of time. His absences from my side are legitimate and I have been able to substantiate them. Mind you, even if I had suspected an infidelity, I would never challenge him with it."

"Why not?"

"Shame, I suppose. Countess Cavendish's book teaches that if we have made our home a pleasant place, our husbands should not be likely to forsake it. And if a wife suspects her husband of adultery, Countess Cavendish admonishes us not to reproach him. We are advised to resign ourselves and let our virtuous behavior serve as a beacon to light his way back to his home."

"I see," he said, even though he didn't. A marriage bed was not meant for three.

"But therein lies my problem. I don't want to drive him to the arms of another. What is it that I am doing wrong?"

He sighed deeply. As a bachelor, he knew he was ill equipped to advise someone on the subject of marriage. The Captain Marshall Hawkesworth of a few months ago might have encouraged Lady Willett to accept her husband's indifference as an advantage in an arranged marriage; at least he didn't care enough to be violent. But Mr. Marshall had discovered that there was far more to a wife than most men are taught to expect. There was her intelligence and audacity whenever she stood her ground; her humor or sensitivity, when she wanted to bring him down or lift him up; her passion and tenderness, which she revealed if he were man enough to inspire them. He smiled . . . Miss Athena McAllister had awakened him to all these things.

"The answer to your problem, Lady Willett, does not lie under the coverlet, but over it."

"Pardon?"

"Clearly, this man has not come to recognize your value. He needs to come to know you better, and you him. Not within the confines of the matrimonial bedchamber, but over the dinner table and across the study desk."

Dismay shifted to puzzlement. "Study desk? But Mr. Marshall, surely you must be mistaken. It is my understanding that gentlemen do not want their wives involved in their business affairs. Countess Cavendish's book forbids us to even inquire about our husbands' ventures."

"You are a member of his family. I don't see why you shouldn't take an interest in your husband's vocation. Like him, you are an investor, so there is your common ground. You can share your expertise with one another."

Hester shook her head. "A wife is not supposed to speak of worldly concerns. It is decidedly unladylike."

"According to whom?"

"Countess Cavendish's book admonishes that if we wish to preserve the connubial affections of our spouses, we must never trespass upon his province, such as in matters of business. We must confine ourselves to that province befitting our sex, namely, to cheer the mind of our husbands, upon whom graver matters depend."

He pursed his lips. "With apologies to Countess Cavendish, I suggest you toss her book out of the window, along with any other notions of prudery and disdain. It is *your* life, *your* family, *your* happiness at stake. You are an intelligent and wise woman, and you mustn't hide these qualities from him, in spite of what is considered proper. You must learn to see each other as you are, warts and all. That is the key to true intimacy."

Hester breathed in her tears. "I shall try that. Thank you, Mr. Marshall. For your wisdom. And for your compassion."

Marshall reached into his sleeve and handed her a kerchief. "I have no experience of marriage, but I hope that when I do wed, it is to a woman just like you, my lady."

"It's so good to have a friend I can confide in. Please . . . call me Hester."

It was a disappointing outing. The students had been uninspired by the paintings at the new Sebastiano Ricci exhibit, and Athena could not get them to appreciate the majesty of the artwork, let alone the brilliance of the artist's technique. Like tethered horses, they were champing at the bit to go shopping at the market, where the stalls were packed with colorful wares. Then the rains came, stranding them all inside the museum.

When the rains abated, they begged Athena to let them go home. By that time, Athena herself had lost her enthusiasm for the museum, and they started back to the school. With their slippers wet and their hems muddied, the ladies complained all the way down Holborn Street, and Athena swore she would never have children if they behaved even half as irritatingly as these women.

They arrived just as another downpour assaulted them. The women stampeded through the doorway, pushing each other to escape the frigid rain. They thrust their decorative but useless parasols onto poor Gert, and stomped up the stairs to change out of their wet clothes.

Athena asked Gert to start a fire in her bedroom and send up some hot tea. As far as she was concerned, she would not lavish any more of her artistic expertise on the students this term. It was beyond her comprehension how a person could be in the same room as a masterpiece and not recognize its intrinsic value. Their behavior today confirmed her supposition: the wealthier the family, the less appreciation they had for art. They derived no enjoyment from the mastery of the art, only from the collection of it.

In preparation for this outing, she had read a book on Ricci, and although the women found the events of his life uninteresting, Athena developed a greater understanding of how his joys and tragedies had inspired his work. She decided to retire to her room with the book for the rest of the afternoon, and went to her sitting room to retrieve it.

She opened the door, and the vision inside stopped her dead in her tracks. Hester and Marshall were sitting on the settee. They were smiling at each other. And he was holding her hand.

A familiar pain stabbed at Athena's heart, one she had determined to forget. It rose from a forgotten chamber of her heart and threatened to choke the life out of her all over again.

"Athena!" smiled Hester. "You're back early."

"A wee bit too early by the look of things."

"Look who's paid us a visit—Mr. Marshall."

"Us?" she repeated with not a little asperity, one eyebrow cocked in his direction.

"Miss McAllister," he said, rising. "I see I was not the only victim of the rain."

"Athena, you're drenched. Come sit by the fire," said Hester, tapping the spot vacated by Marshall.

"I think not. I am sufficiently warm as it is."

"Is something wrong, Miss McAllister?"

Athena glared at him. He looked ever so regal in a royal blue coat with silver buttons down the front. Just like Calvin, unbearably handsome—and unspeakably traitorous.

"I shan't tarry. I just came to get my book. Carry on, do. Just try not to make too much noise as you two make love. The ladies are upstairs."

"Athena!" Hester exclaimed, her eyes bulging. "What *are* you thinking?"

"Only of you, dear Hester. It would not do for the house matron to be caught *in flagrante delicto* with a man off the street."

Marshall's voice deepened masterfully. "Miss Mc-Allister, you are mistaken. Hester and I were only conversing."

Athena crossed her arms in front of her. "It's 'Hester,' now, is it? I see you two have already shed the formalities. Good thing I came when I did. You might have started shedding your clothes."

He took a step toward her. "Miss McAllister, you exceed your own standard of rudeness."

Hester put a hand to her reddened face. "Athena, for heaven's sake! How could you think such a thing of me?"

Athena felt a pang of remorse, but she had already whipped herself into a jealous froth. "How could *I*? Come now, Hester. You've had calf's eyes for this lout since you met him. I'm surprised it took you this long."

The tears Hester had been fighting overpowered her. She ran out of the room, weeping bitterly.

Marshall pinned his fists to his hips. "Why you devilish cat! That was a cruel thing to say and a completely unfounded accusation to make."

She turned her chin up at him. "Names like that won't hurt my feelings."

"It's not your feelings I'm thinking of hurting. You ought to know your own friend is incapable of such wanton behavior."

"Yes, I know Hester. You, however, I don't. Nor do I care to. Be off with you."

His chin jutted forward in offended pride. "I'm no servant to be dismissed like that."

"I don't care if you're the Prince of Wales. In this place, you're nothing more than the hired help."

He strode up to her and planted himself right in her

way. "I have endured your magisterial snubbings as long as I care to. You strut around here acting like the lady of the manor, presuming to be better than me even though it is clear how provincial you actually are. I've been perforated by your prickly demeanor, persuading myself to find it charming. But no longer. Not while you use that sharp tongue of yours to injure someone as noble and beautiful as Lady Willett. You are nothing but a rude and insolent brat, and I'm this close to putting you over my knee. One more nasty remark, and the next thing you utter will be cries of pain."

His eyes flamed like the blue center of an incandescent fire. His fists pumped open and closed, itching to seize her. His whole demeanor practically dared her to be impertinent.

Athena didn't move an inch, meeting his resolute stare. There were a hundred angry thoughts burning inside her. But she soon became aware that her chest, rising and falling in heightened temper, was fanning a painful flame in her heart. Though she scoured every corner of her mind for a scathing rejoinder, her anger began to fade and she was left with deep regret. She was a fool for being jealous over someone she had no claim to, and she shamed both herself and her friend.

Though her stance was brazen and her expression resolute, she felt her eyes mist against her will. Before he could see her emotion, she turned away. "Very well. Please go now."

Behind her, his solid presence moved not at all.

"I asked you nicely." She held her breath, suffocating a sob.

Still he didn't move.

"Athena . . ."

Never had she thought her name could be spoken in so tender a fashion. The desire to have a man speak to her like that, paired with the heartache of its frustrated hope, became too much for her to bear in secret. A sob escaped her.

"What's wrong?"

She could not—would not—show this man her weakness. She would rather take his anger than his pity. "Are you deaf? I said be off with you, you clotheared, dim-witted pillock!"

He moved, but not in the direction she'd hoped. He advanced upon her from behind, and she braced herself. But instead of seizing her, his hand cupped her elbow. "Why do you cry?"

Her chest caved. Yes, she cried. She cried all the time when no one was looking. She cried for all she lacked and all she would never have because of it. She cried for a love lost and trust betrayed. Even now, the scarred memory of Calvin's betrayal bled all over again.

"Go away," she whispered, the loudest she could speak.

"Come here." He clasped her elbow and turned her around. Her head hung between her shoulders, her arms crossed in front of her. He cocooned his arms around her body, and she disappeared in his embrace.

"Did I frighten you? Is that it?"

She shook her head. She could not hold back the tears.

"Pity. I might have known you'd be too stubborn to be intimidated." His voice softened. "What are all those tears for?"

If she answered that question, she'd lose all his

respect. She'd cease being his stern employer, and she'd become a soft-willed, sensitive woman. All the things she'd sworn never to be around a man.

"It is nothing. Truly."

"Come along, you can tell me."

She shook her head. But his arms were strong around her, his chest was warm and comfortable, and his voice was gentle and compassionate. He offered reassurance, and she needed it desperately.

His breath fell on the top of her head. "I promise not to laugh. Too hard."

She chuckled in spite of her misery, but her words were punctuated with emotion. "I'm sorry I . . . behaved so foolishly. I was touched . . . by the way you . . . defended Hester. I just wished that . . . someone had done so for me . . . a long time ago."

"Against whom?"

"No one. That is, no one of consequence. Not anymore."

"What did he do to you?"

"He told me he loved me. And I stupidly believed him. It was all my fault. I should have known better than to fall for a beautiful man. I wish I'd never laid eyes on him."

"Another woman?"

She nodded, humiliated. "On the very day he proposed marriage to me."

He inhaled sharply. "The fact that he didn't love you as you deserve mustn't force you into hiding from all men. One man's ill-treatment mustn't lock away all that beauty."

She pushed away from him and darted to the rain-spattered window. "Beauty . . . that's a laugh. If I had been beautiful he might not have left me for another. I'm no matrimonial prize. I'm not English. I've not got youth, or innocence, or much of a dowry. I'm not even delightful company. To have a man as beautiful and wealthy and highly placed as Calvin Bretherton offer for me was more than I could have hoped for. But how could he resist her greater charms? She knew how to please him with her body, whereas I—I knew how to curtsy." She gasped wetly and wiped her eyes with her hands. "I don't know who I hate more . . . him for deceiving me, or me for needing him in spite of it. Being rejected hurts more than never being chosen at all."

His hands caressed her back tenderly. "Now you make sense to me. All the barbs you wear so as never to be chosen again. Athena . . ."

Her name sounded so different on his lips than on Calvin's. She turned around.

"Athena, you don't have to emulate women you don't admire because they have what you desire. A man is drawn to a woman who knows her own mind, who has the courage to follow her own heart, regardless of where it leads her. Women of loose morals are ten a penny, and they dwell in the darkness of their own choices. But a woman who prizes her dignity has a phosphorescence about her that draws the right sort of man to her like a moth. No matter how pretty the other woman may be, her beauty pales in comparison to the one lit from within."

His words were well intentioned, but Athena knew they weren't true of her.

He grasped her hands. "Do you know who the mythological Athena was?"

"Of course," she replied, her head downturned. "She was the Greek goddess of reason and logic."

He nodded. "She was also the goddess of war. And she never married . . . a virgin goddess. How like your namesake you are."

"You're all warmth, aren't you? Is that intended to flatter me?"

He grinned benevolently. "No. It's intended to illuminate you. Athena was a woman of whom power and wisdom were hallmarks. She is described as the mother of art. She—how does that line from Homer go?— 'she teaches tender maidens in the house and puts knowledge of goodly arts in each one's mind.' She is chaste, fearless, and fair. And she never married because no man, god or no, was her equal."

Athena considered the similarities. And though she had tried to convince herself that she did not need a man in her life, the truth was too great to keep hiding. "I don't want to be like her. I don't want to be unmarried. I don't want to be alone."

"You don't have to be. Come here." He pulled her toward him. His touch was a powerful lure, and she let him wrap her in his embrace.

As she hugged his chest, the self-pitying thoughts began to vanish. Now, she was conscious only of the feel of his hard body, the warmth of his torso, the sensation of his muscled arms on either side of her. The trace of lime-scented toilet water through her stuffy nose.

He rested his chin on top of her damp chignon. "My little stripling goddess. Maybe if you had shot a few of your arrows into him, he might have seen you as I do."

The sound of his speech through his dense chest

gave her more pleasure than the words he spoke. The bitterness that had encased her began to rust, and she started to feel an overwhelming sense of freedom—and warmth.

Above her, his head shifted. One arm slid from her back, and the next thing she felt were his fingertips gently lifting her chin. She didn't want to face him lest her expression show how much she liked—*needed*—this embrace. Her eyes closed against the nakedness, but he waited. When she finally did look at him, she was amazed. It was printed on his face too.

His head lowered, and their lips met. His mouth was soft and tender, giving more than it took. This . . . this was what she had craved—a kiss that branded her a woman worth loving. It felt as if he were shining sunlight onto her wilted heart, and she began to blossom in return.

Wantonly, her hands came astride his face, begging for more. He responded by grasping her waist and flattening her body against his. As his mouth feasted on her neck and shoulders, his large hands slithered down to her bottom and lifted her toward him. A yearning came into full bloom inside her. Desire burst forth from her, and it threatened to engulf him completely. He was oblivious to the danger, foolishly feeding her want with his wayward hands and lips.

Her whole body blazed to life at once. She threaded her fingers into his golden hair, balling it into her fists. Her aggression spurred his own, and his right hand wound around to the front of her dress and swallowed her breast. Her lips fell open in a wanton gasp, and she arched her back to receive him. His hungry mouth descended onto her dress, closing over her breast right through the fabric.

She gloried in the sensation from his mouth, infusing her whole body with heat. Her eyes closed to hold in the pleasure. To her dismay, his mouth departed, and she waited anxiously for it to land somewhere else. But there was no more.

Reluctantly, she opened her eyes. Through the haze of lust, she became aware of his self-recriminating expression.

"What's wrong?" she whispered.

He shook his head, forcing himself to dispel his pleasure. "I'm sorry."

"For what? Don't stop, please."

"I mustn't." His hands, which just a moment ago had pulled her hips to his body, now pushed them away.

"But . . . but . . ." She didn't know what to say or how to say it.

"Please forgive me. It got too far. I . . ." He stood up, though her body was still pressed against him. "I must go." He placed a brief kiss on her lips, and pushed past her.

She stood in mute bafflement, unmet need still swirling in her body, watching as he closed the door behind him.

THIRTEEN

"Thank heavens you're home," Aquilla Hawkesworth called down from behind the second-floor balustrade.

Marshall handed his hat and cloak to the butler. "What is it, Mother?"

Aquilla began the long descent down the curved staircase. Although nearly sixty, she was a woman who radiated elegance and decorum. The train on her dress swept the steps behind her. "A man was just here. He wanted to speak with Justine."

"With Justine? Who was he?"

"He said his name was Nance. Awful, common person. He said he was a journalist with the *Town Crier.* I told you this would happen. That man you chose to be her fiancé will plunge this whole family into a scandal."

Marshall heaved a sigh, hoping that his mother would choose reason over hysterics. "Mother, please tell me the facts. What specifically did this Nance fellow want?"

"Isn't it obvious? No doubt he wanted to ask about the dissolution of her engagement. Didn't I tell you that this humiliating attention would come?"

Marshall cursed silently. Indeed, he had almost expected it. A dissolved betrothal was prime fodder for the scandal pages, especially if it concerned a girl of Justine's rank. "I trust you didn't let her speak to him."

"Certainly not."

Marshall walked through to the library and poured himself a large brandy from the side table. His mother followed behind him, closing the door so they could speak in private.

"You know what's going to happen, don't you?" she said, patting her flawless gray-blonde coif. "If our name is printed in that scandalmonger's smear rag, Justine and I will lose our voucher at Almack's. We'll be ruined socially."

The golden liquid seared as it went down his throat. He didn't drink hard liquor often. He knew better than to try to drown his troubles in drink. Like turds in seawater, troubles float.

"What I can't fathom," his mother said, folding herself into a chair, "is how the papers discovered it so quickly."

He sat down opposite his mother. "I can. Stanton must have tipped them off."

"But to what end? What does he gain by besmirching our Justine?"

He took another swallow. "There's something you ought to know." Circumspectly, he explained the real reason for Stanton's breaking off the engagement, without explaining where Justine learned all she had. His mother reacted just as he had anticipated—and hoped to avoid.

She bolted out of her chair and paced the carpeting like an angry, imperious queen. "Why didn't you tell me this before? I will have words with Justine! The nerve of that man! How dare he insult my daughter! Look at what he's subjected us to! Her reputation will be called into question! Wait until I get my hands on that girl. She's ruined us all!"

He rolled his eyes as she rained blame on everyone around her. "Calm yourself, Mother."

"And you! Keeping this from me all this time!"

"Mother, please sit!" His voice cracked across the room.

Aquilla sank into the chair, her mood dissolving from outrage to devastation. "To think of our names in that fish wrapping of a newspaper. What will people say? Marshall, fetch me a drink."

Marshall listened to his mother whimper as he went to the side table and poured her a glass of brandy. He put it into her outstretched hand.

"Thank you, my dear. I just don't understand it. Why on earth didn't that man just let Justine call off the engagement, like every other civilized gentleman would have done?"

Marshall rubbed his tired face. "I don't know. I can only surmise that after he sent me that letter, he realized that he could actually get sued for breach of promise. Perhaps that's why he set the journalist on us . . . to gather evidence of Justine's improprieties and strengthen his position in case I decided to file suit."

She nodded slowly. "You must go and speak to Herbert Stanton. You will make assurances you won't sue if he will renew the betrothal to Justine. We'll have a physician examine her and testify to her virginity. We'll pay the man to swear to it if we have to. Just tell him to call off the journalist."

Though he inhaled deeply, the air did not seem to

enter his chest. "I don't know if that's the right thing to do."

"Oh? And why not?"

Thoughts of Athena filled his head. "Well, for one thing, Justine doesn't love him."

His mother looked at him as though he were speaking a foreign language. "What possible weight could that have on this decision?"

His words felt unfamiliar, but they also felt *right*. "Don't you want your daughter to marry out of love?"

"Preposterous. A slip of a girl like Justine can't be counted on to choose the right man to marry. She doesn't know her own heart."

It sounded like something his father would have said. "Did you?"

"Did I what?"

"At that age . . . did you know your own heart?"

"That's irrelevant."

"Did you love Father when you married him?"

She shook her head. "No one marries out of love. Marriages are supposed to be orchestrated so as to benefit each family. I gave your father a generous dowry, and he gave me the title of marchioness. We were an ideal match."

Marshall recalled all the arguments that, over the years, turned into chilly aloofness. His mother didn't attend his father, even when he was on his deathbed. "Did you stay that way? An ideal match?"

She turned her head away. "Love is one thing. Marriage is another. I did my duty. So did your father."

For a long time, Marshall stared into the empty glass in his hand. "If you had it to do over again, would you choose love over my father?"

His mother's gaze disappeared through the darkened window. "I wish I could say I grew to love your father. But I never did. Your grandmother said I would, but—" Her voice lost its characteristic self-assurance and aristocratic veneer. "In many ways, my life—our life—grew more unbearable once we were married. But I do not regret our marriage . . . it brought you and Justine into my world. And I gave you all the love I could not give him."

The candlelight glittered off the etched crystal, forming a dozen false stars in his glass. He was sorry his parents had suffered such a hollow union. Better dead than wed, he used to tell himself, and now he understood why. His father had never encouraged in him much esteem for the value of women, and his mother had never done anything to prove him wrong.

But Athena did, and she proclaimed it loudly. She had brought fresh eyes to him, showing him the myriad surprises and adventures a woman has to offer. He discovered in Athena a world far more intriguing than the hazy landforms at the horizons of the sea, and he found himself wanting more. A great deal more.

He leaned over and covered his mother's hand reassuringly with his own. Her hand was frail and papery, and the veins showed blue between the skeletal joints. It was a shame that her joy came finally at this stage in her life, now that her spouse was a year in the grave.

He didn't want that for himself. And he didn't want it for Justine.

FOURTEEN

"Send him away." said Athena. "Preferably at gun-point."

Gert blinked in disbelief. "Miss?"

"Go out there and tell Mr. Marshall I won't have a visit from him."

"But Athena," drawled Hester from her settee, where she was finishing her needlepoint. "He's come to see you."

Athena didn't bother looking up from her ledger. "The day I'll see that man again I'll be sure to have a crossbow and a quiver full of arrows at my side."

Gert bit her lip. "He's most insistent, miss."

"Gert, you have my permission to kick him out. I'd kick him out myself, only I have my best shoes on."

Hester sighed. "Athena, I know you're hurt over the way he left you, but perhaps you should consider this from all angles."

"I've already considered him from all angles. And I have a nude sketch of him to prove it."

"Why must you be so surly? He's really very pleas-ant."

"So is a Shetland pony, but I don't want one in my sitting room."

Hester raised her voice, something she didn't do well without it wavering from emotion. "Athena, Mr. Marshall showed me great kindness the other day when I imposed my *crie de coeur* upon him, and he gave me invaluable advice when I needed it most. Now, you apologized to me for insulting me that day, but I'll not forgive you if you make me go out there and tell Mr. Marshall he must leave because you won't see him."

Athena set her quill down roughly, creating a large blue blotch on the page. "Oh, very well. Show him in."

Gert slinked out through the door and returned a few moments later with Marshall.

"Good afternoon, ladies."

"Good afternoon, Mr. Marshall," responded Hester.

Athena closed the ledger and stood up. "Mr. Marshall, if you're here seeking a post, I'm afraid there is none to offer you. We are fully staffed."

"Thank you, no, Miss McAllister. I'm here on another matter. How are you, Lady Willett?"

"I'm well, Mr. Marshall. We both are, aren't we, Athena?"

Athena glanced at Marshall, her chin jutting forward. Marshall's expression was apologetic. Unspoken words hung between them.

"Lady Willett, I wonder if you'd be good enough to allow me a private interview with Miss McAllister?"

Athena glanced at Hester and nodded curtly.

"Certainly," said Hester, her dress whispering as she exited and closed the door behind her.

Marshall held his hands up. "Athena—"

"Don't speak to me again."

"Hear me out."

"I'd rather throw you out."

"Please understand . . . you're the only woman in the world I would have walked out on at a moment like that."

Sarcasm dripped from her lips. "Thank you very much! I don't know if I can withstand any more of your compliments."

He hung his head. "You know what I mean. I respect you. I wanted to safeguard your honor."

"Sod my honor. What about my pride? One moment you're cheering me up and making me feel beautiful, and the next you're tossing me over like a wheelbarrow full of cow pats."

He had to chuckle at the imagery. "I didn't mean to upset you. Truly. But it was important to me not to take advantage of you in your fragile state."

"Well done, Mr. Marshall. High marks for gallantry."

Marshall sighed. "I'm sorry. I shouldn't have started a fire I couldn't control."

"Don't flatter yourself. This fire has gone quite cold."

"That's the last thing I want. Athena—"

"If you've come to make an apology, you've done it. You may go now."

"Don't dismiss me like that," he said, the edge returning to his voice. "Please . . . I have a request to make."

"You have a request to make of me?" Athena sat down and crossed her arms at her chest. "My, this promises to be fun."

"It's a serious matter, Athena. I need to speak to Countess Cavendish."

She chuckled. "That's out of the question."

"Why?"

She leaned forward over the desk. "Because I handle matters concerning the staff."

"It's imperative that I see her."

"Tell me what is so important that it warrants troubling the countess."

"I can't. With all due respect, this matter goes over your head."

Athena's nostrils flared with indignation. "Well, let's hope this doesn't go over yours. Get out!"

Marshall stepped out into the street. The day was sunny and cloudless, but he could not dispel the shadow that lay across him.

He fully expected the stubborn Athena to refuse him admission to see Countess Cavendish, but even the gentle Hester was unwilling to help.

It was time he raised his voice a little. The countess had to be told of the imminent danger of the journalist's interest. He knew it was only a matter of time before the school's misconduct would be exposed, and many young ladies, his sister included, would be vilified. He couldn't reveal his true identity to Athena and Hester, but he could appeal to Countess Cavendish as himself.

He had tried consulting *Debrett's Peerage* for the countess's residence, but he couldn't find any mention of a Countess Cavendish. He was frustrated by the dead end, but it was not uncommon for some nobles to be left out of the book. Some people with new titles, or even Continental peers, were sometimes left out of the book altogether. He decided to try one more tack.

Marshall rapped on the door to the offices of Messrs. Stewart and Newman, publishers of Countess Cavendish's *Feminine Excellence, or Every Young Woman's Guide to Ladylike Comportment.* It didn't take long for him to be ushered in to see Mr. Hadley Stewart, the editor. All he had to do was say that he himself was a journalist for the *Times,* and that he was writing a piece extolling the virtues of that manual for the edification of women. Marshall found Mr. Stewart practically panting for the increased revenue such an article would surely bring.

Mr. Stewart was effusively jovial, if a bit obsequious. Light flashed off his small round spectacles as he animatedly discussed, in exaggerated terms, the success of the book. He was quick to draw attention to his shelves, where books printed under his signet were perched like trophies.

"But it's of particular interest to the paper that I interview the authoress," explained Marshall. "My readers will no doubt want a few words from her to learn the inspiration that spawned such a great volume. Would it be possible for me to meet her?"

The man smiled broadly. "I'm certain she would not object to a very brief visit, especially in light of your willingness to write a favorable review in the *Times.*"

"Why only briefly?"

"The countess, as I understand it, is not a well woman. Concerns for her health have kept her in seclusion in the country."

Marshall could not conceal his surprise. "Do you mean to tell me that Countess Cavendish is not residing in London?"

"I'm afraid not. But it isn't far to her home in Surrey."

Confusion creased his brow. Athena gave him the impression that the countess was practically in residence at the school to which she had given her name. "Are you certain that the countess is not even visiting London? For the Season, I mean?"

Grizzled eyebrows hovered over the spectacles. "Quite certain. I had a letter from her just last week, return address Kingston Lodge, Shepherds Green, Surrey. When you see her, perhaps you will be good enough to invite her once more to London. I've been most anxious to meet her."

"You've never met her?"

He shook his head. "I've never been offered the pleasure, no."

"What about the school?"

The eyebrows drew together above the rims of the spectacles. "School? What school?"

Marshall rose quickly. "No matter. Thank you for your time, and for her address. I shall of course convey your good wishes."

He stepped once more onto the curb. The city was practically teeming with pedestrians enjoying the lovely weather, but despite the cheery disposition infusing all of London, Marshall's mood had distinctly stormed over.

FIFTEEN

Marshall's carriage rumbled through Surrey. And for each of the bum-numbing miles between London and his destination, his anger at Miss Athena McAllister mounted.

Mentally, he counted off the indictments against her. She was a liar. A fraud. A contrary minx. She was running a business under a stolen standard, using someone else's name to bring in money for herself. School for the Womanly Arts indeed! It was just shy of being a bordello, one that pandered to women instead of men. And Athena was its Mademoiselle! He wanted to punish her for her deception—and for her abrasiveness. Her ready insults skewered him at every opportunity, and he withstood it as a gentleman would. But each time he thought up ways to tame that sharp tongue of hers, he inevitably wound up fantasizing about putting it to more pleasurable uses.

As he drew near the village where Countess Cavendish resided, he was overtaken by suspicion. Shepherds Green was exactly that—a cluster of hills dotted with sheep, and at the center of it was a rustic village of tanners, blacksmiths, and ostlers. He rode through the high road on the way to Kingston Lodge, expecting to find a palatial estate at the end of his journey. As Marshall's carriage trundled up the unpaved road, it led him to a weathered country house at the crest of a hill.

The house was baronial and impressive, but had a particularly unloved look to it, as if the inhabitants had neglected to recognize its grandeur. The knocker squeaked loudly in complaint as he rapped. After a few moments, a man came to the door.

"Good afternoon, sir. My name is Marshall Hawkesworth, Marquess of Warridge. I'd like to see Countess Cavendish, if she'd be so good as to oblige me."

The stout man looked him up and down in disbelief. "Countess Cavendish?"

"Yes, sir. I don't have an appointment, but I'd be most grateful if she'd grant me an audience."

The man looked askance at Marshall. "Who told you she lives here?"

"Someone in London gave me this address. May I come in?"

"There's no countess here."

His eyebrows drew together in puzzlement. "But I'm sure this is the address I was given."

"You've been misinformed. Goodbye." He swung the door.

Marshall stopped it with his forearm. "Sir," he began, holding his temper against the rudeness. "I've driven all the way from London. I don't wish to impose upon your patience, but it is a matter of great importance. Her good name and fortune are at stake."

The man's eyebrows drew together. "What about her fortune?"

"May I explain inside?"

The man sighed, but held open the door. Marshall stepped through, and was led to the front sitting room.

The room was comfortable but had a distinctly masculine expression to it. The air was thick with pipe smoke, and the walls were heavy with mounted heads and racks of antlers. Great leather chairs flanked a dead fireplace, between which stood a table made of an elephant's leg.

Marshall despised hunting. Though he was not above enjoying a generous plate of venison or pheasant, he was averse to the perspective that killing animals was some sort of sport. There was a vile, bloody aspect to it that he found distasteful. It was bad enough that men celebrated when they killed an animal, but he became disgusted when they gloated over wounding one. He couldn't abide suffering, and leaving an animal wingless or with a bullet in a flank was abhorrent to him. On his estate, game for the table was trapped, not hunted.

He studied the man who poured him something from a decanter. He wore no coat, and his waistcoat stretched over the expanse of his back. A horseshoe of graying hair ringed his head, and the overgrown sideburns at each cheek failed utterly to compensate for the missing hair at his crown.

"May I presume you to be the earl?"

The man chuckled. "No, I'm not the earl."

"Might I ask your name, sir?"

"Straiter. Jules Straiter. Now, what is this about the countess's fortune?"

"Mr. Straiter, I don't wish to appear rude, but this is a matter of great delicacy. What I have to say is for the countess's ears alone. May I be permitted to see her?"

Once again, the man looked Marshall up and down, sizing him up. He upended the glass into his mouth and swirled the liquid around before swallowing it. "You're here about the book."

"Why . . . yes, I am."

He snorted derisively as he served himself another drink from the decanter. It seemed to Marshall that the man had already had a few before Marshall knocked on his door.

"You may as well tell *me* what you have to say. There is no Countess Cavendish."

Marshall's brows drew together. "I'm so sorry. I'd heard she was ill, but I was unaware that she'd passed on."

"She didn't 'pass on.' The bitch never existed."

He blinked in disbelief. "I beg your pardon?"

A sheen broke out on the man's face. "Do you have children?"

"No, but—"

"Don't bother. Enjoy women as pleasurable pursuits. But don't saddle yourself with a wife and children, especially when those children are girls. They represent a loss of time, money, and above all, peace."

"Mr. Straiter, you're not making any sense."

"Neither do women. I proved it by writing that joke of a book. But now, it seems, the joke is on me."

"Wait . . . *you* wrote Countess Cavendish's book?"

The man gave a sarcastic smile. "I *am* Countess Cavendish. I, a landowner from the country, am the one who's decreed how women in polite society should act and talk and think. How's that for a lark?

I've become the ideal of female comportment, and I'm not even a woman!"

"Why?"

Mr. Straiter's glass rattled the tray as he set it down roughly. "Because young girls today don't know how to behave! They're lazy, vain, self-indulgent, and disrespectful. Women today are not being taught to recognize the superiority of our sex. We treat them like porcelain dolls—we pamper them, flatter them, and show self-restraint around them. And what do they do? Flout us. Disobey us. Make demands. And God forbid they reproduce. Insubordinate wives inevitably bear insubordinate daughters."

He went to a drawer in a desk and pulled out a sheaf of papers. "You see this? This is how that book started. As a long and scathing letter to my daughter, that bitch-in-heat who went off and married some Irishman against my express wishes. So I told her. A decent woman would be modest. And virtuous. And parsimonious. She should respect her father and obey him in all things. I outlined to her in no uncertain terms how proper women should behave." He began to pace the floor, his unsteady voice booming across the room. "And after I had written that long letter, it occurred to me. This is something every woman should learn. Wives, mothers, daughters . . . every woman should be made to follow these precepts! So I sat down and expanded that letter into a manual, a book for the instruction of all women. I knew as soon as it was finished that it was perfect. But I also knew no one would buy it if it came from Jules Straiter. So when I sent it to London to be published, I signed the manuscript 'Countess Cavendish,' knowing that every rattle-pated goose out there would do whatever some skirt with a title told them to do."

Marshall's reaction shifted from disgust to bafflement to anger. Athena, that little trickster, was herself tricked. She and every other female who thought they'd profit from the opinions of an "expert."

Mr. Straiter wiped his face with his shirtsleeves. "I'd hoped the book would sell well, but I certainly didn't want it to become as successful as it did. Just now, I had a woman over—some widow that lives outside the village. We shared a few drinks. I spent the entire afternoon feigning interest in all the insignificant minutiae of her life just to get her into the mood. I almost had her on her back, when all of a sudden she gets up and spouts off some platitude about purity being the hallmark of a woman's character, and how without it no man would want to marry her. 'A woman must imagine herself a tightly furled flower, its petals protecting her delicate heart with a fragrant blush of beauty,' she said. I wrote that! That antiquated hausfrau, who should be glad of my attentions, actually used my own words against me! As if I would marry a troglodyte like her."

Marshall had heard enough. He set down his glass, untouched.

"Sir, you're a charlatan and a hypocrite. You expect women to be ladies—or not—only when it suits you. You're right about purity being a hallmark of a woman's character, but you don't know a thing about what makes a lady." Marshall picked up his hat and headed for the door.

"Wait! You told me you had something to tell me about my fortune."

Marshall turned around. "Countess Cavendish is about to be defrocked as the fountainhead of feminine virtue. My advice to you is to take a page from your own book and start implementing some parsimony. In other words, act like a lady."

Armed with the knowledge that there was no Countess Cavendish, Marshall marched back to the school ready to wage war. His adversary was none other than one feisty, intractable—and foolish—woman.

He shouldered past Gert at half past ten. The evening lecture was still in session, the ladies all assembled in the parlor listening to a young American poet. The man was freshly handsome, with a youth's smooth face and dark eyelashes surrounded sparkling hazel eyes. But his unkempt brown hair and eccentric clothes lent him a rakish, Gypsy quality that held the ladies in thrall.

His deep voice was smoky. "Her twisting body to his manhood pin'd, like a tulip's stem tossed to and fro in the wind." His smoldering eyes alighted on each of their faces, as though he were wooing each one in turn. "A fire stirred by stroking flesh, his thrusts provoked her pleasure afresh."

Marshall strode to the lectern and closed the young man's book. "The reading is over. Class dismissed."

"Who the devil are you?" the poet demanded.

"No one to be trifled with."

"Do you know who I am? I am Clint—"

"I know who you're going to be—one sorely bruised American. Take your salacious limericks and get out." He took the book and shoved it into the poet's chest.

"This is an outrage! I'll have an explanation from Miss McAllister."

Marshall seized him by his red neckcloth. The young man, dwarfed by Marshall in both height and breadth, had the sense to tremble.

Marshall muttered into the wide-eyed face, his words meant only for the younger man's ears. "I shall give you just one moment more to take your soft words and hard cock and get the hell out of here."

The terrified man nodded vehemently, then flew out the door when Marshall released him.

Holding a cream-colored letter in her hand, Athena pushed her way through the students. "How dare you come in here and disrupt my class! Who do you think you are?"

He met her fiery gaze. "I want a word with you." Without giving her a chance to respond, he turned to the students. "The rest of you . . . to bed. Now!" His command had the effect of a gunshot in a room full of startled cats. They bolted up the stairs.

She whirled upon him, her eyes blazing hot fury. "Why, you despicable Visigoth! You've got a bloody cheek coming in here and spouting out orders like some deranged schoolmaster."

"Sit down. I want an explanation from you."

Her eyes squinted with venomous rage. "You asked for this. I'm sending for the constable."

"Good. Then perhaps you can explain to both of us why you stole Countess Cavendish's name."

Athena froze halfway through the doorway. "What?"

"You heard me. You brandished the name of Countess Cavendish to give your 'School for the Womanly Arts' some credibility. But the truth is, Countess Cavendish has no earthly idea what you are up to."

"What are you talking about? I have a letter from her lending her patronage to the school."

"A forgery."

"How dare you," she repeated in indignation, though it was said with significantly less vehemence.

"You've defrauded dozens of prominent families. Charged steep tuition under the false pretenses that the renowned Countess Cavendish oversaw the education of their innocent daughters—when in fact, Countess Cavendish has patronized this school about as much as Napoleon patronized Buckingham House."

Athena's face flushed to the color of her hair. "That's not true."

"Oh, but it is," he countered, walking steadily toward her. "You're a swindler and a cheat and a liar. A magistrate will hold you accountable for operating under the auspices of Countess Cavendish without permission. It is a crime punishable by hanging."

Her chest caved, but she steadied herself. "Nonsense. Countess Cavendish will be flattered by the homage."

He smiled wryly. "I have a feeling he won't."

"Yes, he w— He?"

Marshall walked around behind her. "A lesser known fact of your exemplar. Countess Cavendish is, in fact, a rather embittered old man with an ax to grind against women. I met him this afternoon. He authored that book of yours to prove his premise that women are not only stupid, but brainless. And after discovering your orchestration of this farce of a school, I'm tempted to agree with him."

Athena's jaw dropped. "It's not possible. I don't believe you."

Marshall leaned his frame upon the back of the settee. "Kingston Lodge, Shepherds Green, Surrey. Feel free to pay him a visit."

Athena began to pace the room, the cream-colored paper strangled in her fist. "Oh, I ought to take that book and bash that man's head in!"

"Just a moment, my little hypocrite," he said, stopping her in her tracks. "Before you go exacting retribution from someone who cheated you before you cheated others, perhaps you'd be good enough to explain to me what made you decide to peddle the countess's teachings in the first place."

She jerked her arm from his grip. "I don't owe *you* any explanation."

"The hell you don't! Was it just a sham to cover up for these lessons on being a demimondaine?"

Athena straightened. "In the first place, they're informative practicums on relations between the sexes. And in the second, I may have been exposing these ladies to sexual matters, but at least I was equipping them to face the real world . . . a world where husbands are permitted to keep a bit of fluff on the side, but a woman who does so would be disgraced, divorced, or beaten. I had to teach them that they didn't have to resign themselves to sitting at home in a corner like some ruddy spider, waiting for their husbands to return from the beds of their kept women. I had to teach them how to steal their husbands back from their mistresses."

"You should have taught them to be their own person, not a harem seductress." His mind turned to Hester. "Sex holds a man's interest only so long. We want a companion, a friend, a consort, and a love. Are you so uninformed that you do not understand what *we* desire?"

Athena shook her head as her chest rose and fell over the bodice of her turquoise dress. "Men desire a skilled lover."

"Yes, Athena, but not a tutored one. If a woman is to know how to pleasure me, it is in *my* bed I want her to learn it."

"Don't be ridiculous. If I didn't learn how to please a man, he wouldn't notice me in the first place."

His expression blackened with jealousy. "You little fool. No matter what you do, Calvin Bretherton will never want you back."

The earnestness was struck from her face as if by some invisible hand. But the shock was quickly replaced by fury. "Is that so? Well, here!" she cried, throwing the rumpled parchment at him as her eyes misted over. "See for yourself! Who's the fool now?"

He picked up the paper off the floor. "What is this?"

"It's a letter from Calvin Bretherton," she crowed, "begging for my forgiveness and asking me once more for my hand in marriage. He wants to publish the banns at the earliest opportunity. What do you think about that?"

Bewilderment overtook his features. His brows drew together as he read the letter.

"Ha! That's done you white!" she continued, swallowing back the tears. "Where's your grand talk about men now? You posture and pose, boasting about how much you know about love and courtship, and you're nothing but a fraud yourself. That'll put you in your place!"

It was as she said. Bretherton was proposing

marriage all over again. Marshall should have been happy for her, but he wasn't. The thought of seeing Athena as some other man's wife set off an alarm inside him that he found impossible to silence. But there was something else that disturbed him, and it made him anxious not just for his own sake, but for hers.

"What about his love, Athena?"

A kink appeared in her self-satisfied expression. "What?"

He held out the bruised paper. "Where does he say how much he loves you? I couldn't read that anywhere in this letter."

She snatched the paper from his hand and pored over it. "I . . . he . . . it's implied."

"Is it? Or is his offer of matrimony enough for you?"

She was silent.

Marshall shook his head, a weak chuckle shrugging his shoulders. "He won you over with just a few words."

"No! He loves me."

"How do you know?"

"Because why else would he—" Her voice disappeared like smoke.

"Why else would he what? Bretherton can't express his love even in words, which are far easier to offer than actions, and you assume that he must love you because he asks to marry you?"

Though her eyes were still glued to the paper, her expression mercuried into something he'd never seen before—vulnerability. "He loves me because I became the woman he wanted."

He shook his head, his eyes shutting to the meaning

behind her words. "How can you value yourself so cheaply? Athena, can't you see that despite your flaws—legion though they are—you are worth all a man can give and more? You don't have to buy his love with saucy words or furtive touches . . . you already deserve it."

She turned her face to the parchment in her hands, her eyes glassy with tears.

He lifted her face with his fingers, and the look in her eyes wounded him deeply. Her eyes were searching for the truth . . . pleading for it. He was sorry she'd experienced such unscrupulous men. As he looked deep into her expectant eyes, he saw the hazy expression of a young girl, disappointment distorting her pure heart. He wanted to restore her faith in men. He wanted to bring hope back to that dreamy young face.

Slowly, his face lowered until his mouth hovered within a hairsbreadth of hers. If she had the audacity to hope again, he would show her that it would be worth it.

SIXTEEN

She had been towering with confidence only moments before, and now she felt as if she had fallen off her own shoulders.

Please, her heart cried, but she didn't know what it was asking for. She was in freefall, and there was nothing to grab onto.

He was offering her something she wanted desperately—faith. She wanted to believe in the possibility of Cinderella's prince again. And here was a man promising her that the ideal still existed, a man who would love her and not hurt her, and never deceive her.

A kiss. He wanted to seal the promise with a kiss. She wanted that promise. And his lips were so tantalizingly close . . .

Their lips met. The kiss was gentle and earnest, and in it he seemed to declare feelings she never thought to receive from a man. Truth, strength, affection, commitment. The clenched fist her heart had become began to unfurl.

He inhaled sharply, as if being infused with new life. She neared him, her hands gripping his lapels. Closer she drew, taking the step he asked of her. In response, his arms enfolded her in his embrace, so close that the light between their bodies disappeared.

His kiss grew more insistent, more desperate to explain. His tongue darted out to taste her lips, and this time, she was ready for him. Her tongue stretched out and met his, answering his need with an admission of her own. The wet hotness of his mouth called to mind another organ that also cried for attention, and she felt it taking on a life of its own.

The hands that caressed her back awoke a sleeping craving she felt unable to control. Her hands lifted to the crown of his golden head, and she curled her fingers through the silken strands. The intimate gesture seemed to send him into a fury of want. He groaned, and his mouth broke free of her lips. His lips began a descent down the column of her neck, and the erotic sensation pulled her toward a descent of her own into uncharted depths of pleasure.

Farther down his kisses went, and she arched her back to let him pass. A large hand cupped her breast, lifting it to his hungry mouth. It mounded over the neckline of her gown, like a ripe fruit stretching to fullness. She buried her cheek into the soft waves of his hair, inhaling the warm scent. The kisses on her tender skin were scratchy from the day's growth of beard, but when his hot tongue licked at her breast, pleasure exploded over her entire body. Her fevered mind begged him to show her what she had been missing all these years. She didn't know if words came out of her mouth, but somehow he understood her wishes. He bent down and snaked his forearm under her knees.

She felt him lifting her body into the air. Frightening and liberating at the same time—that was the feeling of being no longer in control. Though they were of one mind, she surrendered to his greater resolve.

And his greater strength. It took a man of great vigor and might to carry a woman as substantial as she up the stairs. She stared into Marshall's handsome face, gritty with willpower. He looked back at her, imparting what was about to happen. Not asking . . . telling. And she'd be damned if she'd put up a fight.

"Which one?" he growled. She liked the rumble in his voice.

"End of the hall," she rasped back.

He pushed through her bedroom door, and laid her down on the needlepointed bedspread—a gift from the first-term students. Her heartbeat began to pound in her ears. In this vulnerable position, the colossal impact of what she was about to do slammed into her. All her life, she had dreamed of a Cinderella wedding and a prince's nuptial bed. Life had dealt her a severe blow that crushed her fantasies and skewed the course of her life. Nevertheless, even at her age, there was the nebulous hope that she could still marry . . . some women of her years did. But if she allowed this man in her bed, it was final. To lose her virginity now would obliterate those chances. There would be no wedding, no husband, no children—forever a spinster. Was this man worth all that?

She looked up at him. He had one knee on the bed, and between his legs the fabric of his trousers stretched over the hard shape. Moonlight from her open window illuminated him from behind. His golden hair haloed his head, and his silhouette filled her senses. He stared down at her, his chest expanding raggedly. In the half dark of her room, his eyes were cast in shadow, but the jut of his chin revealed his resolute purpose.

"You're a mistake," she said, hating her own confession of stupidity almost as much as the imminent disappointment of interrupted pleasure.

"So are you," he said, ripping off his coat.

His answer lit a flame of anger. "Then get out."

"No. I'm going to make you mine tonight," he said solemnly, tugging at his cravat. "But once you belong to me, you shall belong to no other."

Her mind rebelled at the thought of belonging to somebody. But not her heart. Those words were music to her lonely soul, and it drank them in like a withered plant takes in life-giving water. His words were almost a profession of love. Almost, but not quite. And not enough.

She propped herself up on her elbows. "I'll belong to no man."

"We'll see about that."

He leaned over her body and melded his mouth to hers. Irritated that he would force a kiss upon her, she tried pushing him away. It had no effect. Her hands just slid across his silk waistcoat.

His hot mouth enveloped her frightened lips, coaxing them to open for him. A moan escaped her, letting loose a passion that had for too long been suppressed. Her lips parted, swallowing his mouth in hers. The shadow that had formed around his mouth scraped the softness of her moist lips, but the masculinity of it inflamed her feminine senses. Her womanhood ached within her, warming her body like hot breath on a frosted window.

His cheek scraped hers as his lips wended down

her jaw. He took her earlobe in his mouth, and half her body blazed to life with that one sensation. All along her right side the tiny hairs on her skin stood on end. In that sensitive spot behind her ear, the breath from his nostrils fanned a new awareness of her body's capacity for pleasure.

His hand circled round the base of her neck, making her gasp at its feel on her naked flesh. It trailed down the exposed part of her chest, coming to rest on her breast. His palm found her nipple, rising through the fabric of her dress. Slowly, the fleshy palm smoothed over her breast, intensifying her passion exponentially.

She heard herself moan, and instantly hated her own confession of desire. But before she could stop him from inciting her body's betrayal, his fingers curled into the fabric of her dress and rent it from her shoulder.

The sound tore a surprised shriek from her. She didn't recognize the hot-blooded expression on his face, but somehow exulted in it. The turquoise muslin fell away, exposing her breast to him. Her mouth hung open as he took what he came after. The scorching mouth locked onto her breast, and laved fire onto the tender flesh.

His sunlight-colored hair whispered over her face. She eased her fingers through the glossy waves, losing them in the thickness. The intimate contact of his body at each point filled her with sensual bliss.

But a rogue thought splintered through her pleasure. Calvin.

How many times had she lain on this very bed, fantasizing this very scenario? A man's body stretched over hers as she spread herself to his invisible manhood. Her fingers would give her the pleasure that the daydreamed lover could not. But sometimes, though she would never admit it to anyone, the imaginary face above her own would materialize into Calvin's. And even though the thought of him hastened her body's pleasure, it would almost always be followed by a stab of shame.

There was a real man over her now, and his hands traveled down her leg and balled the fabric of the skirt in his fist. Her rational mind, dulled by the haze of pleasure, now raised its scolding voice. There was a letter downstairs from Calvin, and it effectively asked her to save herself for him. And although Calvin's proposal brought forth a host of turbulent thoughts, at least it would end her spinsterhood. The man in her bed, on the other hand, would seal it.

"No," she breathed. The word sounded foreign, her body shouting its resentment. It was as if her body and her mind were at war with one another.

"Don't fight me, Athena," he said in a heavy whisper intensified by emotion. "If you become mine, I shall also become yours."

If her rational thought could take physical form, it would be standing in front of her with its hands on its hips saying, "I told you so." This man was so skilled at manipulating her into giving him what he wanted. And even though at that moment she wanted it too—more than anything—her pride would not let her stand for the presumption.

"Get off my bed."

He raised himself up, his hair rumpled from her hands. "Don't be absurd."

She knew her will could only stand so much before breaking, and if she didn't stop this now, she'd be lost. She drew back her hand and slapped him.

He remained frozen in that position, face turned in the direction she hit him. His eyes closed tightly, his slack jaw absorbing the shock of her strike.

His eyes slowly refocused on her face. "That is enough, Athena."

She slapped him again, this time on the other cheek.

"That is *more* than enough." He placed one foot on the floor and brought himself to a kneeling position. He jerked her up and wrapped an arm around her waist. Effortlessly, he tossed her over onto her knees facing the headboard. And knelt behind her.

"All right, my little cat," he said, jerking her back into place as she tried to escape, "your claws will do you no good in this position." He bunched her gown and her shift in his hands and tossed them over her waist.

"Let me go! I don't want you! I love Calvin!" In spite of the humiliating position, a familiar stab of shame skewered her heart.

He held her like that as he unfastened the buttons of his trousers with one hand. "You can lie to others and you can even lie to yourself, but you won't lie to me."

"Don't," she said halfheartedly.

From above her, she heard him growl. "I won't force myself on you. If you want me to stop, I'll stop. But admit that I'm the one for you, Athena, and I'll be yours."

She remained there panting, reason shattered by the tide of her urges. His thighs between her thighs provoked a resurgence of passion. She couldn't see his face, and maybe that was a blessing. She shut her eyes, trying to imagine Calvin as the man behind her, but the fantasy failed her utterly. The truth was that she wanted the lovemaking not from Calvin, but from Marshall.

"Yes."

There was no turning back now. Athena, sandwiched between the soft bed and his hard body, found herself imprisoned between the comfortable and the dangerous. She braced herself for the pain.

He shifted behind her. He brought the tip of his manhood to her glistening curls. There was a gentle pressure at her opening, as though she had leaned upon a bedknob. But the roundness pushed farther, making her wince and cry out. As it advanced slowly, the pain grew until he was sheathed entirely inside her.

She had not expected such pain. She didn't know if it was because she was too old or he was too big, but she didn't care. Before she had a chance to demand it, he began to pull out, relieving her discomfort a little.

"Breathe," he said, and she did so. But instead of coming out of her, he pushed himself back in.

She whimpered, feeling the tightness all over again.

Again he slid out and thrust back in. There was a different feeling now, not so much of stretching but of fullness. The pain took on a different dimension, transforming into perverse pleasure.

His hands caressed her arching back as she accepted his movements easier. Slowly, she started to enjoy the thrusts, as they began to fuel the fire between her legs. Her fists balled the sweaty sheets as his pushing sped up. Her breasts rocked back and forth by the force of his body. Against her naked thighs, she felt the soft fabric of his fawn breeches, and she derived a corrupt pleasure from the wantonness of their position. It was so animal, so dirty, so different from her youthful fantasies. It wasn't supposed to be like this, and yet, right now, she wouldn't have it any other way.

Above him, she heard him groan. As his pleasure began to mount, so did hers. But suddenly he stopped, and she moaned in protest.

"Not like this," she heard him say, and he slid out of her. She felt him easing her onto her side. "Lie back."

She lay down, and he descended onto her. He kissed her fervently, inciting her forgotten lips to passion once more. He drew himself onto one forearm. Instinctively, she raised her legs on either side of him, and he entered her from the front. It had been torture to have him absent from her body, and joining to him somehow made her feel complete. The warm, solid body rocking above her, and the smooth silk of his waistcoat rubbing against her bare breasts, acquainted her with an unknown height of eroticism. In no time, his movements on top and inside her accelerated the onset of her quickening.

He moaned, and the sound felt glorious to her ears. She had not been the only one subjugated by the pleasure of the night. It pleased her to be the object of his desire as much as he'd become hers. Though she enjoyed seeing the raw expression on his face, her orgasm approached and she closed her eyes to receive it. Her mouth fell open, her breathing grew more ragged, and her body exploded in a flash of erotic delight.

Her tight womanhood clamped onto his muscle, her legs folded over his hips like wings. As the spasms subsided, she realized he was no longer thrusting. She opened her eyes, and found him looking intently at her.

"I'd love to spend a lifetime bringing that look to your face."

She smiled through the fog of her private pleasure. Once more, he began to move inside her, at his own rhythm. Her lust dispelled, she now regarded him through dreamy eyelids. He was a kind man, a noble man, a handsome man. How could she have been so blind? And as he allowed himself the luxury of enjoying his own explosive orgasm, she fell in love with him all over again.

When he opened his eyes, the expression on his face was completely different from anything she had seen before. His eyes held a serene joy as they looked down at her, and that became the single, greatest moment of her life. He lowered his head, and their foreheads touched. During that silent, intimate time, as he caressed her face, she burgeoned into something beyond herself, like an oasis in full flower.

Outside the window, the moon drifted higher into the night sky. She lay curled against his side, unable to take her eyes off him.

"Did I ever tell you what a beautiful man you are?"

He chuckled. "Just the opposite. When we first met, you questioned the species of my parents."

"Did I? That was a peculiar thing to do."

"You are a peculiar person."

"I don't mean to be."

He kissed her temple. "Oddly enough, your sharp manner is part of your charm."

"I take umbrage at 'sharp.' Determined, perhaps, but not sharp."

"What on earth is someone like you teaching females how to be ladies? You're the least ladylike woman here."

"Why, you miserable, fetid—"

His body rocked with laughter. "No, no, I didn't mean it like that. I just meant that you don't have much to offer them in the way of drawing room decorum, that's all."

She glanced sidewise at him. "I shall ignore that remark."

"I was always taught that ladies don't go into trades."

"Why not? I've a mind for it. If I were to marry, I'd probably end up squandering my intelligence."

"I see. Better to be the head of a mouse than the tail of a lion, is that it?"

"Precisely."

"Do you still want to?"

"Want to what?"

"Marry."

She exhaled. "It's not a question of wanting to. I know I'm a bit ancient to be a debutante. Put in my place, how would you feel?"

"I don't know. I'm not a debutante."

She punched him on the shoulder playfully. "I meant old."

"You're not old. Of course, you're not exactly an adolescent."

She stiffened. "You're not an adolescent either. Why aren't you married?"

"I don't know. Never found the right girl, I expect."

"You make it sound like a scavenger hunt."

"I suppose it is, of a sort. All the women I seem to meet are more concerned with the condition of their hair than the condition of their character. I can't bear to spend more than twenty minutes with any of them. I seem to have gone right off brainless women."

"Oh? Too smart for you?"

He narrowed his eyes at her. "One of these days, I'm going to teach you a better use for that sassy mouth of yours." He began to stroke her hair tenderly. "The kind of woman I'm drawn to is intelligent, humorous, kindhearted, brave. Redheaded . . ."

Athena blushed, her eyelashes pressing against her cheek.

He grinned wickedly. "I don't suppose you know anyone like that you could introduce me to?"

"Oh!" she cried, and drove her fist into his abdomen.

"Oof! You won't get a proposal out of me by pummeling me."

"Ha! As if you had many other bridal prospects. For one thing, she would have to be receptive to marrying into gentlemanly penury. For another, she would have to be a fairly forgiving woman to allow her husband to model nude and kiss women on a regular basis."

Marshall's expression sobered. "Ah. I've been meaning to talk to you about that." He stood up and walked to the window, silently staring into the blackness for a long time. "Athena, I want you to close down the school."

She sat up in bed. "What?"

He turned around to face her. "The school, Athena. It needs to be shut down."

He said it with such solemn gravity that the blood drained from her face. "Why?"

Marshall had considered various ways to confess to Athena who he was and what he knew about the potential for scandal. But the question of *when* he would do it was more of a mystery—and now was certainly not the right time. "Athena, do you trust me?"

Her eyebrows drew together as she absorbed all his words. "No. I can't say I do."

Now it was Marshall's turn to be surprised. "After all we've just done together? You've just given yourself to me . . . how can you say you don't trust me?"

Athena's breathing quickened. "Why would you want me to close down my school?"

"For your own good. For the good of your students. For their families. And for me."

"You're not making any sense."

"I know. I'll explain everything, I promise. But not tonight, Athena. Tonight is our special night." He sat upon her bed. "Tomorrow, though, I must ask that you send your pupils home."

She backed away from his outstretched hand. "You've got a bloody cheek. First you storm in here and send my lecturer home with a flea in his ear. Then you ravage me like I'm some sort of street harlot. And now you tell me in no uncertain terms that I'm to give up my school just because you say so. Who the hell do you think you are?"

"Athena, I—"

She narrowed her eyes at him. "What are you trying to do . . . take over my school? Did you seduce me just to get me to give up my business? Is that your game?"

He held his hands up. "Steady on."

She bolted out of bed, clutching the coverlet to her

chest. "No, *you* steady on! I would no more give up my school than I would my left arm. And certainly not in deference to a *subordinate*."

He rose, bristling at the way she spat out the word. "What I'm trying to tell you, or rather keep from telling you, is that there is a newspaperman who is making inquiries into this place. And I don't want him to discover what truly goes on here."

"That is none of your concern, Mr. Marshall. In this place, *I* am in charge, not you. I will determine the course of this school. I don't give a damn what some newspaperman writes about. And don't think you can use blackmail over using Countess Cavendish's name to get me to do your bidding. I answer to no man, least of all you. Get out!"

He knew he had smashed into that brick wall of hers. He was going to get nowhere tonight, not in her present imperial mood. He leaned over and picked up his coat from the floor. "I will go. For now. But remember this in the coming days: duty does not always lie in our best interest." He threw his coat over his shoulder and walked out of her room.

SEVENTEEN

The street was dead.

Recent rain had made the cobblestones sleek, and an unopposed blanket of fog had begun to nestle between the buildings. At that hour, not even a dog could be heard. Even the perfume of London, far different to the one created during the bustling day, seemed colorless and still.

Marshall closed the front door of the school gently behind him. He had handled that badly. Athena was not a woman who responded well to demands, even if they were in her own best interest. He shook his head. What a handful she was. She was uncharted territory— independent, clever, and yet strangely vulnerable. Her badinage always left him exhilarated, and her beauty kept him in a state of thorough arousal. Half the time he wanted to fence with her, the other half he wanted to spend wrapped in her limbs like he did tonight. Of one thing he was certain . . . Miss Athena McAllister took his breath away, and he'd never get it back again.

"Lord Warridge."

Marshall turned, startled more by the form of address than the unexpected voice. "Who's there?"

Through the fog, he saw a flicker of light. A man

broke through the mist, his cigar glowing in the night.

Marshall looked him up and down. He was a slender man, dressed in a weathered coat and worn pants. His hat hung askew, and his face was shiny with dew. Whoever he was, he'd been sitting out in this fog for some time.

"Edward Nance, at your service."

The man extended a hand, and Marshall took it. He hoped he heard the name aright, distorted as his words were with the thick cigar between his teeth. "Do we know one another, Mr. Nance?"

"Not yet, but I'm hoping we'll become discreet confidants. I'm a journalist, and I'm working on a story for my paper."

"Ah. Mr. Nance. I understand you've been to my home. Are you following me?"

"Consider it a desperate act born of an urgent need to speak with you."

Marshall's scowl blackened. "I don't take kindly to having my steps shadowed. And I don't particularly care for having my family hounded either. If you wish to have an audience with me, you can write me to request an appointment."

Nance smiled down into the cigar between his fingers. "I'm afraid that would be quite impossible. You see, I have time constraints, and my paper demands my story soon."

"Then I'm afraid I cannot help you. Good evening."

"Wouldn't you like to know what it's about?"

Marshall stopped in his tracks. A sickening feeling rose up inside him.

Nance laughed. "Don't worry. It's not about your sister. Not directly, anyway."

Marshall turned and faced him. "Mr. Nance, have a care what you print about my family, or I will haul you into court so fast—"

Nance waved his cigar in denial. "No need to worry, Lord Warridge. I'm not after your family. Just answer me this . . . what were you doing in that school across the street?"

Marshall's fists clenched. "None of your damned business."

"Now, now. I'm not dim-witted. A gentleman like you . . . leaving a school for women at an indecent hour . . . with your coat in your arms . . . What's a worldly man supposed to think?"

"I don't give a damn what you think."

"Yes you do. Let's not play games, Lord Warridge. Your shows of outrage don't move me. Quite frankly, if I had your kind of capital, I'd be in there myself."

"I'm warning you, Nance—"

"I apologize. I don't want to offend you. I need you. More to the point, we need each other. I want your co-operation for my story. If you help me, I promise to keep any mention of you or your sister out of the article."

"What do you want from me?" he growled.

"It's this school I'm after. I've heard there are disreputable things happening behind that door. Things that wouldn't shock the likes of you and me, but to the public, it would make for very interesting reading. Unmarried ladies learning sexual promiscuity? It's an outrage. All I want from you is a little information. Tell me what goes on in there."

"What makes you think I know anything about a girl's school?"

His eyes became hard slits. "People I know have told me what you've been up to in there. Men being paid to teach ladies how to kiss. Oh, I know all about it. If I were a handsome man like you, I'd be first in line for that sort of job. But to the decent and moral people of this city, it's depraved. Corrupt. I wouldn't be surprised if a trial ensued. Indecency, debauchery . . . male prostitution. Who knows?"

Marshall went cold. If the school was exposed, the ensuing storm would leave Athena ruined. She was a strong woman, but she wouldn't be able to keep the wolves at bay before they completely devoured her. He couldn't stomach something like that happening to her.

"Look, Nance. I understand your need for a captivating story. But there is no need to create intrigue where it does not exist. There is no prostitution at that school."

"So what does go on in there?"

"It's a school for women. They teach embroidery and needlepoint, nonsense like that."

His dark eyes sparked to life. "And sex?"

"No!"

"Come now, Lord Warridge. At least give me the truth so I have a choice what to print."

Marshall shifted his weight from one foot to the other. "I give you my word that nothing untoward goes on in there."

Nance shoved his cigar into his mouth, snarling his lips. "Not good enough. I want the facts."

He expelled a labored breath. "You and I both know that you are not interested in facts. You want a titillating read. Nance, reflect . . . you could do a lot of damage by casting aspersions on these women. There are a lot of lives at stake. Spinster women and old maids, guilty of nothing. Assassinate their character and they'll be damaged for life."

"I don't assassinate character, Lord Warridge, I just reveal it. Help me to get my facts correct. Tell me what you know. You don't have to say much. I've already got most of the details I need."

His head jerked back. "From whom?"

"I'm not at liberty to say. Suffice to say that my source has a firsthand knowledge of what's been going on in there."

A stormy expression clouded over his face. Rutherford! He'd stake his life that the blackguard was doing what he did best . . . pitting people's actions against their reputations, forcing them to compromise everything they hold dear to protect the only thing they value. The bastard probably threw Athena to this wolf Nance when Marshall snatched Rutherford's lucrative position away from him. A tide of guilt engulfed him. He had inadvertently set in motion the events that threatened to bring about Athena's downfall.

"All right, Nance. I know what this is about. How much do you want to keep from implicating this school in a sordid scandal?"

Nance crossed his arms in front of his chest. "Must be considerably salacious what you did in there. The fact that you're willing to pay a blackmailer's fee confirms everything my source has told me."

Marshall had had enough. "Damn you and your source! If you've got all the information you need, what in blazes do you need me for?"

Nance took his cigar and jabbed it in Marshall's direction. "I need you to give my story credibility. When this story breaks, legions of prominent and wealthy families are going to descend on the paper en masse clutching sheaves of lawsuits in their hands. I'll be the first to admit that the word of my source alone isn't going to be enough to repel those sticky accusations of slander. But a gentleman like you—marquess from an upright and noble family, an officer in His Majesty's Navy—your imprint of truth will carry a lot of weight."

Marshall gave a mirthless chuckle. "Then the devil take you. I'll not be a party to this, this . . . stoning." He turned on his heel and started down the street.

"Story's going to run anyway, Lord Warridge. Whether you put your seal upon it or not."

Marshall faced the man once more.

Nance turned to stare at the school, his cigar casting a red glow on his shiny face. "Once the constabulary investigates, my story will be corroborated by their investigation anyway. I'm giving you a choice. You can either appear in my story as a witness . . . or as an accomplice." He gave Marshall a meaningful look. "Think it over."

And then, like a cat that has tired of toying with a mouse, Edward Nance disappeared back into the fog, leaving Marshall to bleed worry onto the rain-soaked street.

EIGHTEEN

"Look what I bought yesterday," exclaimed Hester, bouncing into the school clutching a bundle of hair ribbons in a rainbow of colors. "We can give them to the ladies next month when the term ends as a farewell pres— Athena, what's wrong?"

Athena had been sitting alone on the settee in the parlor, nursing a cup of coffee while the ladies took breakfast in the dining room. Her glazed eyes had been staring into the empty fireplace when she glanced up at Hester. "Why do you ask?"

"Well, for one thing you're as white as a sheet. And for another, your dress isn't."

Athena looked down at her lap. A large dark brown stain had spread across the front of her eggshell-colored dress.

"Oh, dear!" she cried, putting the cold cup and saucer down on the table. She grabbed the linen napkin and dabbed at it, but the coffee stain had thoroughly dried in. "Oh, dear!" she repeated, her voice sharp with anxiety.

Hester went to ring for Gert. "Lemon water will get that stain out."

"If only it were that simple," Athena shrieked, and crumpled into the chair.

"Whatever's the matter with you?" Hester knelt in front of Athena, staring up into her face.

Athena's hand pressed against her chest, as if she could somehow still its pounding. "Oh, Hester. I've done an awful thing. Last night, after you left, Mr. Marshall came here." Athena described everything that had happened in accurate detail—even to the moment that they made love.

"Athena," breathed Hester, her hand obscuring her mouth. "What were you thinking?"

Her eyebrows tented in dismay. "I *wasn't* thinking. I was just sort of *doing*. It wasn't really my fault, except . . . well, he was so handsome, and it was all so passionate, and then . . . it just happened."

"Here? With all the girls around?"

"Well, they weren't in the room with me," she said defensively. "Oh, I knew the moment that man set foot in this house that it would mean disaster. Look at me now. He's ruined me." Athena, the goddess dethroned.

"He'll offer for you, surely."

"I don't want to marry him!" Athena exclaimed, rising off the settee. "Do you know why that lout seduced me? To get my school! He only wanted me to fall for him so that I would do his bidding."

"I can't believe that."

"It's true. After he made love to me, the first thing he told me to do was to close down my school!"

"But why?"

"I don't know . . . maybe he wants to start a school

of his own and he's trying to close down the competition. Maybe he wanted a portion of our income. Maybe he wanted to assume more authority here. What does it matter why? He took my virginity and then he demanded my obedience. He is a blackguard and a cad, and I can't believe I was foolish enough to think I loved him."

Hester breathed a deep sigh, and sat in a chair. "I don't see you have a choice. If he's sullied you, you're not fit to marry anyone else."

"Don't be absurd. I can't marry a penniless gentleman. What would my grandfather say? Oh, Hester," she said, her tone changing to panic, "what *would* my grandfather say?"

"Your grandfather dotes upon you. He'll love you no matter what your condition."

She bit her lip. "I do have a condition, don't I?"

"Calm yourself."

Athena started pacing the room, worrying her moist hands. *Women of loose morals are ten a penny,* he had once told her, *and they dwell in the darkness of their own choices.* She had given herself to this man, but what did she really know about him? His whole life was a mystery to her, and she had deliberately kept it that way. Now their relationship had advanced far ahead of its time. "Oh, Hester, I feel such a harlot. I don't even know that man's first name."

"I think you ought to—"

"Lady Ponsonby was right. The forbidden fruit isn't shaped like an apple. It's shaped like a banana."

"Athena!" Hester rarely raised her voice, as she was practically incapable of doing so. "Sit down so we can talk rationally."

Athena perched herself on the edge of the settee, her eyes desperate. "Tell me, please . . . what must I do?"

Hester clasped Athena's hands. "You must accept Calvin's proposal."

Athena pulled her moist hands away. "These are my choices? Calvin or *him*?"

She nodded. "Calvin knows he hurt you, and he knows how he hurt you. He should jolly well be the last person to judge you."

"I don't want to marry Calvin."

"No other gentleman will have you. And don't think you can deceive a man after he's wed you. That will bring irreversible shame to you and to your grandfather. The only other choice is to remain a spinster, which is almost as disgraceful."

Athena's shoulders slumped as she contemplated the courses of action. "Either way, I'm to live happily never after."

A polite knock sounded on the door. Gert entered. "A letter's just arrived for you, miss. The messenger said it was urgent."

Athena tore open the letter. "It's from Grandfather. He asks me to return to Endsleigh Grange straight-away. But he doesn't say why! Oh, I hope nothing's happened to him. Gert, put some clothes in a valise for me. And I'll need to change into something else. Hester, could you stay with the girls for a day or two? I'll be back to the school as soon as I can."

It was almost a relief. Now that the focus of her anxiety had shifted from herself to her grandfather, she felt quite her old self again.

* * *

Endsleigh Grange was ensconced in a cramped dell between two wrestling hills. The house was indicative of her grandfather's reduced circumstances, far different from their former residence at Tigh na Coille, where she had grown up. Her Scottish home had been a flourishing estate that provided meat and vegetables for the entire household with enough left over to sell at the village. In summer, wild strawberries were everywhere. And the fruit orchards were so plentiful that Athena could lean out of the kitchen window and pluck the pears right off the branches.

By contrast, the house at Endsleigh Grange was isolated, hemmed in by trees and bushes overgrown to the extent of some years. A single servant tended to the cleaning and cooking, and half the house was shuttered up for lack of capital necessary to restore it to its former usefulness.

Having lived in London these past months, Athena had almost forgotten the disrepair the house was in, largely unreversed since she and her grandfather had moved in. The front garden was a jungle of green foliage, completely bereft of flowers. A crippled carriage still leaned against one side of the house. Chickens scrambled from her approaching feet as she made her way to the front door.

The woman from the village who looked after the place opened the door. "Hello again, Miss Athena."

"Hello, again, Mrs. Tassel. You're looking well. How's my grandfather? Is he all right?"

"Fit as ever! He's in the ballroom with his guest."

With characteristic good humor, her grandfather had named the house's smallest living space "the grand ballroom." It served as his study, which he kept piled with ancient tomes on his favorite subject, the exploits and quests of knights errant. Athena puzzled over the affirmation of his good health as Mrs. Tassel took Athena's valise and spencer.

"Can I go straight in to see him?"

"'Course. He's been expecting you. Mind you, he's in a temper. Word to the wise—have a kind remark on your lips."

What could have put her customarily genial grandfather in a foul mood? Athena's mind swiftly ticked off all the possible causes without settling on one. She wended her way to the ballroom and knocked on the door.

"Come in."

Athena walked through. "Grandfather! How wonderful to see you!"

He rose slowly from his chair behind the desk. "Athena," he responded tersely. His grave tone was like an invisible arm holding her back from running into his embrace.

Her eyes darted to the man sitting across from his desk, his back turned to her. He was dressed in a navy blue military uniform, and her frantic mind immediately turned to bad news from the war.

The man stood and faced her. Athena could not possibly have been more shocked. The man wearing the crisp blue coat was none other than Mr. Marshall.

Her round eyes swept over the gold braid edging the high collar, lapels, and cuffs. Gold epaulettes ridged his shoulders, and gold buttons marched down the front of his coat. Though her fractured mind failed to absorb the incongruence, it was *him*. The man she thought was an impoverished gentleman desperate for work was standing in front of her in a hero's mantle. Here, in her home, standing with her grandfather, was the man who had secretly shared her bed the night before.

"Good afternoon," he said. There was a significant look on his face, but she couldn't make out what it was she was supposed to know. How much had Mr. Marshall told her grandfather? Her eyes darted back to the older man.

Her grandfather's lips pursed. "Captain Hawkesworth came to see me this morning. He's told me all about it."

Captain Hawkesworth? Athena's eyes jumped from the man's gleaming black boots to his white breeches to the sword hanging from his belt. Mr. Marshall was a naval officer?

"All about what, Grandfather?"

"You know perfectly well what!"

Her eyes flew to Mr. Marshall's face. His expression was grave.

"I informed Lord Penhaligan of our discussion concerning your school, Miss McAllister."

"School!" spat her grandfather. "It's a bawdy-house . . . a seraglio. Except that the women pay the men!"

Athena grew livid. "What has this man been telling you?"

Mason leaned over the desk. "He told me that your school has been instructing ladies on lovemaking. Is that true?"

She glanced sidewise at the man in uniform. If her grandfather weren't in the room, she'd run him through with his own sword. "It's true."

Mason banged on the surface of the desk. "I couldn't believe it of my own granddaughter. I thought you had a sound head on your shoulders. But now I see that you've been given far too much freedom. Are you aware that a journalist is going to investigate and expose the lewdness that's been going on there? You've pitched this family headlong into a scandal. I'll be very surprised if you can even still marry after this." Mason fell into the chair, shielding his eyes with a wrinkled hand. "I'm at a loss. Captain Hawkesworth, I can't apologize enough for my granddaughter's actions. I hope she hasn't completely corrupted your sister."

"Your sister?" she asked.

He shifted his sword and sat down. "Justine Hawkesworth."

Illumination dawned on her. She remembered that Justine was the daughter of the Marquess of Warridge, who was now deceased. As she was one of two children, that made the man in front of her his successor.

"Does the Duchess of Twillingham know what's been going on at your school?" her grandfather demanded.

Her mind reeled from all that they had spoken of and done with one another. "No, Grandfather. She doesn't even know I started the school."

"Damnation!" shouted her grandfather. "Captain Hawkesworth, the fault of all this lies with me. At first I thought it wholesome—amusing even—that a former bordello would be turned into a schoolhouse for virgins. But now I see I was wrong. Clearly, that blasted Pleasure Emporium never truly ceased to exist. I just don't understand it. Athena has always been a levelheaded and intellectual girl, not prone to lasciviousness. Now she's done this foolish and detestable thing."

She stood before the two men like a miscreant child whose shameful actions were being discussed. She could no longer look at either of them. Her face fell to the floor.

Captain Hawkesworth crossed his legs. "I didn't want the scandal to befall your granddaughter or indeed any of the other students, some of whom are from noble families. I thought the best course of action to be to disband the school immediately, which might hinder any investigation by this unscrupulous journalist. He seems out for blood, and he will ruin anyone in his path. I therefore came to you, Lord Penhaligan, in the hope that you might use your influence over Athena to bring her and her students out of immediate danger."

"Of course, Captain. I'm in your debt. I'm very glad that someone is looking out for Athena's welfare. I realize now I may have been too indulgent with her. When her parents were murdered . . . I was beside myself with grief. After their death, I found myself feeling obligated to give Athena whatever she asked—to compensate for the loss of her parents, I suppose. But I gave her too much freedom, too much independence. I shall have to consider very carefully what is to be done with Athena now."

Athena's gaze was riveted to a spot on the carpet, which began to blur as tears filled her eyes.

"What about marriage, sir? Has any thought been given to that?"

Mason gave a hollow laugh. "No one will have her. She's pretty enough, but too obstinate, too opinionated.

I thought that book would have transformed her into a more tractable sort of girl. To think she was supposed to be modeling that behavior to her students! Clearly, she was teaching them to be more like her. I can't apologize enough."

Tears fell from her eyes, and she did nothing to hide them.

Her grandfather shook his head. "I can't have her fend for herself. She'll need to be betrothed at the earliest opportunity."

"Sir," she heard Captain Hawkesworth begin slowly. "May I have Athena's hand?"

She blinked, birthing new rivulets of tears. Slowly, her gaze drifted upward to Marshall's face. The earnestness in his eyes was evident.

"I realize that it is customary for a gentleman to ask the guardian first, and as Athena's future is being contemplated, I thought now would be the best time to present my intentions."

Mason drew back in disbelief. "Sir . . . you shock me."

"Is my suit unwelcome? I assure you I am able to provide for her."

"Not at all, sir. Not at all." Mason smiled broadly and reached over the desk to shake Marshall's hand. "You do us too much honor. But I had not expected that you knew Athena well enough to offer for her."

He glanced over at her. "We've had a few run-ins— that is, we've run into one another several times."

Her grandfather turned to her. "Well, Athena? What do you say to that?"

She sniffed and wiped her face. "What do I say? Why, I'm speechless. I can't seem to find the right words to express myself fully, and yet there is only one sentiment that comes to mind."

"And that is?" asked her grandfather.

"Bollocks."

Mason sank into his chair. Marshall was not too surprised.

"I wouldn't marry him if he were the last man on earth. Grandfather, this man has been after my school. He knows what a lucrative enterprise it is and he wants it for himself. By fair means or foul, he intends to assume control over it. Even if it means he has to marry me to get it."

"That isn't true," Captain Hawkesworth said.

"Isn't it? Then why do you want to close it down?"

"I've told you. A journalist wants to expose you."

"Ha! You'll say anything to get me to shut it down. First that folderol about Countess Cavendish, and now some fiction about a newspaperman."

"Both those things are true."

"You're just like all the rest. Traitorous to a man. Like a field of Scottish thistles . . . lovely to look at but covered in sharp prickles. I wish you and the devil together!"

"That's enough! Now sit down and listen."

Athena's chin started to wobble, so she stopped ranting and sat down. She'd be damned if she was going to start bawling in front of these men. Anger was infinitely more dignified.

"Sir," began Captain Hawkesworth, "please allow me to speak with Athena alone. I believe I can make her understand the practical wisdom of accepting my offer of marriage."

"Practical wisdom?" she retorted sarcastically.

"Please continue. Your profession of eternal love and devotion will surely overcome my tender heart."

Her grandfather shook his head. "Athena, marriage doesn't work that way. It should, but it doesn't. I know I filled your head with fairy tales and the romantic escapades of medieval knights and their ladies, but this is the nineteenth century." He threw his arms open. "This is the real world. Men and women don't marry for love, they marry out of duty. And the time has come for you to do yours."

"I won't marry *him*," she said, jerking her head toward the adjacent chair. "I'd rather marry Calvin."

"Calvin Bretherton may end up retracting his offer of marriage," her grandfather said.

"What?" A horrible sinking feeling went through her. In her stomach and in her heart. "That's impossible."

"Bretherton came to see me last night in a state of distress. He told me that although he had renewed his proposal to you by letter, the only reason he had asked to marry you was that he had made certain assurances to the Duchess of Twillingham. But he confessed last night that he wanted to marry someone else, and he begged me to speak to the duchess on his behalf in order to acquit him of his offer of marriage on the grounds that you did not want him."

Athena wished the ground would swallow her up. It was bad enough that Calvin didn't want her, but to have it admitted in front of Captain Hawkesworth was more than she could bear. And yet her options were perfectly clear. If she didn't marry Marshall or Calvin, she'd remain a spinster. It was the best choice by far.

"Then I shan't marry anyone."

Her grandfather clasped his hands on the desk. "Athena, if you don't want to marry Calvin, then please reconsider Captain Hawkesworth's offer."

She turned to look at him. He was even more handsome in his uniform. But he had presented himself fictitiously, and she had no idea how much of what he told her was true and how much was a lie. She doubted she could ever trust him again. "I have considered it. My mind is made up. No."

Marshall turned to Mason. "I'm afraid I must insist upon my suit."

Mason's grizzled eyebrows knitted together. "Captain?"

"I claim Athena for my wife . . . on account that she is already mine."

Athena turned in Marshall's direction, her reddened eyes wide with incredulity. She couldn't believe what he was about to say.

The wrinkles on her grandfather's face deepened. "What calumny is this? Are you claiming she has already given herself to you?"

"It wasn't her fault, sir. I seduced her. But I never meant to dishonor her. I still don't. It is one of the reasons I am offering for her now."

Mason leaned back in his chair, his face ashen. "Is this true, Athena?"

Her heart turned to water. "It was a mistake."

Her grandfather covered his face with both withered hands.

She felt so utterly despicable, so far removed from innocence. She looked guiltily at his hands, which she loved to watch as they turned the pages of the books of romance and heroism that he read to her after dinner each night. Now, those hands, spotted with age, kept his face from even looking at her.

Finally, he stood. "Captain Hawkesworth, you have denigrated my family by your thoughtless actions. If I were a younger man, I would call you out, sir, the law be damned."

Marshall came to his feet. "Yes, sir. I apologize for the insult to you and to your granddaughter. I feel my guilt keenly, having left her wingless and wounded. I can only hope that you'll accept my sincere apology by allowing me to do the honorable thing. I will give Athena my name, and pay the bride-price you name. And if you accept my gesture, you may rest in the knowledge that our marriage will keep Athena safe from criminal prosecution—should the events at Athena's school come to light and an investigation en-sue, no one can compel my testimony, as a husband cannot testify against his wife."

Disappointment marred Mason's features. "Very well. Athena is yours."

"Grandfather!" she yelped.

The old man turned his face to her, and he looked considerably older. "You chose him, Granddaughter, not I. When you took him to your bed, he became in-extricably part of you, and you of him. Now you are damaged. If you're upset, you have only yourself to blame. You let him rob you of the privilege to choose your husband." With slow, weighted steps, Mason left the room.

Athena left too, fleeing to her room as swiftly as her feet would carry her.

NINETEEN

Marshall raked his anxious fingers through his hair before knocking on the door. Despite Athena's reluctance to marry him, there was an even bigger obstacle to their union—Aquilla Hawkesworth.

His mother's boudoir was one of the largest rooms in his home. At the far end of the room, a bronze bath was hidden behind a screen. Adjacent to the fireplace were two couches upholstered in a darker shade of pink than the floral wallpaper. Three long windows breathed light and warmth onto the comfortable furniture. Aquilla's boudoir was her sanctuary, and she spent a great deal of time in it when there were no guests in the house.

He found her writing at her desk underneath one of the windows.

"Ah, Marshall. I've been giving some thought to the matter of Justine. Her birthday is approaching. I was thinking to hold a supper this Friday. We can invite Herbert Stanton, and perhaps get him round to our way of thinking."

Marshall perched himself on the arm of one of the couches. "Mother, I'd like to talk to you about another happy event in prospect."

"Oh?" she remarked absently, scribbling onto another sheet of paper. "What?"

"My wedding."

The quill stilled, and she gasped. "Cordelia said yes?"

Marshall shifted uneasily. "I didn't ask *her,* Mother. I proposed marriage to Athena McAllister."

Aquilla paused. Marshall detested those frigid silences of hers, because it implied her intense displeasure. "The headmistress of Justine's school?"

"Yes."

"But she's no one."

His jaw tensed. "She's someone to me."

"I mean she's no one of any real consequence."

"She's the granddaughter of Mason Royce, the Baron Penhaligan."

His mother snorted delicately. "I don't even know who that is."

"Well, that's neither here nor there. The Baron Penhaligan is a noble man, in every sense of the word."

"Then why did his granddaughter go into business? Granted, Miss McAllister and her curriculum are sanctioned by Countess Cavendish, so naturally I sent Justine to be educated there. But just because there's a title in her family somewhere doesn't make her a marriageable prospect for you."

The entire sordid truth flashed in his head like cold water on sizzling oil. "Are you telling me that she's good enough to teach your daughter but not good enough for me to marry?"

"Of course. She's little more than a glorified servant."

It was his mother's disdain that he had to battle. "I

urge you to reconsider your position. That 'servant' as you call her is going to be my wife."

"Don't be absurd. She's Scottish."

"Her father's Scottish. But her mother's English."

"Half a Scot is half too much. Besides, the whisper is that the Duchess of Twillingham only sponsored her as a favor to Miss McAllister's grandfather. The whole family is absolutely impoverished. Is this who you're thinking of marrying?"

"Yes."

There it was, the mortal silence. His mother's face was a mask of refined contempt. "Well, I'll not have it."

"Mother—"

"You expect me to tell everyone that the Warridge line will now be muddied by thin Scottish blood?"

He bolted from his chair. "Dammit, Mother, why must you be so disparaging?"

"For heaven's sake, Marshall. Haven't you had your fill of common girls on your travels?"

He pulled out a fire iron from the tool rack along the hearth. "She's not common, Mother. She's Viscount McAllister's daughter."

"A Scottish viscount. She may as well be common."

He grunted, stabbing at the shrinking fire.

"Dearest Marshall, why don't you marry Cordelia? She's titled, wealthy . . . a union with her would go far for your descendants."

He stood, gripping the iron rod in both fists. "I won't marry Cordelia. I want Athena."

"But why?"

He could never make his mother understand. Since

he had met Athena, he had learned something that changed his life. He had discovered that a hero isn't just the man at the head of a ship with an upraised sword in one hand. A hero is also the man who is able to transform the heart of a woman. "Because she needs me. And because . . . I think I love her."

Aquilla stood and walked straight up to him, a thing most men would cower from doing. "You listen to me very carefully, Marshall. You have a duty to your family, both the one you have and the one you'll sire. You don't have the luxury of marrying out of love. None of us do. Marry Cordelia. She is your ideal match."

The cold poker heated instantly to the temperature of his skin. Anger burned within him, partly because she stood up to him, and partly because he knew she was right. But she was treating him just as he had treated Justine, dictating to him a spouse not of his choosing, and he was too honest not to recognize his own words to Justine coming from his mother's mouth.

Marshall looked down into Aquilla's gaunt face, a shadow of the beauty from the painting in the hallway. Marrying her "ideal match" had made her leather-hearted, and brought decades of misery to all of their lives. He would not allow the same fate to befall himself.

"Athena will be at your supper on Friday. Upon Sunday, the banns will be published." He took a step toward the door, then turned around. "And don't bother inviting Herbert Stanton. He's not welcome in Justine's life anymore." Marshall tossed the poker onto the upholstered chair near the door before closing it behind him.

Aquilla's eyes remained fixed on the gray ash stain the poker left on her white-and-gold-upholstered chair.

The fireplace was not the only thing that smoldered.

TWENTY

As the carriage rumbled toward Ashburnham Manor, Athena stared quietly out of the window.

Hester cast her an anxious glance. Her friend had had three continuous episodes of bad luck. First, she lost her virginity to a man not her husband, inheriting the shame that such a thing entailed. Next, her beloved school was forced into hiatus, and her students sent home only midway through the term. Now she was headed toward a dinner—absent her grandfather—in honor of her betrothal to a man she wanted to hate. Her luck was bound to change soon, but Hester couldn't make Athena accept it.

"That emerald dress is very pretty, Athena. Did you order it especially for tonight?"

No answer. Hester fidgeted, growing increasingly uncomfortable with the tense silence.

"This is a lovely carriage that Captain Hawkesworth sent for us. Don't you think so?"

No answer. Having exhausted all of her small talk, Hester gave up trying. "Athena, do be sensible. It will do you no good to start your betrothal in a difficult frame of mind."

Athena turned to Hester. "I have no intention of

being difficult. I intend to be positively impossible. If Captain Marshall Hawkesworth thinks he wants me for a wife, he's in for a great surprise. Tonight, he's going to get Athena McAllister. Every infuriating facet of her."

"Athena . . . what are you up to? Are you trying to get back at Marshall for forcing his suit upon you?"

"Revenge is too commonplace, and will profit me nothing. I have in mind something infinitely more subtle and yet just as sinister. Sabotage."

"Athena, I hope you're aware that Captain Hawkesworth's mother is renowned for her intolerance of people of lower birth."

"Good. Then that shall make my job much easier."

The ancestral seat of the Hawkesworth family was revered for its grandeur. The house sprawled across acres of verdant land, its buttery limestone façade contrasting sharply with the green carpet of lawn. With the light of the setting sun falling upon its face, the house looked like a giant gold brick. Intricate gardens, replete with fountains and statuary, extended from the house like vast outdoor rooms. On the approach, the façade glassed itself in the broad lake.

A dozen carriages were already entrenched along the side of the house when the crunch of the driveway gravel announced Athena's arrival. Two liveried footmen approached, one to hold the horses still while the other handed the ladies down.

"It appears as if the party is a bit larger than I imagined," whispered Hester.

Athena harrumphed. "For my purposes, the more the merrier."

The interior of the manor was more like a palace

than a country estate. Statues lined the circular foyer, which opened onto an expanse of hallway. Pedestal candelabra illuminated the way to the ballroom, which was rumbling with the chatter of guests.

The man she now knew to be Captain Marshall Hawkesworth materialized from the crowd, dressed in full military regalia. Against her will, the sight of him made Athena's heart flutter. He was so handsome in that uniform that Athena momentarily forgot her quest. It fit him so perfectly that she could not remember him dressed otherwise. In fact, he seemed to wear the Navy from the inside out. Nevertheless, Athena steeled her heart.

He took her hand and bowed curtly over it. "Welcome to Ashburnham Manor. Athena, you look ravishing."

"Spoken like one who knows the true meaning of ravishment."

He cocked his head, pondering her meaning. "Y-yes. And Lady Willett, how very fetching you look. What an honor to have you visit our home."

"Thank you, Captain Hawkesworth," she replied.

An older woman walked up behind Marshall. She was dressed in a dark blue dress in a gossamer fabric. Bright blond hair graced her head, the same shade as Marshall's, though hers had faded with gray.

"Ladies, may I present my mother, the dowager marchioness, Lady Aquilla Hawkesworth. Mother, I believe you've met Athena . . . my fiancée."

In an instant, Aquilla's sharp blue eyes raked Athena up and down. They had first met when they discussed the course overview for Justine's education. The interview had been brief, and Aquilla had agreed to Athena's terms without dispute. And when Aquilla had delivered Justine and her luggage to the school, it was as if she were doing no more than bringing in a dress for alteration. Now, although Aquilla presented a smile, Athena could sense her intense disapproval.

Athena curtsied. "My lady."

"Welcome to Ashburnham Manor, Miss McAllister. I do hope your ride wasn't too difficult."

"Not at all. Your son provided an adequate mount."

Aquilla was puzzled by the response, but Marshall's profound inhalation revealed his irritation. "Lady Hawkesworth, may I present Lady Willett."

Aquilla extended her hand. "Lady Willett, it's a pleasure to finally meet you. Your husband is known to us."

"Thank you, my lady. I did hope you wouldn't mind if I accompanied Athena in place of her grandfather."

Aquilla, who was a tall woman, peered down her nose at Athena. "I had hoped to meet your grandfather. Was it lack of health that kept him from joining us?"

"No, my lady," replied Athena. "Lack of sobriety."

"I see." Aquilla cast a disapproving glance at her son. Exactly what Athena wanted to see.

Marshall cleared his throat. "Miss McAllister is only funning, Mother. She has an impious sense of humor."

Athena smiled. "Captain Hawkesworth knows me too well. And with the passage of time, I have finally come to know him quite well too. Seeing you both side by side, I can now see where he gets his good looks. Although where he gets his sense of honesty is more of a puzzle."

Marshall had heard enough. He took her by the elbow. "Ladies, do excuse us while I have a word with Athena." He didn't wait for a response from any of them before he led her away forcefully to the hall.

His voice was a low whisper, but his tone bellowed. "May I ask what in the hell you think you're doing?"

"I'm doing exactly as you asked. Meeting your family and friends."

"You know perfectly well what I'm talking about. Why are you acting like a little doxy?"

She narrowed her eyes at him. "I think you'll find that as the evening wears on, the diminutive will not be necessary."

He straightened. "Are you trying to sabotage this betrothal?"

She put on her most innocent face. "Sabotage? Why, all I'm trying to do is to show everyone in there precisely who it is you're intending to marry."

He squared up on her. "I'm warning you, Athena. If you think you're going to appeal to the court of public opinion to be spared from marrying me, you're in for a big shock. None of the people in there have absolutely any influence over me. And in case I haven't made myself perfectly clear, you're going to marry me, whether you like it or not."

She pinned her fists to her hips. "See? That's exactly what gets up my nose. Ordering me about like I'm one of your soldiers."

"Sailors."

"Whatever!"

"*They* understand that I have a heavy hand for insolence, and you would do well to learn that. Carry on the way you're doing, and I'll make you regret your folly." He took her hand, placed it on his out-stretched arm, and led her back into the ballroom.

A knot of men stood in a corner with drinks in their hands. One of their number was a rotund man with a jowly face, and he was dressed in a uniform similar to Marshall's. As they approached, she caught the tail end of his story.

"So the French damsel whom the old Englishman rescued said to him, 'Oh, monsieur, I regret I have nothing with which to pay you.' The old man replied, 'No, my dear, you have something with which to pay me, but I regret I have nothing with which to charge you!' "

The three other men burst out in deep-throated laughter.

Marshall cleared his throat. "Excuse me, Admiral. I wondered if I might introduce my fiancée, Miss Athena McAllister."

The man turned around, his sparking blue eyes beaming down on her from beneath twin white clouds of eyebrows. "You certainly may! Miss McAllister, how very delightful to meet you."

"Athena," continued Marshall, "this is Admiral Jasper Rowland of His Majesty's Royal Navy."

Athena curtsied. "Sir."

"You're even prettier than Hawkesworth described you."

Athena had to blush at that. "I wasn't aware I had become a topic of discourse."

"Ho! The only other female I have heard him talk about with as lively an interest was his ship."

It was hard for Athena to scowl at such a rosy-cheeked smile. "His ship?"

"The HMS *Reprisal*. Hawkesworth here was her captain for many years."

"I see. And did she chafe under his control too?"

"Athena—" There was a smile on Marshall's face, but a warning on his lips.

"Oh, hardly," replied the admiral. "His men would follow him to the gates of Hades. By Jove, on occasion they have done."

Athena chuckled behind her smile, casting Marshall a sidewise glance. "Too bad they didn't leave him there."

The admiral tossed back his head and laughed. His heavy jowls shook like a plate of calf's foot jelly.

"By Jove, you were right about her, Hawkesworth. She's just as dangerous as any battleship."

Marshall sighed. "And just as difficult to command, sir. If you'll excuse us."

The admiral reached out and grasped her hand. "No, sir, I will not. We're just getting to know one another. You carry on. I want to learn more about this delightful creature. Come, my dear. Let's get a drink in your hand."

Marshall stood rooted to the spot as the admiral swept her away. She threw him a glance over her shoulder, and his face returned a multitude of warning looks.

"I must say how utterly surprised we all were by the news that Hawkesworth had finally chosen a bride. I never thought that a crusty old nautical cove like him would ever sprout roots on land."

"No?"

The admiral handed her a glass of champagne from a passing salver. "Life aboard a ship is never

pleasant. Particularly a warship. The smell of un-
washed bodies, the dry bread, the rotten food, the bad
drink. The . . . loneliness for a woman's comfort. It
takes a man of stern stuff to even endure that sort of
life, let alone choose it."

"Choose it?"

"Yes. Look around you. This is where Hawkesworth
grew up. Enveloped by wealth and circumstance. A
lesser man would have nestled into this life of privilege, secure in his fortune and titles. But not your future
husband. He's a patriot. A man devoted to serving king
and country. Never afraid to put himself in harm's way
for a worthy cause. It is sufficient to most men to be
protectors of their homes. Hawkesworth is a protector
of his *homeland*."

Athena turned toward Marshall, standing in profile
amid a gathering of people on the opposite side of the
dance floor. The first time she had seen him in uniform, all she could see was deception. It was as if he
were wearing a new identity, one foreign to her. Now,
the uniform he was wearing began to mean something
to her—something true and good, and it touched her
deep inside.

"He's the finest officer His Majesty commands,"
the admiral continued. "All who know him are loyal
to him."

Maybe that was the problem. She wasn't sure that
she *did* know him.

"And you, my dear, were the one to finally charm
him. I simply had to steal you away to see if you would
have the same effect upon me."

"The mystery must stand unsolved, Admiral Rowland. I don't profess to be a tender woman. In fact, quite the opposite."

"Oh, I never expected you to be tender. Marshall has always been repelled by milky women. I just knew you would have a lot more pluck."

Athena nodded slowly, fueling a spark of illumination. "Repelled, you say?"

"Absolutely. Take that lady over there." The admiral used his glass to point to an elegantly dressed woman in the corner talking to two men. "That's Lady Cordelia Renville-Hope, the duke's daughter. She had her cap set for him for years. A gentle woman, in the strictest sense of the word, and a diamond of the first water. But that sweet disposition of hers, which has those two chaps circling her like flies, is like vinegar to Hawkesworth. Never understood why. But I suppose the great democracy of love is that all may have it, even a man like Marshall."

Athena took a long draught of the champagne. If Marshall was repelled by soft women, it was no wonder he had been so attracted to her. Clearly, she had been going about this all wrong. She had to go meet the woman who could curl Marshall's lip so. She just might learn how to sour him on herself as well.

Before she had a chance to press the admiral for more information, Justine bounded up to them and embraced Athena soundly.

"Miss McAllister! I'm so happy to see you again!"

"And I you, Justine. Happy birthday."

"Thank you." With an informal smile to the admiral, Justine whisked Athena away toward the balcony at the far end of the ballroom.

It was a cool night, but there was no wind to chill them. Justine dragged her to a darkened alcove hidden behind a large potted plant. "It had to have been you. I just knew it had to have been you."

Athena smiled curiously at Justine's bubbling enthusiasm. "What are you talking about?"

"When Marshall told me he had chosen you for his bride, it all became clear to me. It was you who changed his mind about Herbert Stanton."

"Herbert Stanton? The man you wrote to tell me had become your fiancé?"

"My fiancé no longer!" she tossed back, her gentle brown eyes glowing with gratitude. "Marshall said I didn't have to marry him. And I have you to thank for that!"

Athena shook her head. "Justine, I am happy you aren't being forced into an unwanted marriage, but I assure you your appreciation is misplaced. I said nothing to Captain Hawkesworth on your behalf about Herbert Stanton."

Justine threw her arms around Athena. "You didn't have to. You changed his heart. No one but you could have done that."

Athena patted Justine's slender back. "I . . . I don't know what you mean."

She pulled away and looked into Athena's face earnestly. "Miss McAllister, you taught him the beauty of marrying for love. It was something I couldn't do in all the years since my coming-out. Neither he nor Father ever gave a care as to whether or not I should love my husband-to-be. And then you came along. Now Marshall says that *unless* I meet the man I love, I don't ever have to marry. Can you imagine that? I never thought such words would come out of Marshall's mouth."

Nor did Athena. She couldn't explain what caused such a change in Marshall toward Justine. But whatever it was, he didn't extend it to Athena. He was permitting his sister to stay unwed unless she marry for love, but insisting that Athena marry him whether she loved him or not. It wasn't fair.

"I'm very happy for you, Justine," Athena said begrudgingly. "I do hope you find the man whose wife you wish to become."

Justine leaned in conspiratorially. "That's what I wanted to talk to you about, Miss McAllister. I have already found him."

Her eyes widened. "Oh?"

Worry lined Justine's face. "But I'm afraid he might not be . . . suitable."

"Oh."

"I know Marshall expects me to find a man of rank or wealth to marry. But I've fallen in love with a man who has . . . neither."

"Oh!" Athena swallowed hard. "Who is he?"

Justine looked up with a guilty expression. It was the same expression she wore when she admitted how much she enjoyed the lecture on Sensual Touch. "His name is Elliott Keane. He's our groom."

"I see. Well . . . congratulations."

"Oh, Miss McAllister, you don't understand. Marshall will never allow me to marry Elliott. He's a servant in our household. It'd be too much of a step down, you see."

Athena inhaled sharply. "Well, I shouldn't worry if I were you. You can always accuse him of hypocrisy. Marshall is taking a step down with me as well."

"Couldn't you have a talk with him, Miss McAllister? He'll listen to you."

"Justine, you are laboring under the misconception that I can control your brother. Really, I have very little influence over him."

Justine's large brown eyes focused on hers. "But he loves you."

Those words shattered on Athena's heart. "I can't imagine those words coming out of Marshall's mouth either."

Irritation snapping inside her, she went back inside and looked for her rival. Once, she had to pretend to be someone else to attract a man. Now she had to pretend to be someone else to repel one.

She found Lady Cordelia Renville-Hope talking with a vicar.

Though she was well beyond thirty, there was no outward taint of spinsterhood about Lady Cordelia. Her beauty transcended the blush of youth and dwelt in the realm of womanly charms. A tall, regal-looking woman, she had upswept black hair that revealed high cheekbones and a pale complexion that was only beginning to show the fine lines indicative of her age. The dress that she wore was breathtaking in its elegance, an ivory Grecian frock shimmering with tiny diamonds at the bodice and hem. As rivals go, she presented significant competition. Athena was bent on disliking her.

"Lady Cordelia? How do you do? I am Athena McAllister." She held out a gloved hand.

Athena expected a stiff, reluctant smile, but Lady

Cordelia's expression was conciliatory. "Ah, yes, Miss McAllister. I've heard so much about you."

"Oh? From whom?"

"The marchioness. She has been . . . in anticipation of this evening."

"I see. A pity one cannot outdistance one's own reputation."

"No, indeed. And I hear a happy event is in prospect. I'm very happy for you."

And yet, Athena could see she was not. "Thank you. I know this is indelicate of me to say, but I understand that at one time you had some feelings for Mr. Marsh—that is, Captain Hawkesworth."

"Miss McAllister, I hope you don't think that I would do anything to—"

Athena waved away her protestation. "Not at all. Please forgive me for asking this, but it really is essential that I have the truth. You are much lovelier than I, and of a station far superior to mine, and I simply must know why it is that he didn't offer for you instead."

Her forehead creased as her countenance fell. "Your question wounds me deeply, Miss McAllister."

"I don't mean to cause you embarrassment, my lady, but the fact is, I've had no wish to encourage his suit, and I want to know how I can dissuade him from seeking me. And if you help me, I will do all I can to advance your interest in the matter."

Her frown changed from distress to puzzlement. "You mean you don't want to marry him?"

Athena shook her head. "I'm not fond of arrogant men."

Surprise overtook her features. "Arrogant? Captain Hawkesworth is not arrogant. If anything, he's proud, and he has a right to be. The nobility of his family goes back to the reign of Elizabeth I, and has remained honorable through each successive generation. He is a hero, twice decorated by the prince regent, and one of the most promising officers in the king's service. His accomplishments are legend, as is, in my opinion, his beauty. All his friends are true to him, principally because he always considers others above himself. Say what you will of him, Captain Hawkesworth does not deserve to be called arrogant."

Athena was stunned by her ladyship's defense of Marshall. "You do him too much honor, surely."

"I do him no more than justice."

"I'm sorry. I did not think you would have opposed so vehemently my plan to help you."

"Had I my own interests at heart, I would not have. But the fact of the matter is that he does not love me. He loves you. And if you are the one he thinks will bring him happiness, then I will forgo my own in order that he may have his. It is a pity you do not think likewise." She grabbed her diamond-encrusted skirt and strode off to the far end of the room.

Alone in the corner, Athena had to catch her breath. She felt utterly ashamed of herself. Admiral Rowland, Justine, and now Lady Cordelia—each had made it perfectly clear how unfairly she had regarded Marshall. Was there something warped about her that prevented her from seeing him as others did?

Her eyes scanned the room for him. There he was, talking with another man.

He was everything these people had said. Proud, brave, loving. She looked at him and saw a bronze statue to the image of the gentleman. He preferred personal accomplishments to privileges; family to wealth. Athena to Lady Cordelia.

He laughed then, a hearty sound that carried over the din of conversation, and it filled her with shame. Why was she always so hostile toward him?

It wasn't his deception. She was hostile toward him since the moment they met. Truth be told, he never even lied to her. It was she who had assumed he was someone other than he was. Yet she was always quick to shoot arrows, more inclined to verbal assault than verbal accord.

She had called Marshall a Scottish thistle once, but the truth was that *she* was that terrible plant. No fragrance, no value, no real virtue . . . just an outlaw weed. No one ever picked them because they were so painful to touch.

And yet he had stopped to pick her.

Here he was, at their own engagement party, pronouncing her his bride before all the world. He deserved more from her. Why could she not show him what she truly felt in her heart?

She took a swallow from Lady Cordelia's forgotten glass, shutting her eyes against the awful pounding of her heart. There was only one word to answer that question.

Fear.

Not fear of him. Fear of *losing* him.

Everyone she ever tried to love ended up gone. It was an immovable curse that plagued her since she was a child. Whoever she gave her heart to vanished from her life.

Maybe, she thought, if she kept her heart her own—if she refused to give him her love—he might not vanish.

But protecting her own heart was making her miserable. The thistle's prickles hurt itself just as much.

She rubbed her eyes with both hands. A locked chest. A darkened woods. A masked face. She had grown weary of secrets.

The time had come to reveal.

"I need to speak with you."

Marshall turned to look at Athena. Through the puzzled expression, she saw him . . . the man that everyone else saw, but she couldn't. And it made her ache for his heart.

"Is something wrong?"

"Yes. No." She was panting for air and didn't know why. "I don't know. Is there somewhere we could talk in private?"

"Of course. Come with me." He held out his arm, which gleamed with gold buttons and braiding. For some strange reason, everything about him gleamed. She preceded him out of the ballroom.

He led her down a hallway to a door at the opposite end of the house. The din of music and chattering dimmed as he shut the door.

She gave a cursory look around. They were in a study of sorts—his study. She turned to face him.

"Athena, are you all right?"

Look at him, she thought. Standing there, concerned for her. He was so beautiful, so perfect. There was so much she wanted to tell him.

She started to speak once or twice, but no words

came out. For once in her life, she was speechless. She couldn't say what she wanted to. So she did it instead.

She closed the distance between them and threw her arms around his chest.

Her ear lay flat against his heart. *Don't disappear. Please don't disappear.* The navy wool was rough against her cheek, and the gold braiding pressed against her face. But she could not let go. She would not.

His arms wound around her, though not as tightly. "What did you say?"

She hadn't realized the words came out of her mouth. But the secret was finally out.

"Did you say, 'Don't disappear,' Athena?" He pulled her away and looked into her face.

Against her will, her green eyes began to mist over. "I—I love you." It was the first time she admitted it, even to herself.

The face that looked at her in curiosity softened to something sublimely beautiful. "I know."

"How . . . on God's good earth . . . with all that I say and do . . . could you ever imagine that?"

He smiled, his masculine lips stretching to a sheen. "What I want to know is why you took such pains to hide it?" He sat her down on one of the chairs and knelt before her. "That mask you wear, the one you think hides the scars. You try so hard to conceal them. But they're what make you beautiful. Your paintings spoke it to me. Shouted it, even. What was hidden was buried treasure."

No man had ever been bold enough to see past her defenses. "Why only you? Why has no one else tried to see it but you?"

He shrugged. "Must be the pirate in me. Always looking for buried treasure."

She chuckled wetly, but her face quickly sobered. "How can you look at me and see treasure?"

Blue eyes met green. "When I saw you for the first time, the world as I knew it came to an end. Who I was or what I was after, it all ceased to be important. You changed what mattered to me." He shifted uneasily. "I know I'm not doing a good job of explaining it. All I can say is that when I met you, I wanted to love you. It had nothing to do with a feeling or an emotion. I just felt the need to bring you the love that you had been denied. But then you changed and you began to know your own heart. And when your heart turned to mine, that's when I fell in love with you."

Whatever was said to the rose to unfurl he was saying to her heart. She brought a hand to her trembling lips. "I'm so afraid."

"Of what?"

Her fingers trembled. "Making you go."

Now it was his turn to chuckle. "You can't make me go. Unless you replace me, I won't ever leave."

"It terrifies me still."

"Then give it to me, Athena. Give me your fear. Trust in me to take it from you."

She nodded stiffly. He leaned forward, and their foreheads touched. His hot breath fell on her lips as he whispered her name.

A feeling flickered through her mind, like a forgotten dream traipsing across her dark memory. Though she couldn't name it, she knew she wanted it. She turned her head, and their mouths met.

A soft kiss grew into a desperate one. For once,

she didn't care if she was kissing him right, or using the proper technique. Her heart was begging her to show him how it felt, and she complied with that dire call. He gave it back to her, echoing her devotion. It was a sentence without end, an unfinished phrase that only promised completion but never gave it.

For Athena, it was enough.

TWENTY-ONE

A clock in the hall chimed nine as a bewigged footman in morning livery carried the remaining breakfast dishes on a silver tray. He took slow, measured steps throughout the house, within which all evidence of the party the night before had been erased. The ballroom was empty, the hall quiet, the dining room clean.

He set the tray down on a small table outside the breakfast room. A downstairs maid, who was on the floor lighting the fire in the morning room, nodded her head knowingly and cast him a warning look that said *mind yourself*.

Silently he shrugged and, taking a deep breath, opened the double doors.

The raised voices of Marshall and Aquilla fell to a hush as the footman brought in the tray and set the dishes on the buffet.

"Thank you, Horner," said Aquilla, resuming her formality. "We shall serve ourselves."

"Very good, my lady," he muttered, and effecting a curt bow, closed the double doors once more.

Aquilla sat down at the table and pulled a slice of cold ham onto her plate. "When I think of you eternally linked to that . . . virago . . . It just won't do."

"We've been through that already, Mother. Let's not open old wounds."

Aquilla was undeterred. "Generally, a person is on her best behavior when you first meet her. She acted like a veritable vulgarian."

Marshall went straight for the coffee. "We have to make allowances for her northern provenance. I know her ways may seem sharp. But there's a great economy to her. She says what she means."

"I'm not just talking about her manners. No fruit is found in her trees. She lacks virtue, modesty, decency, birth, beauty."

"*I* find her beautiful."

Aquilla heaved a deep sigh. "You're a man. You'd find a cello beautiful if it put on a dress. We should have massacred all the Scots while we had the chance."

He set the pot down so hard some of the brown liquid sloshed out and stained the white runner. "That joke is in very poor taste and completely beneath you."

"No more than that girl is beneath you."

Marshall sat at the head of the table, raking a claw through his blond head.

Aquilla schooled herself. "I'm not asking you to get rid of her. If you're so drawn to her, then keep her for your own private pleasure. Marry Cordelia, and make the Scot your mistress."

Marshall's blue eyes fixed unblinkingly on his mother's. "I can't believe you're saying such a thing. Have you no consideration for Athena's feelings? Or Cordelia's?"

"No. The only thing I care about is this family. And it would prosper all the more without Athena in it!"

"Good morning." Athena stood in the doorway, her

hand frozen on the doorknob. Justine was right behind her. "Have we come at a bad time?"

Marshall rubbed his face, its expression collapsed
with embarrassment. "No, Athena. Please come in.
Sit down." He held out a chair for her.

Gingerly, Justine gave her mother a soft kiss, as
though the woman would explode from even the slightest movement. "Good morning, Mother."

Athena glanced uncertainly between Marshall and
Aquilla. "It was a lovely party last night, my lady.
Thank you for your hospitality."

Aquilla sat completely erect in her chair, her light
brown dress so stiff it seemed to be made of wood.
"Miss McAllister, please don't take personal offense at
what I'm about to tell you. As you no doubt heard me
tell my son, I do object to this marriage on several accounts, not the least of which is your lack of personal
wealth. As any good mother does, I desire an advantageous match for my children, and you do not present
the best candidate for his wife."

Athena unfolded a napkin and placed it on her lap.
"My word. How refreshing to see romanticism thriving so well among the *ton*."

"You speak the language of sarcasm, Miss McAllister, but I speak the language of realism. Do you or do
you not bring anything material to this union, which
will augment the holdings of my son and his heirs after
him?"

Athena cast her eyes down onto her pale blue
bodice. "We had an estate in Scotland—Tigh na Coille,
in Ayrshire—but my father lost it. He sold all we had
left to acquire some thirty acres in the Highlands . . .
before he died."

"Arable land?"

She bit her lip and gave a brisk shake of her head.

"Am I to understand that your dowry consists of a few miles of mountainous crag in a remote region of Scotland? Is that what you're offering my son?"

Athena straightened. "That . . . and my love."

Marshall covered her hand with his. "Which is priceless."

"And worthless," Aquilla added.

"Mother!" exclaimed Marshall. "Athena is to be my wife. Not because she can augment my holdings or because she can add a lofty branch to our family tree. But because I love her and she loves me. I know you can't bring yourself to comprehend this concept, but marriage is more than a union of assets. Or rather, it should be," he said, glancing at Athena. "On balance, I'd rather be happy than wealthy. So please, Mother . . . either celebrate together with us, or be miserable by yourself."

The silence was broken by Justine's unsteady voice. "Marshall, I'm very happy to hear you say what you just did. About marriage, I mean." Athena tensed. She threw an anxious glance at Justine, wordlessly shaking her head, but Justine plodded forward. "Because there's something I have to tell you."

"Oh?"

"I'd like your blessing to marry."

"Whom?" Aquilla exclaimed.

Justine's nervous gaze wavered between Aquilla and Marshall. "Elliott Keane."

Aquilla bolted out of her chair and faced the window. "Preposterous."

Marshall heaved a profound sigh. "Justine—"

"Preposterous," repeated Aquilla, facing Marshall. "Do you see what you've started? A girl worth twenty thousand a year . . . married to a stable servant? The answer is no."

"We shall talk about it," Marshall stated with finality.

"It's bad enough my eldest is bringing shame upon this house. I won't have both my children humiliate me." Aquilla swung open the doors and let them slam against the wall. The footman, who'd been dutifully waiting to be summoned outside the room, gripped the vibrating doors and closed them softly.

Athena gripped his forearm. "I'm sorry, Marshall."

He leaned over and kissed her. "You have nothing to be sorry for. That is my mother. She buzzes about like an overturned beehive."

"Yes, but I'm the one who poked at the beehive with a stick."

"I shouldn't worry about her. She's always been more concerned with what people might say about her family than how we actually feel. If I walked in here after a lion had mauled my arm off, she'd say, 'Just look at the state your coat's in.' "

Athena giggled.

"As for you," he said, turning to Justine. "You picked a fine time to bring your news, didn't you?"

Justine shrugged. "In for a penny, in for a pound?"

He nodded. "Hmm. More like 'people who live in greenhouses,' eh?"

"Something like that," she said, her pale face coloring.

"I shall want to know more about this Keane fellow. But it shall be *your* job to pacify Mother."

She walked round the table and gave her brother a hug from behind. "Thank you, Marshall."

"Go, before I change my mind," he quipped.

Once they were alone, Athena stared at him across the table. "Justine was right. You really have changed, haven't you?"

He shook his head. "Not so much changed as . . . enlightened. By a very good teacher." He took her by the hand and reeled her in until she was sitting on his lap.

If ever there was a moment she wanted captured in time, it would be this one. Blue eyes that glowed brightly with declared affection, a sly grin edging his mouth with sensual awareness, arms that embraced her tightly against the firmness of his own body. These were not mere visions, but feelings she could not capture except in her heart. He was more than she could see. He was more than money and titles and good looks . . . he was kind and funny and disciplined, a brave adventurer with the scars to prove it. Even if she could attempt his likeness, she knew she would fail. He was more than the length and breadth of her canvas— he was the depth behind it, that which she could not paint or conceive, only discover.

"What are you going to do now?"

He raked his eyes across her mouth. "One or two ideas do suggest themselves."

She rolled her eyes. "I meant what will you decide about Justine's marriage?"

His eyebrows drew together, but the smile never left his lips. "Justine's? I haven't even made up my mind to marry you, yet."

"I suppose you think that's fun—" Her words were

smothered in a hot kiss that caused a hum of arousal in her.

His freshly shaved skin smelled of lime-scented water. Everything about him was clean and pressed and starched, and yet her fevered brain could only imagine him standing in the middle of the art room without a shred of clothes.

Dangerous. He was a man she couldn't control. What's more, she even lost control over herself when he was around. Now he was kindling erotic sensations that she knew to be ungovernable.

"Stop," she said when he finally freed her lips to kiss the hollow of her throat.

"No." His voice was round and deep, seductive and powerful. His lips wandered across her chest, and she began to melt into his embrace. There was no way she had enough discipline for both of them.

"Mmm. Strawberries and cream." His lips vibrated against the slope of her breast, and his golden hair tickled Athena's own lips. One more kiss, and she would have to have him.

"Oh, dear," came a voice from the doorway. Athena's eyes flew open, and saw Hester looking flustered. "I'll come back."

"No, no!" said Athena, scrambling off his lap. "Come in. We were just . . . That is, we were about to . . ."

"Have breakfast?" he offered.

"Yes," she said, smoothing out her skirt. "Have breakfast."

"I see," Hester said, gingerly stepping inside the room. "What is being served?"

"Strawberries and cream," he said.

Athena whacked him on the shoulder. "Sausages. I smell sausages. Shall I serve you or will you help yourself?"

"Sausages," repeated Hester. Marshall chuckled while Athena's face colored even more. "No, I think I shall content myself with the ham."

Athena sat on her own chair and buried her burning cheeks in her cool hands. "Yes. I think I shall join you."

Marshall stood and walked to her side. He leaned over and placed a kiss on top of her head. "It's all right, my sweet. We all know what you really want for breakfast." And with those humiliating parting words, he closed the door behind him.

Although they had planned to stay until Sunday, Athena thought it best, given the current atmosphere, to leave immediately after breakfast.

Marshall saw them to the driveway, and helped them ascend the carriage. He bid Athena farewell with a chaste kiss upon her hand. As his carriage drove them away, he glanced up at the window of his mother's boudoir. She peered down at him, and closed the curtain before disappearing into the room.

He shook his head. He knew his mother too well to think she would come round to his way of thinking. It might have been different if his mother remembered falling in love—that is, if she had ever done so. Sometimes, he thought his mother was born ancient.

The carriage turned onto the road into town and disappeared beyond the trees. He looked up into the sky. The day, which had dawned so sweetly, had begun to grow hostile.

Just before he turned to go back into the house, he

noticed a carriage, coming from the opposite direction, turn onto the road to his property. He wasn't expecting visitors, so he watched as the matched pair of white horses cantered toward his driveway. The exquisite, black-lacquered carriage, bearing a crest on the door, came to a halt in front of the steps leading up to the house.

Two people got out of the carriage.

Marshall's jaw tightened. The weather wasn't the only thing that had suddenly grown hostile.

TWENTY-TWO

A half hour later, after the guests had left, Marshall yanked on the bell cord in his study. He grabbed a sheet of paper, scribbled something on it, then folded and sealed it. The butler appeared, and Marshall gave him terse instructions to pack a valise.

His boots hammered on the marble floor as he made his way through the house. He went out to the stable and looked around until he found Keane, the groom.

Elliott Keane was the newest member of his staff. He was a slender man, though Marshall knew he had a strong back on him. Perhaps it was his sun-browned complexion that had bewitched his sister. Or his gentle temperament, which made him such an ideal handler of horses. Or maybe it was his hazel eyes, which were now rounding nervously as Marshall approached him.

"Mornin', sir," he said, as he tipped his hat to Marshall.

"Keane," Marshall acknowledged, an undeniable edge to his voice.

Elliott slipped off his cap. "If I may be so bold, sir, I'd like an opportunity to explain. About Miss Justine, I mean."

"You will be given ample opportunity, Keane. But for now, pack your bags."

"Oh, sir. Please don't sack me. I've done nothing dishonorable, I swear."

Marshall straightened. "You and I must have a very different view of what's considered dishonorable."

Elliott wrung his hat. "Beggin' your pardon, sir, but we don't. Miss Justine is just as important to me as she is to you. I'd never do anything to harm her."

Marshall crossed his arms imperiously at his chest. "I suppose courting her behind my back is not dishonorable?"

The younger man hung his head. "I didn't realize we were courtin', sir. That just seemed to happen. While she was exercising the horses or taking rides, we'd talk. That's all."

"Nevertheless."

Elliott put his hat back on his head. "Sir, I don't want to create any fuss or friction between you and Miss Justine. I'll be going. But please, sir, let me go on seeing her. Not as her servant, but . . . as a man, like."

"You dare ask me to go on seeing my sister after being sacked?"

Elliott squared himself up under Marshall's gaze, though his voice echoed the uneasiness he felt. "I do, sir. Respectfully, sir. I want permission to court Miss Justine. Not behind your back, but under your eye. That is, after I find another job."

Marshall sized Keane up. It took a brave man to ask him that. More than that. It took a man in love.

"I think you and I need to do some more talking, Keane. I want you to come with me on a trip up north. But first I want you to take this note to Miss Athena

McAllister at Endsleigh Grange. Wait the night there, and then bring her and Lady Willett back to Ashburnham in the carriage tomorrow morning."

Elliott eyed the note, more confused than ever. "So . . . I'm not sacked?"

Marshall laid his broad hand on Elliott's shoulder. "I wanted you to pack for a few days, not forever."

Elliott's broad smile lit up his young face, and it suddenly became clear to Marshall just what had bewitched his sister.

"Thank you, sir!"

By eleven o'clock the next morning, Athena, Hester, and Marshall set out from Ashburnham in the coach, with Elliott Keane at the reins.

Athena had had trouble reading Marshall's note. The penmanship looked only slightly clearer than if a pigeon with ink on his feet had walked all over the paper. But she made out the words "trip" and "Scotland" just as clearly as if she'd written them herself, and she practically jumped for sheer joy. Hester dashed off a note to her husband, despondent that he probably wouldn't miss her at all if she remained away from home to serve as Athena's chaperone.

"You'll love it once we get there," Athena kept saying, and her elation buoyed the others in the carriage during the long ride there. "I haven't set foot in Scotland for twenty years, but in my mind, the memories of Tigh na Coille are just as fresh as if they were rememberin' yesterday."

Marshall cocked an eyebrow. "I'm not sure if it's my imagination, but is your accent returning?"

"Och, no," she said, making him chuckle.

The weather blessed them all the way to the border of Scotland, and they made good time. In only four days they crossed into the town of Jedburgh.

They were greeted by the sight of vast rolling hills sprinkled with black-faced sheep grazing tranquilly on emerald grass. The air was brisk and fresh, perfumed by the fragrance of moist earth. Tiny cottages slept at the edge of the farms, each with its own crop, which from a distance looked like a vast patchwork quilt in varying shades of green.

Athena stuck her head out of the carriage. The furious northern wind whipped her hair from its pins, and she couldn't care less. Here she felt alive, free of constraints, each of her senses heightened. She felt drawn to this land like a compass needle points true north. And now that she was here again after so long, her entire being hummed as with the quickening of a night before a storm.

The carriage came to a fork in the road. But instead of going west toward Ayrshire, where Athena came from, it continued to travel north toward Edinburgh.

She turned to Marshall. "Elliott is guiding the horses in the wrong direction."

Marshall heaved a tense sigh. "We're not going to Tigh na Coille. We're headed for the Highlands."

Athena's expression deflated with disappointment. "Why?"

Marshall took some time before he answered, and when he spoke, his tone was circumspect. "Your parents passed away in the Highlands, didn't they?"

"Yes, but—"

"In light of our upcoming nuptials, I . . . felt sorry for you, not having your father or mother to take part in the wedding. So I . . . thought it would be a fitting tribute to their memory by visiting them where they . . . passed over into the next world."

Athena's face softened as she placed a hand on his cheek. "Oh, how sweet!" she cooed. "Hester, isn't he the most thoughtful and considerate man you've ever met?"

"Few men would have contemplated such a meaningful gesture, Captain Hawkesworth."

Marshall smiled nervously, wiping the perspiration from his upper lip. The less Athena suspected, the more peaceful the rest of the trip would be.

The next day, as their carriage rumbled up the unpaved drover's road toward the Highlands, the landscape changed considerably. As they traveled northward, their eyes beheld roofless ruins, the skeletal remains of thriving villages, with nothing but scorched earth to mark that the cluster of homes were not archaeological remains, but recent reminders of abandoned homesteads.

"What is the cause of all this desolation?" remarked Hester, aghast at the sight.

"The rich and powerful," answered Athena, "removing all the crofters from their homes—even burning them out."

"To what end?"

Athena's nostrils flared with indignation. "To become more rich and powerful. Landlords have thrown decent hardworking families off their ancestral land to make way for sheep runs."

Athena recounted the brutality of the stories she had heard. Tenant farmers were told that the land would be cleared for "improvements," then expelled from their homes, rescuing what little they could before their houses were burned to the ground—sometimes with the elderly and infirm still inside. Many families emigrated to England, some to the Americas. An unhappy number were replanted along the coast, forced into the unfamiliar work of subsistence fishing, living under the open canopy of heaven while they rebuilt their homes one piece of timber at a time.

They spent the night in Golspie, precisely one of the fishing villages Athena had talked about. In the morning, however, Hester was too weary to embark on the final bone-jarring leg of their trip into the mountains. Athena insisted she remain behind. Marshall paid the innkeeper's wife to look in on her, and ordered Elliott Keane to stay behind to look after her needs.

Once they loaded the carriage with provisions, Athena and Marshall set out for Kildairon, the upland stretch of land where her parents had perished. There were no coaching inns along the way to change horses, so Marshall didn't overtax their horses by urging speed.

They reached the place known as Kildairon by midday. The rugged terrain was harsh but beautiful, virgin land consisting of heaths and deer forests and veined by burns flowing with clear water. They let the horses water at a still, shallow turn in the burn, and walked up the river.

With a hand to his eyes to shield them from the sun, Marshall looked out along the horizon. His expression became one of bafflement. "What were your parents doing all the way out here?"

"From what Grandfather tells me, they wanted to

build a home in Kildairon. My father was a gambler,
I'm afraid, and he lost Tigh na Coille in an unlucky
hand of cards. Grandfather never fails to mention that
foolishness every time my father's name comes up.
Father then asked my grandfather for a small loan to
buy this land, which my grandfather refused. But my
father was very stubborn, and he sold all he had left in
the world, whatever he hadn't lost in the card game, to
purchase it. One day, my father and mother set out for
Kildairon to inspect it for a house. I never saw them
again." Athena's gaze trailed off to a distant point on
the horizon.

Marshall reached his arm around her shoulders
and gave them a reassuring squeeze. "What happened to them?"

"Their carriage was beset by highwaymen . . . ruf-
fians, marauders, God knows who they were. They
were never identified or brought to justice. A traveling
villager found my parents. They were murdered—
shot inside the carriage—their purses and their horses
gone."

He pulled her close and placed a kiss on top of her
head. "I'm so sorry."

Athena heaved a profound sigh. "It was difficult at
first. I was only ten. But it happened a long time ago.
The sadness has faded. Now . . . I just miss them."

Marshall nodded. "My heart still aches for my
father. It's good to know there will come a time when
it won't hurt anymore."

They held each other in that embrace, each drawing comfort from the other. It felt as if they were the
only two people in the whole world. The rushing
sound of the water below them filled their ears.

"Athena," began Marshall, "doesn't it puzzle you that your parents would have chosen such a remote outcropping of inhospitable land to make their home? I mean, the nearest town is eight miles away, there isn't a spot of farming land here, and the timber isn't enough to subsist on, let alone sell for profit. Doesn't it seem odd that they would want to settle here?"

Athena took another look around. "I suppose. I can't say for certain what they were thinking. Maybe Father was trying to reconnect with family. Years ago, a cadet branch of Clan McAllister went up into the Highlands. Perhaps he was trying to unite with our roots."

Unconvinced, his head turned aside. "There's no Scottish heritage for Bretherton to consider."

Athena's eyebrows drew together. "What does Calvin Bretherton have to do with this?"

Marshall revealed a head-to-toe hint of shame. "Ah. I had intended to tell you earlier."

Athena raised a hand to her hip. "Tell me what?"

"After you left Ashburnham the other day, Bretherton came to see me. He came with the Duchess of Twillingham."

"What did he want?" she asked with asperity.

"In a word, you. He wanted to renew his marriage proposal to you. I refused, and told her we were about to publish the banns. Then he asked me—no, he commanded me—to stand down. The duchess insisted that Bretherton's suit came first, and threatened all sorts of retribution for poaching his fiancée."

"I see," she said, crossing her arms in front of her. "And just when did you plan on telling me this?"

"Just as soon as I found out why it is that Calvin Bretherton's suit blows so hot and cold."

"So this trip to Kildairon was not really to honor the memory of my parents, was it?"

He gave a sheepish smile. "Not really."

Her words came out in slow, measured notes. "You thought it was impossible that Calvin Bretherton could want me for myself, so you came to Scotland to see what allure my dowry had."

"You make it sound more sordid than it was."

She was undeterred. "Then tell me, how sordid was it precisely? Athena is too fat and ugly for Calvin to want to marry. Therefore, there must be something valuable in her dowry." Her eyes blazed with green fire.

"Dammit, Athena, can't you be rational? Why must your temper always boil over?"

She closed the distance between them. "Me boil over? You're the one closest to the burn!" With a mighty shove, she pushed him backward over the grassy crag.

His body made a loud splash in the stream. Drenched from head to toe, he flailed wildly to sit up in the freezing water.

"That wasn't funny!" he shouted.

She giggled. "It is from where I'm standing."

He wiped the water from his face, and shook his head. He dragged himself to the burn's edge. He tried to stand, but his legs buckled and he stumbled back into the water.

"Athena, I can't stand up. I think I've broken my ankle."

The mirth drained from her face. "Oh, Lord, what've

I done?" She ran back a few paces toward a slope in the riverbank, clambered down and waded out to the spot where he sat. The water came up to her knees.

"Help me up!" he said, and reached up a hand.

She bent over. "Here, put your arm over my shoulders. Lean on me."

He threw his arm over her slumped shoulders, and helped himself to a kneeling position. Then, with lightning speed, he slid his hand to her bottom and gave it a firm push.

Athena toppled over into the icy water, which quickly saturated her warm spencer and stabbed her skin like sharp knives. She huffed out of the water, long strands of her red hair sticking to her face.

"You were right," he said with a smirk. "It *is* a lot funnier from where you were standing."

Her fists splashed the water. "Why you deceitful, odious . . . Englishman! That was a dirty trick!"

"You started it, Miss McAllister," he said hollowly. "Maybe it'll cool that fiery temper of yours."

The water rushed along her chest. "Just look at what you've done to my clothes."

He scrambled to his feet. "What *I've* done? Ha! It'll be a wonder if we both don't catch our death of cold." He extended his arm to help her stand. "Give us your hand."

"I'd like to give you my foot . . . right up your arse."

He retracted his hand. "Suit yourself."

"Oh, very well!" She reached out her hand.

He grasped her hand and lifted her, but his boot slipped on the rocks below and she crashed back into the water.

She came up for air. "You did that on purpose."

Now he was laughing. "No I didn't," he managed.

"Yes you did!" she sputtered.

He raised a hand defensively. "On my honor. See? Gesture of remorse." He dove back into the water beside her.

"You're as mad as a March hare."

"And you're as mad as a Scotswoman in a freezing burn. What a pair we make." His face softened with a smile, and he leaned over and kissed her.

His wet lips smoothed over hers easily, and she gave in to the seductive sensation. He swept her into his arms, embracing her tightly as he deepened the kiss. Oblivious to the current rushing around them, they felt only the current exchanging between them. Where their bodies touched, the sheen between them heated, gluing them together.

Marshall guided her to the water's edge, hovering over her as he tasted deeper of her lips. The shallow water lapped at her loose hair, making it fan out like a gentle fire over the smooth dark stones. It was an image that radiated to his loins, because his whole body felt on fire for her. He dropped his head again to suck on her sweet wet-strawberry lips, and his eyes closed to revel in the heavenly pleasure.

Her hands grabbed his sodden lapels, and she pushed her tongue into his mouth. The brazen gesture made him smile, and he rewarded it by letting his tongue dance with hers. She moaned softly, and he opened his eyes to see her desire.

Her eyes were seductive slits, inviting him, beguiling him. Her creamy mouth, half open in wanton pleasure, promised more voluptuous pleasures. She was a wild thing, natural and untamed, yet he still yearned to bond with her feral nature. Even her hair spoke danger, igniting the water in burnished whorls that gleamed and glinted . . .

Glinted? He froze, staring at a spot in the rocks under her hair.

"What's wrong?" she asked, her expression changing.

"Don't move," he said, and reached into the water a few inches from her left ear. He pulled something up, water dripping from his fingers onto her neck.

"What is that?" she asked, unable to see with the sun in her eyes.

He turned it over in his hand.

"It's gold."

TWENTY-THREE

"Let me see it."

Athena sat up and took the pebble from his hand. The nugget was the size of her fingernail and shaped like an eagle's beak. It was rough and lackluster. If it *was* gold, it looked as if somebody had chewed it up and spat it back out.

"Look!" Marshall cried, picking up another rock. "Here's another one!"

Athena took it and marveled at the two stones in her hand. "Is this real?"

He cocked his head. "I'd say those two rocks would be worth about ten pounds."

Her eyes grew wide. "Ten pounds? For these two pebbles?"

Marshall scanned the riverbed for more. "Mm-hmm. Your little patch of land seems to be worth a lot more now than you first thought."

She closed her eyes, mentally putting the mysterious puzzle pieces back in their rightful place. "No wonder my parents had to have this land, whatever the cost. They knew there was a fortune here." She shivered uncontrollably, just as much from the cold as from the memory of her parents' stolen lives. "Well, these little rocks won't do me much good if I freeze to death. I'm going back to the carriage."

Reluctantly, Marshall followed. Though the sun was high in the sky, the furious Highland wind was freezing him to his sopping clothes.

She jumped into the coach and wrapped the warm woolen lap blanket around her quivering shoulders. Moments later, Marshall came to the coach and guided it to a grassy spot so the horses could graze. He stripped off all his clothes from the waist up, and hung them on the thill of the carriage.

"Take off your dress," he said through the carriage window.

She frowned. "I beg your pardon?"

He pursed his lips. "If you give me your clothes, I'll hang them out here to dry."

She was pierced by a stab of embarrassment. Even though she and Marshall had already made love, he had never seen her in the nude in broad daylight. Begrudgingly, she peeled off her wet spencer and outer dress, and handed it to him. Modesty forbade her to remove her shift or corset.

A few moments later, he jumped inside the carriage, the picnic hamper under his arm. Athena let her eyes drink their fill of his magnificent torso, a huge triangle of muscle narrowing into a small waist.

"It's blowing up a freeze out there. I haven't felt this cold since the Duchess of Twillingham came to visit me."

Athena inhaled sharply. "To press Calvin's suit."

"Yes. Had you told her of your dowry here in Scotland?"

Athena nodded.

"Who else knew about Kildairon?"

Athena's eyebrows knitted. "Well . . . Grandfather." She began enumerating them on her fingers. "Hester. The Duchess of Twillingham. Calvin Bretherton . . . and his parents. Not counting my own mother and father, of course."

"Did any of them know the land had gold ore?"

She rolled her eyes. "*I* didn't even know it had gold. I'm sure Grandfather didn't know, or he would have told me. Besides, he'd been against the purchase of the land from the start, and has been complaining about it every time he's had to pay the land taxes."

"And Calvin Bretherton?"

Athena shrugged. "As you say . . . if he wanted to marry me, it had to be for my dowry."

Regret twisted Marshall's face at Athena's expression. "Well, if he *did* know about your gold, I doubt he would have ever called off his suit—remember that he told your grandfather he wanted to marry someone else. I doubt he'd have been so cavalier about your dowry if he had known what he was forgoing. Clearly, he only renewed his betrothal at someone else's behest."

"The Duchess of Twillingham? She was trying to help me win Calvin. She was acting on my behalf."

"Maybe she made you *think* she was acting on your behalf. Maybe she was orchestrating this marriage right from the very beginning."

Athena's eyebrows drew together, remembering that the duchess came to offer her unsolicited help in winning Calvin over. "But what would the duchess stand to gain by our union? Upon my marriage to Calvin, my dowry would have become Calvin's property."

"Thus making it easier for him to turn it over to the duchess."

"But why would he do that?"

He leaned back in the seat. "I don't know. Maybe Bretherton is somehow obligated to the duchess. Maybe they struck a bargain that upon your marriage, he gets Kildairon and sells it to her. Whatever the reason, my thoughts are pointing to the notion that there was some sort of scheme concocted between them to get Kildairon . . . before there was a scheme between you and the duchess to get Calvin."

Athena was lost in thought. The thought of a hidden conspiracy dizzied her. "But how did the duchess find out about the gold?"

"I don't know . . . but it really doesn't matter. Because now, the choice is entirely up to you."

He reached over into the basket to pull out the bread and cheese, and she caught a glimpse of his scarred back.

"What choice?" she asked.

"You may still determine what your future will be. These hills are full of gold. Your own personal buried treasure. That makes you a very wealthy woman, once you mine it." He handed her a plate of cold sliced meats. "It also makes you the most attractive prospect on the marriage mart. After all, you are still a free woman. You can marry Calvin . . . or you can marry me." He pulled the cork out of the bottle of wine, and poured it into two rustic pottery cups. "Or you can even choose to stay unmarried, and keep all that wealth to yourself." He handed her a cup. "Now that you're in full possession of your options, what will you choose to do?"

She took the proffered cup and looked Marshall in the eye. "Why are you saying this to me?"

He stared back at her. "I want you to marry me not because I forced your hand, but because it's your choice. I need to know if *I* am the man you want."

She gazed out of the window. Outside, there was a field full of flowers, their petals waving in the breeze. An insect zoomed from one flower to the next, sampling the flavor of each in a restless search for nourishment. Then she saw a butterfly take off in wobbly flight. Her new wings were graceless in movement, but there was direction to her journey. And though it took longer for the butterfly to get to her destination, she knew precisely which bud offered the sweetest nectar.

Athena's eyes traveled back to his. There was an intense look on his face. He held the cup on his knee, frozen in anticipation. There was no bravado, no pretense. Only a nervous quickening of his breathing.

"Calvin was the first man I ever loved. He's the man of my dreams."

Marshall inhaled deeply, his eyebrows knitting together. His gaze fell to the untouched cup.

"But that's all he was. Just a dream. Not like you. You are real. A real man."

A hint of a smile played on his lips.

"When I look at you, Marshall, everything stops. I'm no longer a shattered person. The pieces of who I am come together in such a way that I finally make sense. And that's because I have begun to breathe for you. It's inconceivable to me how you loved me even when there was so little of me that was lovable." Athena leaned forward. "I can't imagine life with Calvin. Or life on my own, regardless of how much money I have.

And when I think of the word 'mine,' I don't think of gold. I think of you."

His expression grew tender and proud at the same time. "Now those are the kind of words I like hearing from your lips."

She got up and sat next to him, and extended her woolen blanket around his shoulders.

He enfolded her in his arms. "Know what else I like hearing from your lips?" he whispered.

She looked up at him quizzically. "Hmm?"

He smiled rakishly. "Something like that."

He touched his open mouth to hers, captivating her with its heated wetness. Slowly, he smoothed his lips over hers, as if he were savoring a juicy fruit, and she melted from the sultry pleasure.

"Mmm," she mouthed absently into his.

He smiled. "That's more like it."

He shifted, and Athena could almost have killed him for taking away the warmth from her back. "Don't move," she protested. "I'm cold."

"I know another way to keep ourselves warm." He pulled her onto his lap, grinning wickedly as he wrapped his arms around her middle. Her thin chemise was pasted to her skin, revealing every curve and contour of her body. One hand went to her back and pulled at the wet strands of her corset.

"What are you doing?"

"Making us more comfortable." As he deftly yanked the strings from their eyelets, the stays in her corset slackened.

He hardly blinked as he watched her face. With each cross-tie unfastened, her breathing became easier and her movements freer. Nevertheless, her heart began to beat faster as she realized that the loosening garment would soon fall away altogether.

He stopped halfway down her back, and brought his mouth to her barely covered breast. The hot lips sizzled on her cool skin, focusing all her senses on that one spot. His other hand drew tight swirls on her back, making her body tingle from the sensation. Again his lips descended onto the ridge between her breasts, searing both of them at the same time. The slow torture was working its effect on her. Her inhibitions were being annihilated, kiss by tantalizing kiss.

The air in the carriage grew progressively warmer as the close heat of their bodies began to steam away the moisture. A scorching kiss on her exposed shoulder made her shudder from warm pleasure.

As he tugged on the last length of her corset's ties, the garment had become an odious barrier rather than a protective covering. The thing collapsed and fell away.

Instinctively, she clutched the blanket to herself. Though she was comfortably free of the constricting stays, her modesty still protested. The sun shone through the carriage window, illuminating her body through the sodden, wrinkled chemise.

He made no effort to remove the blanket. But his blue eyes bored into hers, as if trying to break down the barriers in her mind. He had never beheld her body before, and it terrified her to even consider he might be repulsed by her. The abundant curves that many young men had rejected. The fullness of her figure, which Calvin had abandoned. This body that had helped to keep her unmarried and alone for so many years.

He kissed her tenderly and lovingly, maddening her with the painstaking slowness, helping her win the battle against her own reservations. For the first time, she was able to appreciate the feel of his body. As he cuddled her on his lap, she relished the sensation of his massive arms on either side of her. His thighs, long enough to seat her, pressed firmly against her buttocks. The hard chest against which she lay was molded with muscle she longed to touch.

His kisses wended down her neck, and the vine of erotic sensation descended to a spot between her legs. A single hand cupped her face, and she turned to kiss it. Those large hands, callused from labor aboard ship, were mesmerizing to her. She didn't know which she wanted more . . . to touch them or be touched by them.

But that same hand traveled down to the hem of her chemise, peeling it off her legs. When the air made contact with her skin, the crease deepened between her brows. But that large hand, so warm and strong, caressed a heated path up to her thighs, and her frown evaporated. It felt as if he were slowly bringing her to life . . . and she felt it strongest in the crevice between her legs.

But he was feeling it too. The rising pressure beneath her thigh told her she was not the only one enjoying their closeness. His rearing cock made her believe that whatever the other men had thought of her figure, this man felt aroused by it. Slowly, her reservations were being squeezed out by her growing confidence.

She brushed her hand along his hair, which spiked and curled chaotically. The water had exaggerated the varying shades, exploding it into a prism of yellows and golds. So beautiful, she thought. And yet his vibrant hair and vivid eyes only hinted at the stunning man inside.

"Sit over there," he said, his voice hoarse with leashed passion. She shifted herself over to the seat facing his. He knelt before her, his wide chest nearly spanning the carriage. With one hand, he pushed away her arm that still clutched the blanket, leaving her exposed to his eyes.

She watched his eyes dance down the length of her body. His expression became grave, focused, and his accelerated breathing indicated his mounting arousal. His hands came to rest on her thighs, slowly pushing upward on the tissue of her chemise until the fabric went over her head and puddled on the carriage floor. His mouth fell upon her breasts, devouring the untouched nipples until she was panting for his cock. The remembered sensation of being filled by him tantalized her fevered brain.

Her whole naked body was open to his touch, and he made full use of his hands. There once was a time when she feared what her thighs would look like during lovemaking, but the vanity was drowned out by what her thighs *felt* like at the hands of this man. Between her relaxed thighs he brought his hand, and she gasped at the sensation of someone else's fingers between her folds. Who knew that men could be so gentle? Every caress was itself a profession of love. He kissed her deeply, his tongue tempting hers to spar with him. All the while, his fingers were also dancing inside her, and she nearly swooned from the pleasure of the double penetration.

The skilled fingers gently caressed the pearl

between her legs, experimenting with different rhythms and strokes until he found the one that made her moan. Patiently, maddeningly, he maintained that stroke until her body was begging for release.

As her pleasure mounted, it occurred to her that the first time they had made love, it was an act of taking. This time, it was an act of giving, making it infinitely more enjoyable. But she was not about to enjoy this intense pleasure alone.

"Stop," she breathed, and the interrupted friction from his nimble fingers left the nub throbbing in protest. Panting, she waited to float back to earth so that she could make a coherent sentence. "Sit over there," she repeated.

His intense expression sprouted a smile. With a wonderful economy of movement, his body reversed onto the facing seat. She knelt between his legs, and the wanton position gave her an intense erotic thrill. Slowly, she unbuttoned his trousers, and the rigid pole of his penis pushed aside the flap.

"I've always wanted to touch you here. May I?"

His relaxed grin spread. "Far be it from me to disappoint a pretty redhead."

In daylight, she was able to see his penis so much clearer. The long shaft was covered by veins, just like his muscled forearms, but the skin was infinitely softer. It was a strange dichotomy—something so hard enveloped in something so soft. The knob at the end was amazingly large, and she marveled at the fact that she was able to fit this into her body. She caressed the soft nest of wiry hairs that surrounded his penis, and touched the sack underneath it.

After a few moments, Marshall interrupted her. "Is something wrong?"

The apples of her cheeks darkened. "Well, Lord Rutherford taught us one way to do this, but Mr. Gallintry showed us another, and I was trying to decide which one is right."

With a low growl, he took her by the arms and brought her astride him. "I don't give a damn the way Rutherford or Gallintry would have you do anything. Let me show you what I like."

Her knees fell on either side of his hips. Guided by his hands, her hips descended onto his lap. Reflex made her stop when her soft flesh met with his unyielding staff, but instinct quickly took over. With a force of erotic will, she impaled herself on the thick stake of his body.

Her expression pinched as her body reminded her she was not yet used to his girth. But slowly her slick sheath ceded to him.

"This is how I want you," he said. "Filled by me, just as I am filled by you." He took a long lock of her hair and brought it to his lips.

She rocked on him—uneasily at first, her muscles unaccustomed to such a movement. But soon she found the way to slide over him in such a way that it intensified the pleasure between her legs. Her mouth fell open as she began to excite herself all over again, her passion enraged when he cupped one breast and lifted the plump weight to his mouth, his hot lips sucking on her stiffened nipples.

Her breasts bounced against his chest, and he was enthralled. His jaw tensed as his own instincts took over, and his hips began to buck up into her. Within moments, they were moving together in perfect synchronization. Deep inside his chest, he made the most incredible sounds of pleasure, and it was music to Athena's ears. Lady Ponsonby had once told her that men were to be enjoyed, like rich desserts or fine wine. But she was finding that she derived more satisfaction from eliciting those moans in him than making them herself.

As only lovers can, he communicated his mounting need to her. He increased his speed, thrusting harder, which propelled her to a new level of pleasure. With his hands on her back, her breasts springing against him, and her sex kissing his, her entire body thrummed with sensation. She hugged him to herself, and with one blinding thrust, ecstasy exploded around them like sparks from a firecracker.

He opened his eyes to find her staring at him. His hot breath fell on her face in great gusts.

"I want to spend a lifetime bringing that expression to your face," she said.

He grinned at the memory of his own words. "If you make love to me like that, my lifetime may not last that long."

They remained joined for several moments, each taking part in the other's afterglow. Despite the ebbing of the sexual pleasure, the joy did not diminish. Her caresses continued, her hands studying the feel of his body.

"How did you get these scars?" she said, her fingers rolling over the thickened, jagged lines on his back.

He cocked a sidewise grin and shook his head. "Why must you be so nosy?"

"You loved me and my scars. Let me love you for yours."

He mirrored her seriousness. "Very well. If you must know, it happened ten years ago. The worst day of my entire life." His voice trailed off.

"Go on," she said, climbing off his lap and onto the seat next to him.

He raked a hand over his still-damp hair. "Napoleon was still planning to invade Britain at that time, and . . . he needed to reinforce his naval power. Admiral Nelson had set up an impenetrable blockade at Toulon which he held for some time. You can imagine Admiral Nelson's humiliation when Admiral Villeneuve broke through the blockade with not one but a whole fleet of ships. So Nelson sent the *Vanquisher*—I was her lieutenant then—as a scout ship to follow the fleet and report on its maneuvers. Undetected, we followed Villeneuve's ships from Toulon all the way across the Atlantic to the West Indies. There we found out that Admiral Villeneuve's mission was to attack and conquer the British colonies on the islands. We managed to get the word out in time, and his plans were thwarted. Villeneuve was unable to capture more than the island fort of Diamond Rock. So the fleet returned to Europe, presumably to rendezvous with the rest of Napoleon's fleet."

Marshall closed his eyes against the dark memory. "Midway through the Atlantic, our captain made a tactical error, and the *Vanquisher* ran afoul of Villeneuve's fleet. He was in command of sixteen ships of the line, both French and Spanish, and we were vastly outnumbered. We fought them as long as we could, but our cannons were no match for theirs. Our captain lost his life, along with dozens of our crew. The deck was saturated in blood."

Athena was aghast, living it as he vividly retold the story.

Marshall's eyes glazed over as he opened the door to long-buried thoughts. "With the captain dead, I was now in charge of the ship. And wouldn't you know . . . my very first act of command was to surrender." He was silent for several moments before continuing. "Villeneuve and his men boarded our vessel, and the *Vanquisher* now became a prize for Napoleon. We her crew were taken prisoner and roped to the deck, even the wounded and dying. The admiral was prepared to take us alive, but the captain of one of the Spanish vessels began to gnaw on his ear. That damned Spaniard walked up and down our deck, gloating over his victory. And then he convinced Villeneuve to take only half the crew, and throw the rest of us overboard, bound and helpless."

Athena's blood chilled. Absently, she draped the forgotten blanket around her shoulders.

"I can't say why, but it galled me more that we were to be divided than that we were being denied an honorable death. I tried to reason with the admiral, but the Spaniard poked me in the chest and told the admiral to start the drownings with me. So I spat in his face."

Marshall rubbed his face, as if pacifying a phantom pain. "He backhanded me, hard enough to draw blood. The admiral just shrugged his shoulders and turned the matter over to the Spaniard, which now left me in the humiliating position of pleading with that bastard for the lives of my crew. Finally, the Spaniard made a deal with me. He told me I could buy the lives of my men . . . ten lashes for each man."

Athena's eyes flew open further. "Ten lashes?" she repeated, incredulous. "How many men were in your crew?"

"Two hundred and forty-three."

A hand flew to Athena's open mouth as she calculated the number in her head.

"The Spaniard's men ripped off my coat and shirt, and tied me to the rigging. And then . . . the lashings began. The Spaniard thought that the English were cowards. He thought I would beg him for mercy. But I didn't give him the satisfaction. I was determined to save my crew."

"Oh, Marshall. How many lashes did you endure?"

He shrugged dispassionately. "Forty-seven."

She buried her face in her hand. "You poor man! You must have been in agony."

Marshall only heaved a profound sigh, sparing her the details.

"Does that mean you could only save four of your men?"

"As it turned out, we all escaped capture. The smoke from the cannons during the battle had attracted the attention of a British fleet. While the Spaniard was working me over, the British fleet surprised Villeneuve's ships. Villeneuve and his ships quickly disengaged and headed back for France."

"Thank God. If it wasn't for them, you would have been killed."

He nodded. "And Admiral Rowland has never let me forget it."

She gasped. "It was he who rescued you and your crew?"

"That is how we met, how we became friends. I owe my life to that old man." Marshall put a hand on Athena's ashen face. "So now you know the truth behind the scars. And the only reason I told you is because you finally met both of my conditions: you asked me nicely . . . and you asked me naked."

She smiled in spite of her gloom. His story of heroism and sacrifice endeared him to her tenfold, but her heart still ached for all he had suffered. "I'm sorry that you had to endure such a horrible ordeal."

"Scars have a way of reminding you that the past was real. And that the past hasn't overtaken you . . . you've overtaken it." He placed a soft kiss on her lips. "We've both survived the circumstances of the past. Our scars have become our badges of honor."

TWENTY-FOUR

To their credit, neither Hester nor Elliott made any reference to the state of their clothes when Marshall and Athena returned to the inn. Once they changed into something less damp, they were quite respectable again.

They sat to dinner in the pub, a delicious meal of wood-smoked haddock and potatoes. Quietly, Athena shared the news of their gold find, all to Hester's and Elliott's hearty felicitations.

Marshall downed the haddock with some robust Scottish ale. "The first thing we need to do is to engage a factor, someone trustworthy who can protect our interests on the estate. Keane?"

"Yes, sir?"

"I want you to be my man at Kildairon."

Elliott blinked in disbelief. "Me, sir? But I'm just a groom."

He chuckled. "Keane, I would never entrust such an important job to a groom." He placed a heavy hand on the young man's shoulder. "But I would entrust it to my brother-in-law."

"Oh, sir! Thank you, sir!" He seized Marshall by the hand and shook it vigorously.

"Congratulations, Elliott," said Hester.

"Yes, indeed," echoed Athena. "Justine is a fine woman."

Elliott was beaming. "I can't believe it. I'm marrying Justine! I'll do right by her, sir, don't you worry."

Marshall gave him a warning look. "Don't *you* worry. I'll make certain that you do."

Elliott's surprised smile practically illuminated their table. "Justine is to be mine . . . I can't thank you enough, sir."

A reflective look came over Marshall's face. "My own fiancée told me how much she loved me, Keane. And the effect it had on me . . . every man deserves such happiness. There will be trouble ahead for you. People will talk . . . about you, about her, about me. But you won't get any trouble from me. My sister says she loves you, and I trust that she knows her own heart. I want her to know what it means to marry for love. If she says you are the man to make her happy, then I believe her."

"I will make her happy, sir. I'll go anywhere, do anything, at any cost . . . for her."

"Here we are," Athena bubbled. "All lovers happy."

Gently, Hester pushed her chair backward. "Would you all please excuse me? I'm afraid I'm still not feeling entirely myself."

The two men rose politely as Hester went upstairs to her room. A twinge of concern crossed Marshall's face.

"It won't be dark for another hour. Let's take a walk," Athena said to Marshall.

"Good idea. Keane, we'll set out for England at

daybreak. Make arrangements with the innkeeper, won't you?"

The moon hovered over the western horizon, warring with the setting sun. A fog began to roll in from the sea, like someone pulling a big fluffy blanket over the Highlands to settle in for the night.

"That was a wonderful thing you did for Elliott. For Justine too."

"Well, there's an old song that says, 'Love is love in beggars and in kings.' It wouldn't have been right to deny my sister her happiness just because I am empowered to dictate who she marries. Of course, now I have to explain my decision to Mother."

"I don't see why. Justine is of age. She can marry whomever she wants."

"Yes, but it's different with those of our station. There are consequences to the choice of a spouse. The repercussions of a bad one will last for centuries."

"I'll never understand the English aristocracy. Waving their titles around like some kind of semaphore I'm not meant to comprehend."

"I agree with you. In spite of the war and capture by enemy battleships, things are infinitely less complicated at sea."

"If I was in the Navy, what position would I hold?"

He smiled. "If you were in the Navy, I'd have you kissing the gunner's daughter."

"Oh? Who is she?"

He laughed heartily. "It's the discipline we inflict on insubordinate young sailors who fail to obey their superior officers."

She cocked an eyebrow. "If there was a lesson meant in that remark, it escapes me."

"Oh, no it doesn't," he said, pulling her into his arms. "You are a shrewish, ill-tempered, quarrelsome scold. But now that you've given me your love, you're even more dangerous."

"I *told* you that woman was nothing but trouble," Aquilla Hawkesworth ranted. "Look at what she's done to us!"

The irate woman threw a newspaper across the dining room table, and it slid all the way across to Marshall's hands. He unfolded the paper. And cursed.

A giant headline shouted above line drawings of Athena and Hester. Marshall read the article aloud.

THE LADY PATRONESSES OF ALL-MUCK'S
Lecherous Lectures Lead Lonely Ladies To Lewdness

It has been discovered that Countess Cavendish's School for the Womanly Arts, a finishing academy for the reformation of spinsters and heretofore unmarried women, has been corrupting its pupils with lessons in sexual expression and turning them into ladies of easy virtue. With a clientele that includes female members of the families of England's ruling classes, the school has been functioning as a preparatory institute for the education of courtesans. Miss Athena McAllister and Lady Hester Willett (née Bermondsey), proprietresses of the establishment, hired gentlemen of notoriety to deflower their lady students and instruct them in wanton behavior. Amid accusa-

tions of impropriety, the school was summarily
closed down and the proprietresses are nowhere
to be found.

"Do read on." Aquilla sneered. "Wait until you get
to the list of the names of the pupils. Justine's name
is there, large as life!"

Marshall read the whole sordid piece while pacing
across the room. "That bastard! I warned him not to
print this!"

"You should have seen this house. Slithering with
journalists. To think that *my* daughter should be the
subject of such prurient interest. And this is only the
thin edge of the wedge. Next, we'll be banned from
every salon in England. This home shall become our
cloister . . . our prison!"

"Mother, do try to be constructive. We have to figure out a way to contain the rot."

"Contain it? One can't reverse this kind of damage
once it's been unleashed! It's like tossing a bucket of
feathers in the wind and then trying to catch them all
back again. Words, once they're out, are irretrievable."
She sat down on a chair and stroked her forehead. "My
only consolation is that other families have been impli-
cated too. That lessens our culpability to some degree.
Thank God you haven't published the banns. No one
outside our inmost circle knows about your erstwhile
betrothal to that woman."

He raked a hand through his hair. Aquilla came
from a caste that is not given to fits of emotion, so seeing his mother in this state only exacerbated the situation. "It's not erstwhile at all. I'm marrying Athena."

She leaned over a chair. "Have you gone insane?

You can't seriously be thinking of marrying this person. She is notorious! Her name will forever be whispered as one utters a profanity."

"We are all mired in this mess, Mother. You mustn't be partisan. Athena and Lady Willett are fine, upstanding women."

"Their kind of women are rarely 'upstanding.' Haven't you read that article? They spend all their time on their backs."

"That's enough!"

"Oh, you're a fool. All those years spent with that seafaring rabble has made you a traitor to your class. Can't you for once think of someone other than yourself? I can hardly exaggerate the damage this has done to Justine's marital opportunities. No respectable gentleman will go anywhere near her. What are we going to do about her?"

Her words charred him. "Don't worry about Justine," he said, sarcasm dripping from his voice. "I shall banish her to Scotland with the first man who will have her."

Hester was in her boudoir, grateful to be off that horrible carriage. The jarring motion had made her very sick on the way up to Scotland, but it seemed worse on the way down. She was never fond of long trips, and this one took her from one end of the country to the other. Her lady's maid, Rivers, helped her remove her spencer and frock, and she sat down at her dressing table in her shift to unpin her hair. With a pot of hot tea and some dry biscuits, her queasy stomach finally began to settle—until her husband stormed into the room.

Thomas Willett tossed a newspaper on the dressing table in front of her. "What the devil is this?"

She suppressed a spike of irritation. "It looks like a newspaper."

"Don't be impertinent," he said, pacing the room. Though he was only in his late thirties, Thomas's hair had become prematurely gray. This, together with his gray eyes and square face, lent him a certain distinction that had attracted Hester the moment she met him. But she discovered—after she married him—that there was an imperial attitude to match his regal appearance.

"I would have preferred a more solicitous welcome after being gone for so long."

"Perhaps if my wife were not acting the harlot, I might have been more receptive."

Hester flashed him such a look that Rivers stopped hanging her clothes and discreetly exited.

"I know you will be good enough to explain that slur on my character."

"It is nothing that the world doesn't already know. Read the paper." Thomas turned to look out of the window.

Hester perused the article. "I see."

He turned around. "What do you have to say for yourself?"

She began to brush her hair. "It is not a very good likeness of me."

He crossed his arms at his chest. "How can you be flippant at a time like this?"

"I resent you being masterful in matters that do not concern you."

"How can you say that the utter ruin this will bring does not concern me?"

"I said 'concern you,' not involve you. Nothing I do has ever concerned you, Thomas. Outside of our bedroom, I may as well not exist to you."

"Don't start on that again. I won't be led down that rabbit hole of an argument. I want an explanation for your involvement in that bawdyhouse."

"If you're referring to my investment in the School for the Womanly Arts, then it should come as no surprise to you. You knew precisely where I was and how much time I spent there."

"But I knew nothing of the wanton indecency that was occurring there."

She slammed down the hairbrush. "How dare you make judgments about the activities of the school! Before you go and believe what the newspapers have printed, how about first asking me, your own wife?"

A shade of remorse crossed his face, but indignation quickly replaced it. "Tell me, then. The paper says you were akin to French *salonnières,* receiving men of notoriety to fornicate with your students. Is that true?"

"If you knew me better, then you should be just as outraged as I am by that appalling lie. We were educating ladies with the facts of life. Both its challenges and its pleasures."

He threw his arms in the air. "Pleasures! You allowed men to corrupt these women before they were legally married."

She reached into a silver pot on her dressing table and scooped out some cream. "You should not presume to be any better, Thomas. Had I said 'I don't' before I said 'I do,' you might not have corrupted me before *we* were legally married."

Bafflement contorted his features. "What's gotten

into you? I've never heard you be so fierce before. You never used to talk this way to me."

"You have no idea who I am, Thomas. I do not feel any less the lady for what I have done. In fact, I am becoming the lady I used to envy. I enjoyed having an influence in the lives of our students. But what I truly want is to have an influence over yours."

He quelled his anger somewhat. "How can you say that? Of course you have an influence over me. You're my wife."

"Oh, Thomas," she said, her head shaking slowly. "I am so much more than that."

TWENTY-FIVE

A chill wind began to blow through London, but it did nothing to cool Athena's ire. She stomped up Craig Street toward the printing offices of the *Town Crier,* leaving burning embers in her wake.

Just as she passed an alleyway, a hand shot out and pulled her into the shadowy recess. Athena's scream died as a man's large hand clamped around her mouth. He held her fast against his chest with a massive forearm, his size and strength disarming her completely. She inhaled sharply, the pungent smell of urine and horses assaulting her nose.

"Where do you think you're going?" her assailant growled. It was a very familiar voice. Athena stopped struggling, and the man loosened his hold.

She whirled around and gasped. "Marshall! You scared the life out of me! What the hell are you doing here?"

His lips flattened. "I rode in to Endsleigh to see you. I was hardly surprised you weren't there. Your grandfather told me where you'd gone. And that you'd stormed out of the house before he could stop you."

"Well, you can go back and tell him you found me. Goodbye."

"Just a moment. You mean to tell me that you are seriously thinking of berating that reporter?"

"You have a firm grasp of the obvious."

"And just what do you intend to say?"

"Before or after his funeral?"

He chuckled. "By God, your sharp mouth alone could win England the war. I should set you loose on the local abattoir."

Athena rolled her eyes and turned to leave the alley, but she was halted by Marshall's hand on her arm.

"Not so fast. I want a word with you first."

"Not now, Marshall."

"Precisely now. Come with me." Marshall took her hand and pulled her toward the coaching inn Athena's stage had just pulled in to from the country.

The Mount Olympus was the largest coaching inn in London and the tallest building on Delphin Street. In addition to the pub on the ground floor, there were two floors for bedchambers. A large brick fireplace, big enough for a man to stand in, was roasting a side of beef. The pleasing aroma filled the room.

Marshall led her to a small table in the pub. He ordered some beef stew for them both, and then focused his full attention on Athena.

"I can understand your anger. There wasn't a shred of truth in that salacious article. But poleaxing Edward Nance, despite the pleasure it would give us both, is not the answer. It will just give him fodder for his next article."

She crossed her arms. "All right, then. What do you propose I do? Accept this injustice?"

"Of course not."

"What then?"

He stared at his clasped fists. "I don't know. But there are deeper issues connected to this article than at first glance. I suspected Lord Rutherford of being Nance's source, but now I'm not so sure. Lord Rutherford profits nothing from closing down the school or ruining you. So who does?"

"What does it matter? Nance wrote the article. He can bloody well print a retraction!"

At the next table sat two people: a man with a large mustache, and a woman with a smaller one. The woman looked over at them, aghast. Marshall sharpened his blue-eyed gaze on Athena. "Keep your voice down."

She brought her tirade down to a whisper. "I'm just so frustrated with all of this. That man printed up lies . . . and I don't want him to make away with demolishing all of us."

"But you have to understand that his hand is not the only one against us. Someone put him up to this. Do you have any other enemies?"

"No! None whatsoever." Athena reflected. "You don't suppose it could have been Calvin or the duchess?"

He wrung his clasped hands, their rough texture making a papery sound. "I'm not sure. What do they stand to gain by exposing you?"

Athena didn't get a chance to answer. She was distracted by murmurs at a nearby table where a group of five women sat. There was a newspaper in front of them, and their disapproving faces were comparing Athena's face to the image on the front page. Athena fixed her sight upon them. They said nothing.

But the woman with the mustache at the next table said what the others did not. "Shameless slattern."

Athena's eyes flew open, the air in her lungs escaping her. Shocked, she turned to the table of women, who smiled in vulgar gratification.

She reeled from the table, and made for the door.

"Athena, wait!" Marshall cried out, as he hurried to pull some coins from his money pouch. "Sir," he said to the mustachioed man, "see to it that you govern your wife's tongue, or you may find yourself facing the end of a blade in a duel because of her lack of restraint."

Marshall ran after Athena, finally catching up to her at the end of the street. Tears streamed down her face. He wrapped his arms around her.

"Don't cry," he said gently over her sobs. "Athena, please stop."

"I can't help it." Her words were muffled by his warm chest. "That horrible woman was right."

"Of course she wasn't. She doesn't know the truth."

"But everybody thinks I put men in my employ for sexual congress."

"It isn't true."

"But it is. I paid you, didn't I?"

His chest started to shake with laughter. "So you did. But I'll let you in on a secret. I would have done it for free."

His playful jest couldn't bore through her dismay. "You oughtn't to be seen with me, you know. There's no sense in both of us enduring the humiliation. For your own sake, you should cut me loose."

Gripping her arms firmly, he drew her attention to his face. "I will never—*never*—cut you loose."

The memory of his chilling story aboard ship floated back from his determined stare. His eyes told her . . . there was no price too great to save those he wished to protect.

His kiss snuffed out a sob . . . her very last.

The parlor room at Willett House was a cozy nest, and the room breathed of Hester's warm touches. The dressed limestone walls of the old house were elsewhere covered in plaster, but not here in Hester's parlor where the fawn-colored walls were draped with decorative russet curtains and Hester's own needlepoint. Its detailed vaulted ceiling was painted in royal blue with small gold diamonds. A long sofa and two comfortable chairs were arranged near a roaring fire.

"I'm so sorry I got you into this mess, Hester," Athena said for the fourth time since she and Marshall had arrived. "I had no idea anything like this would ever happen."

Hester shook her head. "If it's any consolation to you, I suspected very strongly that this would happen."

That comment earned her a puzzled look from Thomas, who sat in the chair opposite Marshall. "Then that begs the question . . . why did you do it?"

"Because, Thomas, I believed the rewards outweighed the risks."

Marshall crossed his legs. "A strategy every good captain must subscribe to before entering battle."

Thomas set down his wine glass. "But this school can hardly be considered battle."

"Oh, but it is," countered his wife. "Athena had

proposed to rescue these women from a fate of disgrace and loneliness by helping them to become aware of their own ability to attract a man, an objective that she met with considerable success. The dangers she had to brave were many."

Athena shook her head. "Hester, you make me sound like a hero."

"And so you are. If not to the rest of the world, then to me."

Her cheeks colored. "But I've failed our students utterly. They're going to be ostracized, just as we'll be. I let all of you down."

"Not yet, you haven't. We are not done fighting."

Athena marveled at Hester's pluck as she rose and went to her writing table. She picked up a stack of letters and brought them to the tea table. "These are letters that were delivered today. From our students or their families, demanding answers. It is to them we owe an answer. Before we answer the public."

Athena picked up the sheaf of letters. "I don't know what to tell them."

"The answer will come. But first we must play a game of chess to determine our future, at all times thinking several moves ahead of our opponent."

"But if the adversary is a dishonest press, what do you propose we do?" said Thomas.

She smirked at her husband. "We cheat."

They talked through dinner, during dessert, and into brandies and sherries. They discussed—and discarded—several courses of action. Finally, Hester suggested a bold gambit that was in equal parts risky and promising. But even though they tried to analyze every move and countermove, the variables were far too uncertain. It was a gamble, but then again, the rewards outweighed the risks.

"I don't think I can do it," said Athena. "I just can't see myself being called awful names over and over. I don't want to have to deal with that ever again."

"Athena—" began Marshall, but Hester halted him.

"Athena, you must know what you're up against. People will despise and ridicule you, and those that don't hurl insults at you will shun you. But I will be standing right beside you. We will show them all what women are truly made of."

With Hester's support, what started in Athena as resignation turned into acquiescence. Little by little, she found the courage to once again become headmistress of the School for the Womanly Arts.

It was nearly midnight by the time that Athena and Marshall started to leave Willett House. It was an indecent hour for an unmarried lady to be out, but Athena could hardly consider herself anything but indecent anymore. She was anxious and weary, and she wanted more than anything to return to Scotland, far away from all that awaited her in London in the days to come.

"Thank you both for dinner," said Marshall. "Perhaps the next time we dine together, we'll have jollier things to talk about. Tomorrow will be a difficult day for all. And I think, Athena, that you and I should also make an impromptu visit on the Duchess of Twillingham."

"Why?" asked Hester.

"It's about Kildairon. I want to ask her just how she knew about the gold there."

Thomas's gray eyebrows drew together. "Hester

told me about the nuggets you found in the brook in Scotland. But I'm curious . . . what does the Duchess of Twillingham have to do with your gold?"

Athena closed her eyes. "It's a long story. And we shouldn't keep you up any longer."

"Of course," he responded. "Let me see you both to the door. The duchess seems to be amassing a fair collection of gold these days."

Marshall stopped in his tracks. "What do you mean?"

Thomas shrugged. "Just a bit of gossip I heard at Almack's last year. One of the tenant farmers on the duchess's Lancashire estate had fallen behind on his rent. Her man up there had accepted as payment a small gold nugget from him, and that's what was used to pay the duchess. The whisper was that the man had stolen it from the tooth of a cadaver, but no one knows for sure. Still, he's been making his payments ever since in gold. Digging up corpses just to plunder their mouths seems a horrid way to earn a living, if you ask me. I should stick to farming."

Marshall and Athena exchanged a knowing glance. "I don't suppose you happened to have heard if this tenant farmer was Scottish," he asked.

Thomas shook his head. "Can't say for certain. Come to think of it . . . yes. The ladies I heard the gossip from had teasingly christened the man 'Mac-Graverobber.' "

Marshall looked at Athena. "So that's how the duchess learned about the gold in Kildairon . . . one of her farmers must have stumbled upon the find. Once he started paying his debts to her in gold, she got suspicious and made him confess how he found the nuggets." His jaw tensed. "I think it's safe to assume that Her Grace has known about your little gold stash for some time."

Anger in Athena surged, but it was not directed at the Duchess of Twillingham. It was aimed at Calvin Bretherton. Despite all that had happened, she had still been unwilling to believe that Calvin was romancing her just to get his hands on Kildairon. She foolishly still harbored hope that Calvin had, in his own distorted way, nurtured feelings for her. But now it was a certainty . . . he was the duchess's puppet to rob Athena of her only inheritance.

Calvin's feigned love had made her feel like a queen. But in truth, she had only been a pawn.

She exhaled her shame. Even pawns can topple the king.

TWENTY-SIX

It was nine o'clock in the morning when Athena knocked on the door of Calvin Bretherton's London town house. It did not matter that Countess Cavendish's book of rules prohibited visits at breakfast, and unmarried ladies visiting gentlemen alone. As far as she was concerned, Countess Cavendish could take his rules and shove them right up his arse.

A surprised butler with a weathered face and bowed legs answered the door. Athena pushed her way past him. "I'm here to see Lord Stockdale. Where might I find him?"

"I shall see if he's at home. Whom shall I say is calling?"

"I'll tell him myself." She went to the first door she found and looked inside.

"Miss, if you'd care to wait in the study—"

But he had to finish the sentence at her retreating back as she opened and closed two more doors. The butler protested vociferously but he was too old to catch up to her impassioned search. She ascended the stairs faster than his curved legs could let him pursue.

She flung open a bedroom door. Calvin was inside,

lying in a rumpled bed. He sat up, blinking in shock at her.

Athena was unprepared for the sight before her. He was naked from the waist up, and his body was just as enthralling as the statues of Roman gods she had seen at the museum. Miles of muscle lined his arms, which hung on a wide chest dense with light brown hair. The shadowy beard that darkened his chin, together with the explosion of golden hair tousled from sleep, gave him a savage look. It was a vision she had daydreamed about many times, yet now it left her cold.

The wheezing butler toddled in from the corridor. "Sir, I tried to eject her forcefully, but I had no wish to hurt her."

"Don't blame him," Athena said. "I'm too angry and Scottish for him to catch."

"It's all right, Jansing. Let us have a moment alone."

Calvin regarded her intently as the butler closed the door. He pointed to a spot beside her. "Chair?"

"So it is," she replied.

He sighed heavily, resigning himself to a hostile interview. "To what do I owe the pleasure? Am I right in thinking that you've chosen me over Captain Cuttlefish?"

She smirked jadedly. "You're the one with the preference for lovers who act like lady octopuses."

"I thought you'd forgiven me for that little indiscretion with Lady Ponsonby."

"I shall never forget the sight of the two of you together. If I could somehow scrub it from my mind, I would."

"Aren't you a bit too old not to comprehend a simple act of sex?"

"I don't expect you to understand. If you knew what love I had for you, you'd realize how it forced me to live off only pieces of my heart."

He had the grace to look repentant. "I do know. And I'm sorry."

His expression of remorse dulled the blade of her anger. She raised her chin. "Are you also sorry for conspiring with the Duchess of Twillingham to marry me?"

A look of guilt marred his handsome features. "How did you know about that?"

The confession caused a stab of pain in her heart. "Does it matter?"

Calvin stood up from the bed, tying the bedsheet securely around his waist. He approached her, seemingly growing taller and larger as he neared. His nearness sparked a mysterious flame in her heart that she wished weren't there.

"I never wanted you to find out, Athena. But the duchess . . . I found myself in a hole with her. You see, a couple of years ago I invested heavily in a rather risky American venture, and I borrowed a great deal of capital from the duchess. A lot of time has passed, and there haven't been any returns. Nor, I fear, will there be. But she has demanded to be repaid, and I've been rather embarrassed financially of late. All of my assets are committed, and I haven't the blunt to pay her back. She told me she would consider my debt paid in full if I would just marry you."

It was hard to keep the hurt from her face. "*Just* marry me?"

He shrugged. "Well, that and transfer ownership of Kilkairnon."

She closed her eyes. "Kildairon."

"Right. Sorry. It wasn't that I didn't fancy you. But I just *hated* being manipulated into marriage."

She chuckled mirthlessly. "Did the duchess ever tell you why she wanted Kildairon for herself?"

He nodded. "She said she wanted to pasture her sheep and goats there. She's a rich woman. She has several thousand head of cattle too. I didn't think you'd mind if I used it to pay my debt. I owe her twice as much as those few acres of mountain crag are worth. Besides, you didn't seem to have much attachment to that land. As I recall, you rather belittled it."

"I see," she remarked with asperity. "But I did have an attachment to my school. So why did you expose me to that journalist?"

"What journalist?"

"Nance, the man who scrawled those lies about my school in the *Town Crier.* Just because it was a bordello while in the possession of your onetime paramour, Lady Ponsonby, doesn't make it a bordello still."

"Please don't hold Lady Ponsonby against me, Athena. She means nothing to me."

"Is that so?" said a voice from the back of the room.

Athena's head jerked in the direction of the darkened doorway. A woman stepped into the doorframe, her naked body covered only in the muted sunlight from the shaded window. Large brown nipples covered her small, watery breasts, and her bony hips thinned over a large triangle of black hair.

"Lady Ponsonby." Her name felt like a curse on Athena's lips.

The woman sat on the bed, her back against the mahogany headboard, oblivious to her own nudity.

"Or, as I am otherwise known, Lady Octopus." She picked up a second glass on the bedside table, a detail Athena had missed completely. "Would that I had four more limbs to wrap around your precious lover."

In exasperation, Calvin flew to the bed. "Why didn't you stay in the other room? Athena, I can explain."

"I don't think I need you to, Calvin. I think I understand everything perfectly." Athena would not allow Lady Ponsonby to shock her with her nudity or her words. She brought the chair to the foot of the bed, and sat upon it. "Lady Ponsonby here was not totally frank with me when she told me she barely remembered your last name. In fact, she wanted it for herself, didn't she?"

Calvin perched himself on his side of the bed. "I don't understand."

"Of course you don't. As I said, you don't know what love is, so you cannot understand what it does to a woman."

Calvin looked between the two women, clearly baffled by the silent communication between them.

Athena folded her legs, another of Countess Cavendish's faux pas. "Lady Ponsonby has harbored a deep affection for you for some time, Calvin. She'd do anything to become your wife. Even sacrifice me for it."

"You two have met?" he asked.

The mirth was absent from Athena's smile. "Oh, yes. You see, I begged her once to teach me how to make you fall in love with me. And she taught me what she knew. But she couldn't teach me that. Because the fact was, she didn't know herself."

Lady Ponsonby crossed her arms over her wrinkled

stomach. "And yet, I'm the one in the bed with Calvin, not you."

Athena nodded pensively. "True. You may have mastered his cock. But that's not how you draw out his devotion."

Her angular face adopted a shrewd expression. "It'll do for a start."

Athena shook her head, recognizing her own foolish belief in that sentiment. Once upon a time, she had thought that that's what it took to win a man's love. She had even taught it to others. But she couldn't have been more wrong. *When a man is aroused, the intensity of his words, his embrace, his kisses, could easily confuse you into believing he cares for you.* Marshall had taught her that. *Love begets desire, but desire does not always beget love. When a man truly loves you, you will know it not from his kiss, but from his actions.*

"But it was the end you were looking forward to, an end that never came. Calvin never broached marriage to you. In fact, when you saw that he became more determined to wed me in order to satisfy his obligation to the duchess, that's when you set out to ruin me. Even the duchess could not make Calvin marry me if I was a pariah. So you whispered to Nance what was going on at the school, a school you helped me create."

Lady Ponsonby's large, dark eyes stared into Athena's, eyes that had long ago lost all innocence. "Don't pretend to be some poor put-upon ingénue. You asked for that knowledge, and you got it. But everything carries a price, and you can't expect to acquire the blacker lessons of life without getting stained."

Athena recoiled. The older woman was right. Lady Ponsonby had been Athena's fairy godmother, imbuing her with the sort of beauty she wanted to get her prince. But it was the wrong kind of beauty. And the wrong sort of prince.

Athena rose from the chair and went to the door. "It occurs to me that I never properly thanked you for that knowledge. This then shall be my extension of gratitude—to the two of you. Lady Ponsonby, I shall never—ever—marry Calvin. You may have him. And Calvin, you may have Lady Ponsonby. You both richly deserve one another."

TWENTY-SEVEN

Every week that Athena avoided speaking to Edward Nance was a week that he printed more scandals in the *Town Crier*. An article appeared in which Athena's parents were painted as profligate wastrels who impoverished her and tossed her into the gutter from which her grandfather was forced to take her in. A subsequent article was written casting her grandfather as a drunken scoundrel, whose daughter and son-in-law perished under suspicious and unwitnessed circumstances. The most recent article in the weekly periodical broadcast Hester as an embittered, childless woman whose husband refused to be seen with her in public. They were blatant distortions of the truth, but no one but Athena and Hester were to know that.

Despite the scathing exposé, Athena and Hester went forward with their plan. Together, they paid a visit to all their students and their families. They endured the angry tirade of outraged parents, brothers, and guardians, furious with her for subjecting them to the most humiliating indignations. They were forced to listen to stories of being rebuffed on the streets, snubbed at parties, and denied admission to clubs. Once they spoke their piece, the family members then heard Athena and Hester say the last words they expected to hear: the students should return immediately to the school.

Athena explained that the best way to avoid the taint of bad press was not to run from the questions, but to confront them. Keeping their daughters from finishing out the term was tantamount to an admission of complicity. If the ladies returned to the school, they would show the world that they had nothing whatsoever about which to feel ashamed. If they pulled out, a cloud of suspicion would follow them always.

Hester could empathize with their plight. They were faced with two equally bleak prospects, neither of which offered much promise of protection from public scrutiny. But the only way to combat the prurient inquiry was to band together. A school divided against itself, she said, would bring failure upon all.

On the day the school officially reopened, Athena and Hester sat in the parlor. Patiently, they waited for the students to show. Although they tried to keep the mood light, the mantel clock ticked away their hope. But when the front door sounded, both of them jumped. Without waiting for Gert, they ran to the door and flung it open. Lady Katherine and her mother were at the door, a footman unloading the former's luggage. Athena was so happy she hugged all three of them, one by one.

Within the span of an hour, four more of their students showed up, returning to finish out the term. By noon, all but three of the students had returned. Athena celebrated that night by having a buffet of sweets and engaging a trio of musicians for the ladies to dance.

But Edward Nance would not be stopped. With

each subsequent edition of the paper, he published articles about the school and its occupants. In the days to come, it became evident just how much notoriety Athena had developed. It was impossible to ignore the fact that people on the street rushed past the front door of the School of the Womanly Arts. Or to overlook the whispers behind fans when the students went on an outing to a park. But when she returned to the school and found the front door painted with the words PAYING WHORES, that's when Athena decided that putting on a brave face was no longer enough.

She hired a boy to paint over the insulting red words, donned her gloves and hat, and hired a cab to drive her to see the Duchess of Twillingham.

That night in London, celebration was in the air. Everyone enjoyed the holiday atmosphere, the day that Napoleon Bonaparte surrendered at Waterloo, signifying the end of a long war.

Gentlemen everywhere celebrated at their clubs, and Watier's was no different. Though normally a shade more sedate, Watier's was overflowing with the sum total of its members, and the noise inside was earsplitting. The air was thick with the smell of liquor and smoke, and most of the men stood in tight clusters toasting the victory. Admiral Jasper Rowland sidled up to his friend General Moncrief, a veritable statesman of the British Army, and slapped him on the back. "What do you call a French general who's won the war?"

General Moncrief, a man with a patch over one eye, just shrugged. "I don't know."

Admiral Rowland's florid face widened. "I don't know either. There's never been one before."

The laughter they raised caught Marshall's ear. He could recognize Admiral Rowland's deep-chested laugh even in this din. Marshall squeezed his way through the crowd until he reached the admiral.

The admiral pulled Marshall in, slamming him against his wide body. "Ah, here's my finest officer. Moncrief, you remember Captain Hawkesworth, don't you?"

"Of course," he said, shaking Marshall's hand. "You fought at Copenhagen and Trafalgar."

"Yes, sir. Congratulations on Waterloo. Outgunned, outmanned, outhorsed . . . it was a real triumph for the army."

General Moncrief put a glass into Marshall's hand. "That's all Wellesley's doing. First-rate strategist, that man is. All I ever do is nod my consent to whatever he proposes."

Admiral Rowland elbowed Marshall. "What I wouldn't give to have met Boney in person on the high seas. One look at our newest hundred-gunners and the war would have been over. Say, why do French people always wear yellow?"

Marshall swallowed the liquor hard. "I'm sure I don't know, sir."

"To match the color of their blood!" The admiral guffawed.

Marshall turned to the general. "Sir, would you mind terribly if I had a word in private with the admiral?"

"Not at all. Excuse me, gentlemen."

The club didn't leave anywhere secluded, so Marshall just lowered his voice. "Admiral, I'd like to speak with you about my future in the navy."

The admiral waved his glass. "I thought you might be upset that I pulled you out when I did. You wanted to be in action when the war ended. Not to worry, Hawkesworth. There's plenty of action still to be had. Spain, Ireland, those pesky Americans—"

"No, sir. You see, I . . ." Marshall never thought he would ever speak these words. "I want to resign my commission."

Admiral Rowland smiled softly. "Oh."

Marshall did not expect the admiral's equanimity. "You don't seem terribly upset."

He sighed. "In truth, I had rather hoped you would." At Marshall's indignant expression, the admiral put his hand on the younger man's shoulder. "Don't misunderstand me, my boy. His Majesty owes Britain's military supremacy to men like you. As your commanding officer, I shall feel the loss of your command keenly. No man I know can take up your sword . . . I doubt there ever will be a man brave enough to do it. But as your friend, I can only express my supreme joy at your news. I trust your decision has something to do with a certain Miss McAllister?"

"Yes, sir."

"The navy is a very jealous mistress, my boy. She demands all a man has for as long as he lives. I know. I have given in to her all my life. But the sea robs you of the pleasures of family, and I didn't want you to miss out on that as I have done. You shouldn't be like me, a man grown gray in service to the Crown, with no one to inspire him in his declining years. Not with a pistol of a woman like the one you're lucky enough to marry. Mastering the sea will seem easy compared to mastering one such as she."

Marshall smiled wanly. "She's been characterized erroneously in the press."

"I know. I've read that smut-rag of a paper. Perhaps people's attention will be diverted to the good news about the war for a while."

"I hope so."

"Marrying you might change people's minds about her. I say, Moncrief!" Admiral Rowland waved his drink in the air.

The general turned his head, and walked back toward Rowland. "Yes?"

"You know that lady that's been in the papers, that Athena McAllister? She's Hawkesworth's fiancée."

"Really?" he said, his one good eyebrow lifting in surprise.

"Yes, but don't believe anything that paper has to say. I know the girl personally, and she's as respectable as they come."

The general cocked his head. "You wouldn't think so by the commotion she caused at Almack's."

Marshall's face blanched. "Athena was at Almack's? When was this?"

"Earlier this evening, while I was there. She asked to be allowed in to see the Duchess of Twillingham, but those snobbish Lady Patronesses refused her admittance. She caused the most frightful row. But what was more surprising is that the duchess actually went outside to meet her. And they left together in the duchess's carriage. Raised a few eyebrows, I can tell you."

Marshall's mind raced to figure out why Athena would go see the Duchess of Twillingham without him. "I should go find her. Thank you, General Moncrief.

Admiral," he said, shaking the man's hand, "thank you for your friendship. I shall miss your jokes, sir."

The admiral's white eyebrows lifted. "Not to worry. Do you know where you can find over three million more French jokes?"

Marshall smiled broadly, nodding sagely as he exited. "Yes, sir. In France."

"That's my boy!" the admiral said proudly.

TWENTY-EIGHT

Marshall was unable to track Athena down that night. Or, for that matter, the next morning. She was not at Almack's. She was not at the School for the Womanly Arts. And neither she nor the duchess had been seen at the duchess's home. Athena McAllister had simply vanished.

Marshall was frantic when he arrived at the school again the next day. Fear had worked like yeast in his mind. His wavy blond hair, so naturally attractive, was tortured by his nervous hands. His cravat, which characteristically was tied with military precision, hung askew in his haste to leave the house. Dark smudges appeared under his eyes, bleary from lack of sleep. Despite his determination to believe that there was a rational reason for Athena's disappearance, he couldn't prevent sinister images of evil befalling her from snaking through his head.

Gert showed him into the dining room. Sweet piano music trilled from behind the doors of the parlor, but it collided with his anxious mood. Hester joined him within moments. "Marshall, are you all right?"

"Have you had any word from Athena?"

"No," she said regretfully. "I was tempted to inform

the constabulary, but I was afraid of casting more as-persions on her character if word got to the press she'd been out all night."

He shook his head. "What could have become of her? You're sure she left no note?"

"We've looked everywhere. She just told Gert she was stepping out and then disappeared into the street. I haven't even told the students. Who, incidentally, are inside the parlor receiving a lecture from Mr. Bain-bridge, the dance instructor. I oughtn't to leave them unchaperoned."

"No, o-of course not. You go back inside. I'll . . . head out to Endsleigh Grange. Maybe she decided to go to her grandfather's house for some reason. At any rate, I should alert him that she is missing, just in case she turns up—" *Dead,* he caught himself think-ing, and the idea froze his blood.

The front door opened, and he heard footsteps. Marshall raced into the hall.

The morning sun exploded from the open door, blinding him from gazing upon the silhouette in the doorframe. As she removed her bonnet, burnished hair cascaded down her back.

"Athena! Thank God you're alive!" He squeezed her tightly, grateful to have her soft, yielding body with him still.

She scooped her arms under his. "Gosh, what a wonderful welcome. I wish everyone were as happy to see me as you are."

Hester appeared behind him, relief in her voice. "We thought you'd disappeared."

"What . . . in a puff of smoke?"

Suddenly, like a barrel stripped of its iron hoops, the joy drained from him. He seized her by the arms. "Where *have* you been? I've been mad with worry. How can you leave and not tell anyone where you'd gone?"

The alarm in his voice brought a few curious faces to the parlor room door, where the music had stopped because of the commotion. Lady Katherine brought a hand to her chest. "Oh! Good morning, Mr. Marshall."

Marshall straightened, and turned toward the parlor door. "Good morning, ladies. Please continue your lesson. I hope you'll excuse me while I kill your headmistress in private." He took her by her gloved wrist and pulled her toward the dining room.

"Athena, what happened to you last night?"

"I'd love to tell you, Marshall, but I haven't the time."

"The hell you haven't. I was told you drove away with the Duchess of Twillingham. Is this true?"

"Yes."

"What business did you have with her?"

Athena bit her lip. "Marshall, I really must go. I'm expecting some guests."

He shook his head. "Have you any idea what you put me through last night?"

Her face softened. "I didn't know you'd be looking for me. I'm sorry." She stood on tiptoe and placed a quick kiss on his lips.

His eyes became hard slits. "By God, it will cost you a lot more than that." He lowered his head and consumed her mouth with his own. He drove her head back with his kiss, the surprise of his assault making her cry out into his mouth. Bent over his arm, her waist was crushed against his body, and he sensed her heartbeat quicken with both fear and arousal.

"Don't ever frighten me like that again," he warned.

She shook her head dumbly, her rapid breath fanning his face.

A knock sounded on the door, and Athena jumped. "You have to go now, Marshall."

"Why?"

"Because this will be easier without you."

"Who's that at the door?"

Athena pursed her lips together. "Edward Nance."

Marshall's scowl blackened. "What's he doing here?"

"I asked him to come."

"What are you scheming?"

"A gambit. Queen takes rook."

With a clipped, purposeful stride, Athena walked to the front door.

The man at the door removed his hat. "Miss McAllister?"

He was not at all as she expected. The animosity that Athena had harbored for Edward Nance these past weeks had made her imagine him to be a snarling old man with pinpoint eyes hunched over cheap parchment with his poison pen. Instead, she found him to be tall and rather handsome, if modestly dressed. He was in his mid-forties, with just a splash of gray discoloring his black hair, and his eyes had a caramel-colored hue. But the smell of cigar smoke that clung to his clothes turned her stomach.

"Mr. Nance. Do come in."

"Thank you," he said, his perspicacious eyes darting all around the house. "I hear music. Are you having a party?"

"My students are having a dancing lesson. Won't you come into the front sitting room?"

"Thank you." He followed her into the sitting room, where a bay window looked out onto the street. "I must say I was surprised at your invitation. I've tried repeatedly to get an interview with you, but my requests went unanswered."

Athena sat on the long couch. "Let's just say I've tired of reading fiction."

Nance chuckled softly, sitting opposite her. "Journalism is not a scientific profession, Miss McAllister. Lack of information leads one to a scintilla of creativity. When there are too many holes in a story, the writer must stitch them up as best he can."

Her eyes glinted in pique. "Stitching, perhaps, but you seem to prefer placing patches over yours. Large, incongruous, and totally fabricated patches."

Nance shrugged. "My job is to sell papers, Miss McAllister."

"That's odd. I thought your job was to print the truth."

Nance studied her intently. "Truth is relative—and often uninteresting. Secrets, Miss McAllister—secrets are the birthplace of successful journalism. From them the best stories take shape."

She nodded slowly. "The meaning of which is that the best stories must by definition be scathing exposés."

"Not always, but usually."

"An exposé that is colored by *your* perspective."

"Every journalist is a moralist. It is impossible to report something without adding the writer's personal judgment."

"You mean it's *effortless* to do so. It's far easier to pontificate on a matter than it is to actually explain it."

Nance sighed heavily. "I'm not a scientist, Miss McAllister. I don't explain things. I just communicate them. And that is what I hope that you will help me to do here today—communicate your story."

"How can I be sure that you will report this story as it is, rather than as you see it?"

Nance pulled out a pad and a pencil. "I shall represent the facts as best I can. Tell me about the School for the Womanly Arts."

Athena did so. She told him how she bought the Pleasure Emporium from its former owner, Lady Ponsonby, with the sole purpose of setting up a school for spinsters to learn the art of attracting and acquiring a husband. In addition to the ladylike pursuits of child-rearing, embroidery, and culture, her students would also learn the lessons of the seductress—engaging in intercourse without *intercourse*.

Beads of perspiration broke out on Nance's upper lip as he furiously scribbled onto his pad all that Athena said. Athena could almost read the headlines he was hatching even as she spoke.

"Where did the money come from for this enterprise?"

"Lady Hester Willett provided the capital from her own funds."

"Hester the Investor," he muttered as he wrote. "And Lord Warridge . . . what is his role in all of this?"

"You mean Captain Hawkesworth? He was our artist's model."

"Your model?"

Athena nodded innocently. She went to a cupboard underneath the bay window and pulled out her sketchpad. "See? Here he is."

Nance greeted the sketchbook with saucer-eyed avarice. "Lord Warridge modeled *nude* for all of you?"

"Yes."

Nance was quickly running out of paper onto which his increasingly illegible notes were scripted.

"I realize it's rather early for it, Mr. Nance, but you look as if you could do with a glass of brandy. Would you care for some?"

"Er, yes, thank you."

"I would ring for Gert, but I'm keeping her hopelessly busy now. Could I impose upon you to bring it in?"

"Er, certainly. Where is it?"

"There's a decanter over by the Roman bath."

Nance arose, careful to take his notes with him, and walked to the end of the hallway and down the stairs. A few moments later, he came back up with a decanter and two glasses. He poured some for her and some for himself, downed his glass, then poured himself some more.

"Your students . . . are they all from noble families?"

"No. Some are untitled, from families of modest means, ousted from their brothers' or uncles' homes by intolerant wives. They were working as governesses to keep body and soul together. The only thing all my students have in common is the fact that they have not been able to attract a husband. That is, until they came here."

Athena waited until his pencil slowed over the paper. "So tell me, Mr. Nance, now that I have told the facts as they are, what do you intend to print?"

Nance grinned at her. "Only the most infamous story ever put to paper. This one will beat the Capofaro murders, the assassination of Prime Minister Percival . . . it'll even sell more papers than news of the end of the war!"

"Mr. Nance," Athena said, "you misunderstand my intention. I expect you to print a retraction of everything you've written about me, my school, and all of my students."

Nance's shoulders bucked in mirthless laughter. "With all due respect, Miss McAllister, no one dictates to me what I write in my paper. Least of all someone no better than a common procuress."

The door from the dining room opened and Marshall stormed in, a scowl carved into his features. "Perhaps I can offer some additional inducement." He seized Nance by the lapels and lifted him off his heels.

"Warridge!" Nance smiled. "Can't seem to leave the Pleasure Emporium, can you?"

"Nor will you, except on an undertaker's stretcher."

"That won't be necessary," said a voice from the doorway. "Lord Warridge, release that man at once."

With a growl, Marshall let him go. Nance smoothed his coat and turned around. "Who are you?"

"I am Margaret, Duchess of Twillingham." The duchess folded herself onto a chair, and rested her papery hand on her cane. "And you, sir, will find it in your best interest to recant everything you've printed about this woman in your newspaper."

"Your threats are wasted on me, Your Grace. I don't respond to intimidation." He cast a meaningful glance at Marshall. "Of any sort."

The duchess didn't answer. She took a long, slow look around the room, lost in thought. "I never would have thought I would step through the door of this building. I had hoped, many times, that this place would burn to the ground . . . just disappear from existence. The Pleasure Emporium, it used to be called, but it never afforded me anything but misery. When I stop to think of the number of marriages that have been damaged by the women who have inhabited these walls . . ." Her voice trailed off. "But I admit I have been a shade too harsh on the women who plied their trade, and not harsh enough on the men who gave them their custom."

"Your Grace knows this establishment," remarked Nance.

"And so do you, Mr. Nance. Or should I address you as Lord Essworthy?"

The name was like an arrow into Nance's flesh. "Who is Lord Essworthy?"

"Don't play games with me, Essworthy," she said imperiously. "Your peccadilloes are well known to everyone."

Marshall's gaze bounced from the duchess to Nance. "Essworthy? I know that name. He was an army officer . . . formally charged with desertion and neglect of duty during that business in Ireland. He underwent a general court-martial."

"And was convicted," continued the duchess. "He

was to be imprisoned for a period of five years. But he escaped the clutches of his guards, and disappeared. Until a man named Edward Nance turned up at this very establishment."

"That's a lie. I've never been here before."

"But you have, Mr. Nance," said Athena. "You knew precisely where the brandy was kept. If you had never been here, how would you have known that the Roman bath was in the cellar?"

Nance hesitated. "Most people keep brandy in the cellar."

The duchess opened her reticule and fished out an object. "But only one person could have in his possession this." She handed it to Marshall.

Marshall turned the gold pocket watch over in his hands. "It's engraved. *Essworthy*."

"That isn't mine," declared Nance.

"It was when you gave it to my husband two years ago." The duchess turned to Marshall. "The Pleasure Emporium was an establishment much renowned among gentlemen of the upper classes. It boasted some of the most beautiful women in the world, ladies of quality mostly, who offered their services to gentlemen who could afford them. It shames me to admit it, but my husband was one of that select clientele who patronized this establishment. I found that watch among my husband's possessions two years ago. In the midst of our quarrel, he admitted to me that he had met a man called Nance here, who had given him that timepiece in exchange for the membership fee. He told me that you two prided yourself in sharing the same girl."

"You've found me out, Your Grace," said Nance, a mirthless smile on his lips. "I admit coming to the Pleasure Emporium once or twice. And although I am flattered by the attribution to nobility, I am not this Lord Essworthy you speak of. My name is Edward Nance."

Marshall pocketed the watch. "Then you have no objection to presenting yourself before the judge advocate general who tried the officer named Essworthy just to prove your innocence."

"I don't have to prove anything to you," he said, sneering.

"Do you have any idea what the penalty is for escaping from military detainment? That *merciful* sentence of imprisonment you received would be stiffened . . . to execution."

Nance dashed for the door, but Marshall, who was larger and stronger, grabbed him and tossed him to the floor. "You're not going anywhere. Your days of flight are over. You're about to feel the full, crushing weight of Britain's justice system upon you."

Beads of perspiration broke out on Nance's face. "It was a long time ago, Warridge. Almost twenty years. That business has long been over."

"Not to the military. The Crown has a long memory for deserters . . . and fugitives from the law."

Nance brought himself to his knees. "You can't turn me over to them. I didn't belong in the service. My father bought that commission to give me a future. I was the second son of a second son. I stood to inherit nothing. It was either that or the clergy, and I certainly wasn't cut out for the cloth. But I didn't realize how poorly prepared I was for the army until that war. It was horrible, brutal. And I was so young. So I fled, never thinking the infantrymen of my regiment would turn me over to the colonel."

Marshall's lip curled in disgust. "You're a wretched coward, to be sure. Leaving your own men to face the rebels without a leader."

"We were going to lose that war. It was a bloodbath. There were casualties everywhere. I'm not proud of what I did, but I'd probably do it all again. I haven't even seen my family since my arrest. They probably think I've died or fled the country. Or perhaps hoped I have. I've built another life as Edward Nance. And oddly enough, I'm good at what I do."

Athena shook her head. "You may be good at your profession, but it does no good to anyone else. You're nothing but a verbal arsonist, Mr. Nance. All you do with your stories is set fires in others' lives, and then you sit back and watch them burn. You destroy people's dignity, reducing us to grist for your rumor mill."

Nance looked back at Marshall. "A-all right. I'll do as the duchess says. I'll print a retraction. I'll say the articles were written upon the word of a corrupt and unreliable source."

"Which would be nothing more than the truth," Athena emphasized.

"And I'll admit my error," he continued. "But please, don't remand me to the authorities. It would appease no one and resolve nothing."

Marshall hung his head, weighted by the intensity of his thoughts. His fists pumped open and closed. After several long moments, he straightened. "Very well. I'll let you keep your assumed identity. For now." He bent over to bring his gaze on a level with Nance's. "But know this: if you flee, or betray my leniency, there isn't a square foot in England you can hide in where I won't find you. Do we understand one another?"

Nance nodded. Stiffly, he came to his feet.

"There is another condition, Mr. Nance," said Athena. "The reason I've shared every detail of this school and its students with you is so that you may place it in your vault of secrecy. If I should read about anything or anyone I've mentioned here today—written by you or anyone else—I shall know you've betrayed our confidence. In which case, you can expect us to betray yours. Are we clear on that point?"

"Quite clear." Nance put on his hat, took one more look at the faces in the room, and quietly skulked out.

"What a disagreeable man," said the duchess, rising from the chair. Leaning heavily on her cane, she made her way to the door.

"Your Grace," said Athena, "can I persuade you to take some tea or refreshment before you go?"

She swiveled on her cane. "My dear, this house offers no rest for me. You can call a frog a prince, but it doesn't change the fact that it is still a frog. Likewise, no matter what it says on the door, this place will always be the Pleasure Emporium." A liveried footman was waiting for her at the front door to escort her down the steps.

Athena leaned upon the closed door, a sigh billowing out from the depths of her relief. She looked up. Marshall was staring at her intently.

"You never fail to surprise me, Miss Athena McAllister. So that's where you were all night . . . enlisting the duchess's help."

"As Her Grace likes to say, there is little that is left undiscovered when one frequents Almack's. I decided that if Nance wanted to destroy our reputations, then I should do a little digging into his background.

The duchess secured the information I needed, and I must say I was surprised at just how lurid it turned out to be."

"But the duchess was your adversary. How did you get her to—" Illumination dawned on his features. "Ah. You gave her Kildairon."

Athena shrugged. "Well . . . until a few weeks ago, I didn't even know I had a reserve of gold. Besides, these ladies are worth far more than just a few yellow rocks."

He walked up to her. "I know of one in particular who is," he said, lowering his lips to within a hairsbreadth of hers.

His presence aroused longings she had kept under wraps these many days without him. She raised herself toward him, and their lips met.

Some kisses taste sweeter for their absence. But Marshall's lips awoke dormant yearnings that were anything but sweet. They wanted to possess and consume, and their strength surprised her.

His hands came around her back, pulling her closer. And it was exactly what she wanted. If she could somehow fuse her body with his, she would.

His fingers went to the back of her neck, and the sensation sent shivers skipping down her spine. He released her lips, but his mouth began to press warm, wet kisses down her jaw. "Now that my modeling career . . . is over . . . I find myself . . . in need of . . . employment."

The words barely registered through the fog of her pleasure. "Well, I know of an opening you could fill . . . that is, there is a position you could take . . ."

He chuckled deeply into the turn of her neck. "The

turns your mind takes. Am I to infer that you want me for more than just modeling?"

"Oh, yes," she said with barely concealed enthusiasm.

"That will cost you."

A smile cut across her face. She went to her reticule, still in the foyer, and reached in it. Then she opened his palm, and placed something in it.

It was the two raw gold nuggets they had found in Kildairon. His eyes met hers.

"And for those wages," she said, her eyes glinting, "it had better be good."

TWENTY-NINE

The light in the window of Hester's boudoir grew stronger by the second. Hester looked in the mirror appreciatively once her maid, Rivers, pinned the final curl in place. It was a beautiful coif—Rivers had the brilliant idea of weaving into her dark tresses a pearl necklace that used to belong to her grandmother. The effect was stunning, and it would match her ivory dress becomingly.

"Rivers, help me get dressed. I want to be at the church early in case Athena should become nervous."

The maid extinguished the candles flickering near the dressing mirror. "Little chance of that, ma'am. I don't think I've ever seen Miss Athena anything less than surly."

"Don't let that prickly exterior fool you. Athena has worn a mask for most of her life, shaped by pride and self-protection. But I have a feeling that today we're going to get a good look at the real Athena McAllister, the girl behind the guise."

Just as Rivers held the dress aloft for Hester to step into, a gentle knock sounded at the door.

"Come in," said Hester.

Thomas opened the door, wearing a charcoal-colored coat and a dove-gray waistcoat. With the silver in his hair and the gray-blue eyes, Hester thought he looked a picture, much like he did the day she married him. Except today he was wearing something she hadn't seen before: an expression devoid of pretension.

"Rivers, could you give your mistress and me a moment alone?" With a brief curtsy, the maid placed the dress on the bed and closed the door behind her.

"You look lovely."

She smiled. "Thank you, Thomas. I'm not even dressed yet, so I shall hold that compliment in abeyance until I'm ready for the public."

There was no hint of a smile, as if the gentle joke didn't register. There was something else on his mind, and it weighted down even the air between them.

"Please sit down, Hester. There's something I must tell you."

A thousand emotions went through her head, none of them happy ones. Her pearls quivered as she perched herself on the cushioned bench.

Thomas reduced himself to one knee. She hadn't seen it before, but behind his back he held a package, and he placed it on her lap. "Open it."

Her fingers trembled as she unfastened the bow around the box. She lifted the lid.

"What is it?" she asked, even as she lifted the square, black silk cloth-lined headdress. A tassel hung from the center button.

"It's the mortarboard I wore during my days at Oxford." As she puzzled over this strange gift, he shifted uncertainly. "I know I haven't been the most attentive husband to you. I can't explain myself, except to say . . . I am an educated man, Hester, but some things were never taught to me. Nor, I fear, did I ever show an inclination to learn them. Women, for instance . . . I was brought up to believe that a wife was only slightly more than a beautiful ornament . . . a grown-up child that a husband was expected to indulge. But you have shown me these past few weeks what I had been too ignorant to see. That you are a woman of rarity. Your beauty is but the least of your qualities. I did not fathom the depths of your intelligence, your wisdom, your loyalty, your courage. Even though your name does not have half the alphabet after it as most scholars' do, you have shown outwardly what you possess inwardly. This," he said, holding up the cap, "is for all that you've taught me. My wife . . . and my love."

Hester looked at him with entirely new eyes. He had given her so much more than he realized. Each of his words was like a living seed planted in her fallow heart. Finally, she had more than a husband, more than a lover . . . she had an *intimate*.

Hester brought her lips to Thomas's mouth, and this time, there was more than physical passion in his kiss. Never before had she felt the connection. Finally, she felt joined together with her mate, thinking and feeling as one. Today would be more than Athena's wedding day—it would be hers as well.

Hester's beautiful coif did not survive the consummation.

THIRTY

It was the best present she had ever been given.

As she walked through the now vacant rooms at Tigh na Coille, she was flooded with happy memories. The familiar music of the creaky floors, the sight of the pear trees outside the kitchen window . . . even the smell of the Ayrshire earth seemed to welcome her home.

Marshall walked beside her, enjoying the look on her face as she darted around the house, showing him each landmark of her childhood years.

"How long can we stay?"

"As long as you like. One month . . . maybe two each year. After that, I'm afraid duty beckons. Remember that you're the new lady of Ashburnham Manor."

Athena studied him, so regal in his afternoon finery. His hair shone, as did the gold silk waistcoat and the buttons on his navy blue coat. There was no need for Kildairon. Here was the real gold mine.

"Thank you for buying my old house for me. I can't tell you what it means to be back here again. When I moved to England as a girl, it felt as if I were leaving the whole of me behind . . . as if I were starting someone else's life. Now I feel as if the scattered pages of my life are finally being put together, bound into a single perfect volume."

He took her hand. "And how does your husband figure in this . . . book of your life?"

She smiled. "You're the best part."

He pulled her into his arms. "So when does the climax take place?"

She rolled her eyes heavenward. "We just got here. Let's put a bookmark in it, shall we?"

He ignored her. "In all the years you lived here, I'll bet there's one thing you've never done in this house," he whispered, nibbling on her ear. "What a fitting end to this chapter, eh?"

He started to tug at the sleeve of her beautiful new pink dress, and she chided him for nearly tearing it. "Marshall! I bought this for you."

"I don't want it."

"No, I mean I wore it especially for you."

"Thank you. Take it off."

"What could a man have against this beautiful dress?"

"You mean, apart from his hips?"

His naughty words sparked a flame of arousal in her, just one degree short of dangerous. "Marshall, behave yourself. The servants are just in the other room. If we lock the sitting room door, they may not think us respectable."

His chest shook with laughter. "You establish a school to teach women how to arouse men—within the walls of a bordello, no less—and then go on to become the most notorious woman in London . . . and you're worried about being thought respectable?"

"That was London. This is Scotland."

His eyes crinkled in bemused desire. "Something tells me that before long, you're going to set Scotland on fire too."

Her lips were captured beneath his. Once his heavy arms wrapped around her body and pressed it to his, her whole being thrummed in contentment. By degrees, her pleasure gave way to passion, and the erotic flow coursing through her body obliterated all thought of anyone but Marshall.

Though her life had been filled with hardships and troubles, they were but stepping-stones paving the way to this one perfect man and their life together. It was those very events that had shaped her into the person that this man would fall in love with. And she wouldn't have traded a single one of them if it meant losing them.

His hand crept under her breast, and lifted it to his mouth. The mesmerizing kisses began to inflame her lust. Of its own volition, her leg rose around his hip. Maddened, he lifted her in his strong arms and carried her to the door. Then he turned the key.

Now she was imprisoned between the hard door and his hardening body. There wasn't an inch of her body that wasn't on fire for him. Though the wooden door shook against the jamb with a guilty sound, and their heavy breathing was audible to everyone, there was no going back. The lady in her was subjugated by the woman in her.

And with her last remaining coherent thoughts, just before their bodies became one as their hearts had done, she chuckled at the way their romance had turned out. It wasn't at all like the fairy tales. But it was the way she and Marshall would prefer to live.

Wickedly ever after.

EPILOGUE

The FOR SALE sign was nailed once more to her door—a familiar humiliation, an insulting disgrace.

The ladies who came to learn the art of sex at her lap had graduated to discover the meaning of love. They left her not as courtesans, but as wives.

So few of her denizens ever found the way to true love. It had eluded even her, as the sign so shamefully proclaimed.

But London was a city full of lost women in search of something, they knew not what. There would be others to school, others to seduce. She was not called the Pleasure Emporium for nothing. Soon, someone else would come to gawk, poke around, and maybe purchase. She would let them look, let them touch, let them buy.

A dark-clad figure approached the front door, the person's dark clothes disappearing in the night. Something connected between her and the dark figure, a mutual desire that sprang not from love but from need. This person would do.

The figure lifted a hand and removed the FOR SALE sign, tossing it onto the street. The dim light glinted on the barrel of a key as it penetrated her front door. With a satisfied *thunk,* the lock turned, and the Pleasure Emporium opened herself once more.